DINNER
AT THE
END OF THE WORLD

D I N N E R

AT THE
END OF THE WORLD

by
Antanas Sileika

Mosaic Press
Oakville - Buffalo - London

Canadian Cataloguing in Publication Data

Sileika, Antanas, 1953-
    Dinner at the end of the world

ISBN 0-88962-576-X

I. Title.

PS8587.154D56 1994   C813'.54   C94-931377-7
PR9199.3.S55D56 1994

Published by MOSAIC PRESS, P.O. Box 1032, Oakville, Ontario, L6J 5E9, Canada. Offices and warehouse at 1252 Speers Road, Units #1&2, Oakville, Ontario, L6L 5N9, Canada and Mosaic Press, 85 River Rock Drive, Suite 202, Buffalo, N.Y., 14207, USA.

Mosaic Press acknowledges the assistance of the Canada Council, the Ontario Arts Council, the Ontario Ministry of Culture, Tourism and Recreation and the Dept. of Communications, Government of Canada, for their support of our publishing programme.

Cover design by Snaige
Printed and bound in Canada
ISBN 0-88962-576-X

In Canada:
    MOSAIC PRESS, 1252 Speers Road, Units #1&2, Oakville, Ontario, L6L 5N9, Canada. P.O. Box 1032, Oakville, Ontario, L6J 5E9
In the United States:
    Mosaic Press, 85 River Rock Drive, Suite 202, Buffalo, N.Y., 14207
In the U.K.
    John Calder (Publishers) Ltd., 9-15 Neal Street, London, WC2 H9TU, England

For my mother and Snaige

Acknowledgements

The Hen and the Cock first appeared in *Descant* in a slightly different form, and *Oral Sex* was originally published in *Matrix*.

Many thanks for assistance from Jack David, Max Layton, Mary-Jo Morris, Ed Valiunas, and Jude Waples. Thanks as well to the many readers who commented on the manuscript at various stages. Thanks to Gilbey Canada for the cinzano umbrella on the cover.

Chapter 1

Alban Butler stood in the shade of the Cinzano umbrella with a glass of warm gin in his hand, and he scanned the bay for icebergs. The last one had slipped away three days before when a wind came up during the night. Since then, the wind had gone, and the bay was now a flat blue-green. Gnats circled one another in shifting clouds at the water's edge, and purple martins swept along the shore in swift arcs. Butler dreamed of ice, but for all he knew he would never see another iceberg again. The last great white mountain was now melting somewhere in the middle of a tepid Hudson Bay without being of any use to anyone. All that cold was going to waste. Butler had not even thought of packing an ice-making machine into his four-wheel drive. Even worse, he had forgotten to pack tonic water, and now he took his gin straight. He sipped from the glass and then held it to his cheek as if the memory of ice could evoke a chill.

Butler had forgotten so many items. Small things, like nail clippers. He was using scissors to trim his nails, and paper scissors at that. He could feel the jagged edges of his nails even then, an invitation to hangnails. Teresa had not forgotten her bikini, and

Butler wondered for a moment if she would have sunbathed nude without it. He regretfully ushered the thought out of his mind. It was unfair to the memory of his wife.

Teresa and Dianne were lying on chaises longues beside the spring-fed pool. Each of them was lovely, but Teresa was the one who held Butler's eye. Her face had a pacifying serenity about it, an almost unearthly calm. She was in her late thirties, almost a decade younger than Butler, and her head lay in a halo of her own dark brown hair. Teresa had sung with a band that toured Northern Ontario mining towns until the industry died and the jobs melted away.

"Are you sure you don't have any Coppertone?" Dianne asked plaintively.

"Just baby oil," Teresa said, lips barely moving and eyes hidden behind dark glasses. "We used up the last of the Coppertone three days ago."

Butler's Hawaiian shirt was sticking to his back. He suffered from the heat more than the others because he was a big man. Not fat, but heavy, with the weight distributed evenly over his body. He sweated a lot because of it, and he was acutely aware that his sweat had considerably less appeal than the tiny droplets on Teresa's upper lip.

The heat was bearable during the day when he could wear only his Hawaiian shirt, shorts and sandals. In the evening it was worse. Then, the mosquitos rose up in great clouds from the tundra around them, and he had to wrap every part of his exposed body and sit in the smoke from the barbecue to save his supply of insect repellent. His secret cache of repellent would have been depleted in days if the others found out about it.

They kept secrets from one another; Dianne may have had her own bottle of Coppertone locked in the glove compartment of her car. Margaret, Butler was sure, had boxes of condoms to ward off unwanted pregnancies. Nobody wanted to get pregnant any more. It just did not make any sense. Everyone had secrets, but the longer they were all trapped there at the end of the dry road, the harder it became to keep their caches hidden. It was already impossible for Andy to disguise the fact that he was starting his charcoal with barbecue lighter every night; the great "whoosh" and high flames gave him away immediately while everyone else was trying to use newspapers or twigs. It was true that he was generous with his hot coals once he had cooked his food, but by then the smell of his rabbit, or seagull, or garbanzo burger was making everyone else's mouth water, and it took a while for his hot coals to start the many cooking fires in the camp. No one had had the room to bring along a gas barbecue.

People were not exactly stingy, but careful. Even Leopold was unwilling to lend his books ever since one of them had disappeared two days before. Someone had probably been desperate to start his cooking fire. Leopold had more books than food with him, but he never looked hungry. Short-sighted and ascetic, he lived to read, and he looked more out of place than anyone else in the camp. He was an academic misplaced on the tundra.

The camp was made up of a dozen vehicles parked on a great flat rock where they would be safe if the rains came and turned the muskeg into swamp again. The fear of getting mired kept them where they were. Half a mile away, Stan's one and only folly was a reminder to those who were in too much of a rush to head North. Stan had thought that the muck had dried out enough for him to continue the drive, but his Volvo station wagon had broken through the thin upper crust of dry earth. It was mired to the axles now, and he would have to dig it out when the deeper earth had dried and hardened. All of them wanted to push on, but it took time for the permafrost to melt and then dry out.

Stan was scouting somewhere beyond the horizon on his dirt bike, which was light enough not to break through the crust. Butler hoped he would come back with another rabbit or two that he had trapped in his snares. Sometimes the arctic foxes got them first. Rabbit would be a nice change from the dry cornflakes and spaghetti dinners, but the exchange rate was high. Half a bottle of gin.

Stan was at home in the wilderness, unlike the rest of them, and they admired him for that. He was also a man of means. Besides the Volvo, he owned the dirt bike, which used thimblefuls of gas and let him range around the countryside at will. He had guns and waterproof matches, snare wire and binoculars. Butler regretted that the world had come to this--Boy Scouts were in the ascendancy.

People with campers, pick-ups and full-sized cars formed a kind of aristocracy because of the amount of goods that their cars could hold. Sub-compact car owners were at the bottom of the heap.

At the bottom of the bottom was a family that had arrived in an old Toyota Tercel with two small kids and roof racks filled with disposable diapers. The kids tore around the camp as soon as the car came to a halt; they begged lumps of sugar and bits of melted chocolate with cute smiles or doleful looks. Their father, Simon Waver, was little more than a bigger version of the kids. With curly blonde hair, glasses and a boyish face, he hung around Margaret's camper most of the time, trying to do odd jobs for the price of a freeze-dried dinner or a few bullion cubes. His wife, Alice, looked like she didn't belong with the the kids and father--it was as if she had been attached to the wrong family. The kids were snotty cajers, the old man a goofy blonde, and the wife a vision of what the garment trade could make of a woman. She wore silk dresses, with bits of lace lingerie showing underneath, an antique cameo and a snake-spine necklace. Dressed in this elegant salad, she made watery soups out of the goods Simon brought home, and scanned the horizon from time to time, hoping for the arrival of a carload of kids whose parents might be willing to trade some edibles for a few disposable diapers.

Butler sat down in the shade of his Cinzano beach umbrella and considered how long his stock of gin would last. He still had four cases, but the exchange rate for gin was bad. He would have done better with red wine, which did not need to be chilled at all. He would have done better yet never to have started this crazy trek North. It had given him a sense of hope at first, a sense of fresh start to be heading North with a fully packed car and no clear sense of destination except for some vague other place that was different from the world he saw collapsing around him. He had met others like him along the way, cheerful pilgrims who had decided to leave the past behind them. They met at park benches while there was still highway, and later at fords to rivers. He had met people stuck in potholes, who, with a little ingenuity, had usually managed to get out. This obstacle was different. This could be the end of the line if the muck did not dry out fast enough. There were miles of it ahead of them. And beyond that there was ice, a cool thin layer covering the earth. The thought of that ice made him smile.

Butler saw something on the horizon. Alice Waver saw it too, and she froze in concentration while stirring a pot of Cup-a-Soup which she had been turning into a main course with the addition of bunches of watercress that she had found by the edge of the spring. In the distance, to the South, she saw a column of dust that heralded the arrival of another vehicle. "Car!" she cried out like a kid during a game of street hockey, and the others began to come out from tents and lean-to's where they had been dozing during the afternoon blaze.

Alice Waver did not take her eyes off the column of dust, and the others soon joined her in an attempt to discern the type of vehicle. It was still a few miles away, no more than a spot of reflected light off a windshield at the bottom of the dust column. An imminent arrival was always cause for mixed feelings. It might be a new "pilgrim" with a carload of exchangeable goods, or it might be one of the rumored paramilitary bands that were thieving anything they could under the guise of restoring order. The dust cloud was still a long way off and it gave them plenty of time to think.

Everything started to happen at once. The buzz of Stan's dirt bike announced his arrival from the north, and Alice Waver's daughter shouted "Teddy!" and pointed towards the bay. Nobody would have bothered with the child's call, but the girl tugged at Dianne's bikini bottom until half her rump was exposed and she finally looked over to where the kid was pointing.

"Holy shit. It's a polar bear."

Butler had not thought about polar bears for a long time, and if he had, he would have assumed they were all dead. A polar bear was no more imaginable than a pair of earmuffs. Yet there it was, a great dirty white rump that waddled as the bear ambled towards the waters of Hudson Bay. It looked over its shoulder once at the campers and then continued on, dreaming its dreams of arctic char. Perhaps, thought Butler, as the weather had become hotter and hotter, the bear had burrowed more deeply into the earth to reach the ever-receding perma-frost, but it reached the point where hunger was more pressing than a comfortable temperature and dug its way back out. The bear made him think of steaks.

Stan pulled into the camp, his great brown beard filled with dust and his eyes bright beneath the visor on his crash helmet. He had two hares slung over the back of his bike.

"Mike!" he called, and the only other real hunter in the group was at Stan's side in a moment. Mike Thorson handed a loaded rifle to Stan, and took over the driver's position on the bike. Stan cradled the rifle in one arm and held onto the strap with his other hand as Mike kicked up a cloud of dust. The bear picked up speed when it heard the motor, and Mike turned the bike in a wide loop, trying to herd the creature away from the shores of the bay. But the bear was hot, and it could smell the water. When Mike came in close on its flank, it merely waved a paw in their direction. Don't bother me. Stan usually had a cool head, but the thought of so much meat escaping into the water made him excited, and he started to shoot from the bike, missing wildly as the bike bounced over the rough terrain. Soon the polar bear would be in the water, and then there would be no way to recover the carcass. Back on the rock, the campers cheered.

Butler clutched his glass tightly. Nothing had happened for such a long time that a lethargic impotence had weighed upon him. But now, when the others cheered, he cheered with them.

The dirt bike hit a patch of mud, slid, and fell on its side, throwing the two riders to the earth. But Stan never let go of his gun, took the fall in a roll and then raised himself up to his elbows and fired three fast shots. The bear stopped. It turned around and looked back quizzically. A red patch began to show on its rump. The bear altered its direction for the first time, but instead of charging Stan, it started to amble towards Mike, who was sitting up and holding his ankle between his hands.

"The bear's going to eat him!" Alice's boy said, and she covered his mouth with her hand.

"I'm out of shells," Stan yelled, and Mike reached into his jacket pocket and tossed over a box. Stan snatched it out of the air. He had to reload.

The bear was getting closer to Mike, and various members of the group began to check pants pockets for keys in case the hunt went wrong. The bear stepped up its speed to a lope while Stan opened the breech, blew the dust off a shell and loaded it. There was only time to load one. Now the great white creature mustered its anger and started its charge, and Stan raised the rifle to his shoulder and sighted, aiming for the spot that would take the lead straight to the creature's heart. There would be no time to reload for a second attempt. Mike sat and watched the bear as it came closer.

The rifle cracked.

At first nothing. The charge slowed, finally, to a walk, and then to an unsteady shuffle. The bear was close to Mike, no more than ten feet away. They studied one another and the bear shook its head in disbelief. Its two front legs crumpled like those of a bull in the ring, and it finally collapsed with its head almost in Mike's lap. Red foam came out of its mouth.

* * *

Everyone had known it was coming, but no one had prepared for it, except for the odd meteorologist who bought up the shoreline along James Bay in the hope of developing it into a hotel strip. Even as the greenhouse effect became more pronounced, it took a while for the meaning of the heat to sink in, and when it did, people started to go a little crazy.

Like almost everybody else, Alban Butler had hardly noticed that the winters were becoming shorter and the summers much hotter than before. Until his wife disappeared through the ice, he had only been aware that the gin-drinking season was getting longer and the scotch-drinking one shorter. Even after his wife had gone under, the bigger picture did not really sink in. That only happened three years later when his editor at the fishing magazine called Butler and told him to fly down to New York for a meeting. Butler had not been to the office since his wife died, and he had never even seen this editor before. All their communication was by telephone, or modem or fax.

"I must be getting old," Butler thought, as he looked up at the thirty-three floor glass and red brick Fisherman Tower. Fishing had become big business. Whole blocks of floors were devoted to special items. The first four dealt with the import or manufacture of fish finders, the sonar apparatus that could pinpoint the last smelt in a weed-choked lake and determine the best type of lure to use to land it. Lures and rods were the purview of the next seven floors and after that came outboards, motorboats, and camping paraphernalia. The top two floors were the media side of the enterprise, pumping out fishermen's fantasies as a marketing tool for the floors below.

It had not always been like this. Once the whole operation had prided itself on being "devoid of bullshit." Once editors in checked shirts had sat around an editorial office the size of a bathroom and told fishing stories through a blue haze of pipe tobacco. Butler preferred the old style to the new. Now, beside each button on the elevator, there was a small symbol, an outboard or a boat or a lure, that lit up along with the number of the floor. Fishing had also gone musically upscale. Bach played on the stereo in the reception room.

Butler announced himself to the secretary and then rubbed his shoes on the thick woolen carpet in the waiting room that his stories had helped to buy. It was all the law of unintended results, he reminded himself. He had never really intended to become a fishing writer in the first place. He was supposed to become a priest, and the Basilian fathers still regretted their loss. One of his old professors had showed up at Elaine's funeral - a funeral without a body - and hinted that now was the right time to find solace by returning to the order. "You could be a great teacher!" the decrepit father Abelard remonstrated with him, "instead of writing those corny fishing stories of yours." The priesthood was hardly a temptation any more. He had loved Elaine too much to go back into the order. He longed for her, and he came to love his longing. The priesthood would have meant the end of all that.

"The famous Alban Butler, I presume?"

The new editor was a twenty-eight-year-old Harvard graduate who wore Italian suits and had his hair slicked back like Fred Astaire's. "So you're the legend," he said as he led Butler into his office, shaking his hand and holding his elbow all the way.

"I'm not old enough to be a legend," said Butler, and pulled his hand out of the editor's. "I'm not so sure about that," the editor said, and sat himself on the other side of the desk and leaned forward at an alarming angle. He looked like he was getting ready to bob for apples on Butler's side of the desk.

"Orthopedic chair," said the editor and Butler stood up to take a look at the odd kneeling contraption. "Keeps the back straight. Offer you anything? Pastis? Campari?" Butler took a scotch and the editor returned to his angular position.

"I'm afraid we've got a problem," said the editor, leaning so far forward that it looked as if his nose might touch the table.

"We?"

"That's right. We. Your problem is that the trout and salmon are gone. My problem is that this job won't take me along the career path that I want any more. Without those two game fish, the glamour's out of fishing. Bass might save the day, but don't count on it. This magazine is going to nosedive, and you're the first casualty. I wouldn't be surprised if the television people called you soon."

Trout and salmon preferred cool water, and they had fled the streams of Ontario, or else died out completely. No one was exactly sure whether the trout and salmon had disappeared or died because no one was doing any research on it. Public money went into building up dikes around the cities as the water level rose higher and higher.

"Maybe I could write about carp and sunfish," Butler said, but it seemed like a poor offer to make to a man in an Italian suit who was sipping Pastis.

"Boats are the future," said the editor as he ushered Butler out of the office. "People are going to be running their Johnson outboards past the second floor windows of this tower within two years. Believe me, the water level's rising that fast." A final firm handshake, and Butler was standing beside the elevator.

The fishing journalist was an early career casualty of the greenhouse effect, but most people eventually lost their jobs for one reason or another. Snowmobile manufacturers, ski makers and the other winter-driven industries disappeared within months of one another. The textile industry lost its entire fall and autumn market and collapsed without a sigh. As in most crises, however, some people did well. Makers of air conditioners earned fortunes until the electricity supply became erratic, and lifeguards and ice cream manufacturers could never keep up with the demand.

*   *   *

Butler's career as a fishing journalist had been an unlikely one in the first place. He had originally intended to be a priest, but a combination of food and love had taken him to another calling. He had been in his third year at the Basilian seminary and was already wearing a white collar from time to time. Then his priestly career began to unravel. The seminary was part of the downtown Catholic university, and

Butler liked the old houses, shady streets and donnish atmosphere. The Basilians were a teaching order, and he could expect to spend the rest of his career in the leafy academic surroundings that attracted him so much. He had liked the idea of being both a teacher and a priest, with the emphasis on the former. At least, he liked the idea until the seed of doubt started to grow in him. His doubts began in the seminary refectory, and had nothing to do with the existence of God.

The food was awful. Pale roast beef in gelatinous gravy, sticky spaghetti, and the greatest abomination of all, fish sticks. Butler liked the taste of fish fried in butter or barbecued on a grill, but he could not bear fish masquerading as putty. He was not exactly crazy about the refectory atmosphere either. The seminarians were mostly young and spirited. They were always trying to show one another what a good time they were having at the dinner table, and so they broke into bread fights or noisy laughter at too many meals. Butler was young too, and at first the refectory table had been amusing, like a fraternity. But most men left their fraternities after they graduated from school. Priests, especially teaching priests, just moved to other refectories. Butler imagined all of them at a table in the home for aged priests, still throwing dinner rolls at one another fifty years later.

Food was a problem, but the serious doubts about his choice of career started after Elaine began inviting him to dinner in the parking lot shack. She was a student working her way through university by running the parking lot across the street from the seminary.

"Where you going, Father?" she had asked him one day after he left a meal of turkey a la king in the seminary and went for a walk instead. Butler was not even wearing his collar, so he was surprised to be called "Father". And she had a way of saying it that made him feel embarrassed. It was early September, and she had the door of her glass-walled shack open. She was sitting on a chair in jeans and a white, man's shirt, smoking a cigarette. She was smiling at him ironically, her eyes wicked beneath a head of curly brown hair. It crossed Butler's mind that the devil could be an ingenious fellow.

"Aren't you a little old for this kind of job?" Butler asked. He used his frumpiest Father Alban C. Butler voice. Elaine was in her late twenties, and by campus standards that was old.

"That's what my boss said," Elaine answered.

"Your boss?"

"At the stockyards. He told me I was making good money and going back to school was a mistake."

"Was it a mistake?"

"No fucking way."

Butler was not exactly sure he had heard her right. She was still smiling her ironic smile at him.

"I see you out walking whenever the other priests are eating. Food bad?" Elaine asked.

"How did you guess?"

"You look unhappy. Care to join me for dinner? Cold chicken with homemade mayo and carp in aspic."

"Carp in Aspic?"

"My mother was Polish. Hey, you've got to try it before you decide."

Elaine had two chairs, and she set them outside the parking lot shack on the asphalt. It would have been too close inside for Butler to feel comfortable, especially when half the windows of the seminary overlooked the lot.

Carp in aspic turned out to be pretty good.

"There's no reason to eat shit," said Elaine. "We can get anything we want in this country. We have good produce, and then we turn it into shitburgers and Kentucky-fried puke fingers."

"How come your language is so bad?" Butler asked.

"I don't know. Always has been. Gets me in trouble sometimes."

"What are you studying?"

"Everything."

And she was. All the other students had their career paths plotted by the end of their first year, but Elaine leaped into her collage of study the way a girl might leap into a swimming pool.

"I hated being stupid," said Elaine. "At first I wanted to learn the name and date of everything just so I wouldn't feel stupid. But there's too much to learn, so I don't worry about feeling like a jerk any more. Now I'm getting into Anglo-Saxon poetry." She worked an errant chicken bone loose with her tongue and tossed it to a pigeon that had been strutting warily around them. "Those rhymes give me a tingle up my spine."

Butler was feeling a tingle as well, though he would have been embarrassed to locate it.

"Come around again sometime Father," Elaine said when it was time for him to go. "I've always got something good to eat and I can use the company. The rest of the students around here are too young for me, and the few that aren't keep trying to squeeze my tits."

That was the beginning of the end for Butler. He was somehow ashamed that he was not included in the tit-squeezing group.

"Have a nice chat with a lost soul?"

Father Abelard was manning the reception desk during dinner, and the office window overlooked the parking lot. He was a retired priest who did not believe in eating after lunch, an old-time flesh-mortifier. He perched on his high stool and gave Butler a piercing look.

"Not a lost soul," Butler said airily. Father Abelard raised an eyebrow. "Just someone who needs a little help."

Father Abelard snorted, and returned to his *Lives of the Saints*.

Butler's room was just over the reception area, and it too overlooked Elaine's parking lot shack. Butler kept a sharp lookout for tit-squeezers. He ate with her whenever he could get away. The seminary actually encouraged that sort of thing, much to the disgust of Father Abelard. The priests were supposed to be sure about their vocation in the face of Temptation.

Butler was so close to Temptation that they were almost nose to nose.

*   *   *

Stan started to gut the bear beside the spring, and Dianne organized them all into work details. Some of them had to help Stan, and Butler drew the unenviable task of burying the guts. He did not exactly like the idea, but he did like the coming party. Simon and his kids were out looking for wood and gathering offerings of charcoal to make a big fire, and Dianne was sharpening her Henkels knife and racking her brains for bear meat recipes. Alice Waver sang to herself while she laid out dishes on the dry Muskeg, happy that her kids were going to get some meat into them for a change. Teresa put a Eurorock tape into her ghetto blaster, and soon the music was blaring out over the tundra, playing out across Hudson Bay where the last few seals were swimming North. The air cooled a little in the late afternoon, and Margaret dug out some paper napkins, and then hurried back to take care of Mike. She took his foot, the one with the sprained ankle, nestled in her lap like a baby, and kept examining it as she were a doctor trying to locate a hairline crack in the bone. At least, she tried to look serious, but she could not resist running her hand over the foot, and Mike kept blushing.

"There's that column of dust again," said Alice. It was getting closer now, and they could make out the vehicle. It was a truck or van of some kind, much heavier than any car in the camp.

"He'll be lucky to make it this far," said Mike, "with all that weight on his wheels." Stan stood up from his butchering job, and wiped the blood off his hands.

"I hope it's not a military vehicle," said Gary, and the others shuddered. The military had swollen over the years as people needed jobs, and the army had recently declared its intention to "guard the frontiers and honour of Canada." No one could argue with the former, because American wetbacks had been stealing over the border for years in order to escape their drought-ridden states. The honour of Canada was a little more ambiguous. Recently it had meant soldiers on street corners, and not the kind of soldiers that Canadians were accustomed to. They smoked cigarettes and carried automatic weapons and seemed to shave only one day in three. They had a way of looking at you that made you feel uncomfortable and guilty. And there were rumours about them too, rumours of drunkenness and looting that never made it into the newspapers or on the few remaining TV channels. The media just kept on talking about what a fine job the troops were doing, but to most people it did not look like they were doing any job at all, unless acting like pool-room toughs was a profession.

"Too big to be a tank," said Butler.

"Personnel carrier, maybe."

But as it drew nearer, it became clear that the vehicle was civilian. It was a Winnebago, and the biggest, most top-of-the-line, all-accessories-included Winnebago that had ever been built. It was two-tone blue, sky and navy, and it had chrome ladders that led to the roof. There were three small motorcycles, a mountain bike and an inflatable rubber raft tied to the sides. Six car-top carriers were strapped to the top and there were packages and boxes tied to the top of those. The Winnebago had a smoked glass picture window on the side, racing stripes and chrome trim. "Here Comes the Beef" was painted in fancy scrolled letters above the windshield. Five brass horns on the driver's side honked out the tune that played at horse races before the announcer said, "They're at the Post!"

"I've got to be dreaming," said Margaret, one hand on her hip and the other shielding her eyes from the sun.

The great vehicle pulled right up to the big rock where the cars were parked, and honked out its tune one more time. The driver cut the engine, and then his door swung open and he stepped out onto his running board like a president stepping out onto a balcony.

He was the strangest human being they had seen in a long time: a midget with a strawberry birthmark across half his face and with ears that stuck out like flaps. He wore a candy-stripe jacket and had Walkman earphones slung around his neck. The hand that reached into his breast pocket for sunglasses was big, and his voice was deep and rich, like that of a much bigger man.

"Tammy Odds and Ends is my name, but most people just call me Odds," the midget said. "Road not dried up yet over there?"

"Nope," said Stan. All the others did not say anything at all. Odds could have been be a military spy, or one of the growing number of freaks who wandered the land. With a few old nuclear power plants spewing out steam and land-fill sites leaking mutation-inducing cocktails, there seemed to be a lot more strange people around than before. Sometimes they looked normal, but acted funny. The friendliest situations could turn ugly.

"Well, if I can't go North, then this place will be just fine," said Odds. "I see you've got yourselves a bear. Lovely specimen too, one of the finest specimens of Thalarctos Maritimi I've ever seen. Going to have a party?"

"Maybe."

Stan did the talking. The rest were still unsure. The midget sounded friendly enough, but even if he were normal, maybe he was just a gate-crasher.

"Well, don't let me hold you up on that. I'll just pitch a tent in some quiet corner and I won't get in your way."

How much could a man that size eat, thought Butler. Someone ought to invite him to join the party.

"Unless..." and here Odds paused for a long time and put his finger against the side of his nose. "Unless, of course," he continued, "I might have something that you want."

It was the right thing to say. A ripple went through the crowd gathered around the running board of the Winnebago. Everybody wanted something, and this midget had the air of a game show host with goods to pass out. Not that Odds would ever pass a screen test, but he smiled and seemed ready to announce the winner on the Sixty-Four Thousand Dollar Question.

"Just what have you got to offer?" Margaret asked.

"What have I got?"

Even though Odds was wearing sunglasses, you could tell that his eyes were rounding with incredulity. It was as if someone had asked him how many red blood cells were floating in his veins or wanted to know the number of hairs on his head. "It would be easier to tell you what I haven't got," Odds finally said. "Inside this wheeled retail establishment you'll find just about anything that has ever been made by the factories on this continent. I've got everything that's ever been grown on this earth and a little more besides."

He got down off his running board and walked around to the back of his Winnebago. He chose a key from the bunch attached to his belt and pulled it forward on its spring-tied cord to unlock a small door. He shut the door behind him. They could hear him moving through the Winnebago, and it sounded as if he was moving machinery, and knocking down tins and stepping on glass as he worked his way forward through the camper. And then they heard him fumble with the latch of the picture window and finally swing it up the way a flap on a fish and chip wagon opens. On the underside of the window the following words were written in metallic gold letters: BARTER! I HAVE WHAT YOU WANT AND I WANT WHAT YOU HAVE!!! The last exclamation mark was squeezed in to fit on the window. Behind the midget, who stood on a wooden box behind the counter, there were shelves filled with plastic bags, boxes and packages. Familiar words like "Kellogg's" and "L.L. Bean" and "Sony" glittered from within. The interior of the Winnebago was crammed with goods, and there were low, tunnel-like passages through the piles of stock that seemed to lead to other storerooms.

"Odds is the name and I'm a trader by trade. As this is the end of this road, I'm going to have a sale, a kind of 'end of the world sale'. Of course, we all know this isn't the end of the world, but the road ahead is muddy and I can't afford to carry too much weight. I've got everything you need, and I'm willing to trade, because what you've got, others want someplace else. No item too big or too small, Odds is the name and I deal in them all." He put his hands down on the counter and leaned forward, ready to do business.

"Tonic water," thought Butler.

"Coppertone," thought Dianne.

But it sounded too good to be true. The end of the world would be the opportunity for a slam-bang sale, that was clear enough. But for one thing, none of them really believed it *was* the end of the world. And for another, the midget was a little too weird for them. He sounded like all the Crazy Harolds and Wacky Willies they had seen on TV hawking fridges and Lay-z-Boy chairs, but he didn't have the same screen presence as the shysters they had seen before.

Simon shuffled his feet and Margaret looked at the ground. Butler carefully studied the sky for cloud formations.

"There's no such thing as a free lunch, mister," Stan finally said. "What's in this for you?"

"Free lunch? Who said anything about a free lunch? I'm not giving anything away, but I'm willing to trade. You've got something I need. Look, you're going to have a barbecue. No secret about that. Nice spit you've got rigged up over there. Now I haven't been to a good barbecue since the water filter broke down on the backyard pool ten years ago. And you've got bear meat, which is the tastiest, but toughest meat there is. I'd sorely like an invitation to your little feast, but I'm new here. Nobody knows me. Fair enough. Man's got to bring something along too. So here's my offer. Invite me to your barbecue, and I'll give you this!" And he reached behind the counter and pulled out the biggest container of Adolph's Meat Tenderizer that anyone had ever seen before.

"That's my man!" Dianne shouted, and she took the bottle from his hands. "You've got yourself an invitation!"

"You got any use for disposable diapers?" Alice Waver asked next.

"Disposable diapers? Why, people have been asking me for disposable diapers from Temiscaming to Moose Jaw! You think they're making those any more? Mothers are going out of their minds boiling diapers over wood fires these days, and they'd just love to have a disposable or two, if only to put on the kids at night so they don't wet their beds. Sure I need disposable diapers. What do you want in exchange?"

"Food."

"That word is kind of vague. Doesn't mean too much to me. It's kind of abstract, and I'm not an abstract kind of man. Give me a brand name and I'll see what I can do."

"Pop Rock candies," said Alice's daughter.

"Pop Rocks it is. I got a box from a dentist who felt bad about having them, and I'd say one diaper is worth two packs of Pop Rocks any day. But child does not live on pop-rocks alone, so what else does her Mom have in mind?"

Alice was quick to calculate what would go the farthest.

"Uncle Ben's Rice," she said, "long grain. Bird's Custard Powder, puffed wheat, soda crackers, One-A-Day vitamins and Maille Dijon Mustard."

"No sooner said than done. All you've said for two dozen Luvs or thirty Pampers."

"Coppertone?"

"Every number except six, including waterproof. What do you have to offer in return? Baby oil? Wonderful. The exchange rate is two for one."

"Tonic water?"

"I've only got Schweppes, if that's all right with you. The rate is three bottles of Schweppes to one of gin, and I'll throw in half a bag of ice because the ice machine has been running for days and I've got no place to put the stuff."

"How about K-Y jelly?" Margaret asked, ignoring the stares of the others. She whispered in his ear when he asked what she had to offer.

"I need those. People are still falling in love all over this continent, and those things are practical. Kids can use them for balloons too."

Odds paused.

"Hey you. What can I get for you?" He pointed to Lionel, who was smirking from the edge of the crowd. Lionel had long blonde hair that fell on both sides of his face, and he and his wife Eve hung back from the others most of the time.

"Organically grown tomatoes," Lionel said as if it were a challenge.

"Well of course I've got tomatoes, but only in cans. Now don't worry about the organic part, because there haven't been any pesticides for three years at least. The last were used for the plague of locusts at the end of the last decade."

Car trunks opened, glove compartments were unlocked, and goods changed hands faster than it took for Jiffy-Pop popcorn to expand to a gleaming ball of silver paper. Stan finished the butchering, Dianne got the fire going and Gary had the spit ready. It was going to be some party.

*   *   *

"I think maybe we should go away for a weekend so we can talk things out," said Butler.

"Mmm," said Elaine.

"There's somebody watching us," Butler said.

"Should give them a big thrill."

"I wish I wasn't in my collar."

"Take it off, then. Slip it off... slip it on... slip it off... slip it on... slip it in....."

"I don't think I'm ready for this."

"You're ready all right. You're just too shy to admit it."

It would only have made matters worse to take his collar off now. He and Elaine had gone to tour the art galleries. More specifically, she had discovered he was an artistic illiterate, and wanted him to see some wood and cloth installations at an uptown gallery. One of the installations was set up outside in the late June sun, and it looked like there was a second one at the side of the building. The second sculpture turned out to be a pile of junk that was left over from the first one, but once Butler and Elaine made it to the side of the building, they saw that there was an alley that led behind the gallery.

"Let's explore," said Elaine.

"There's nothing here," Butler answered. "What's to explore?"

"Plenty."

He might have felt less guilty about it if she had taken the lead after that, but she did not. He was definitely the one who took the initiative. It was Butler who put his arms around her and pressed his lips to her warm mouth.

"Mmmmph!"

"What?" Butler asked, pulling his mouth away reluctantly.

"I'm interested in your lips, not your teeth. Didn't any girl tell you that in high school?"

"I went to a boys' school."

If only he had not worn the whole priestly outfit. The alley had apartment buildings around it, and dozens of windows looked down on them. He was damning not only himself, but all other priests as long as he continued to neck like this. And anyway, he had intended to tell Elaine that he could not see her any more. That was not the message his lips were giving. While he was kissing her, Butler hit on the idea of "working things out." They would go away someplace for two or three days and "work things out."

Butler quickly learned another thing about necking. From time to time, both man and woman had to come up for air.

"I know just the place where we can go to work things out," said Elaine.

"So do I," said Butler.

"I was thinking of the Royal York Hotel."

"I was thinking about a retreat the parish is organizing at Lake Pagunda."

"I'd retreat with you any time."

There would be time to explain about retreats later, Butler thought. Just then, it crossed his mind that Elaine's neck could be kissed as well as her lips, and that the curve at the base of her neck led naturally to her shoulder, which lay beneath her easy-to-remove light summer blouse.

*   *   *

"Rolaids! Do you have any Rolaids on that Winnebago of yours?" Gary's stomach groaned and rumbled as he said it. The bear had been eaten and more than a few bottles of liquor drunk. The fire was sputtering low and Stan got up and threw a few more dry sticks on it. Dianne hacked up the remains of the bear to put into pots for the next day's stew. In a fit of generosity, Butler had brought out an entire case of gin, and there were still half a dozen bottles left in the carton. Nobody could ever remember eating so much. Bear meat with No-Name Macaroni and Cheese on the side. Stan had traded Odds a spare tire for a gross of Fauchon Truffle Surprise Cupcakes. Gary traded one package of orange drink crystals for one package of Rolaids.

The mosquitos were out as usual, but since everyone was wearing Butler's repellent, it was not too bad to be sitting outside. Alice Waver's two kids were sleeping with their heads on her lap. Far above them all, a thin haze covered the starlight, but no moon shone. The lights from a few fireflies blinked in the darkness beyond the pilgrims at the fire.

The night air, so pleasantly warm, had filled with Teresa's voice as she sang Eurorock hits from early in the decade, when there had still been something of music scene. Now it was getting late, and yet they lingered by the fire, hoping for something more from the night. Their contentment bordered on melancholy, the sweet romance of a moment all the more precious because it would soon pass. If only there were some way of extending the moment, of freezing it.

"The wheels of commerce are going to keep this country afloat," said Odds from the stone where he sat. He had taken off his candy-stripe jacket and now wore suspenders and rolled-up shirt-sleeves as he stirred the embers at the edge of the fire with a stick. "All that stuff about the Renaissance pushing out the Dark Ages is just nonsense, I say. What got things rolling was commerce. First people came in from the farms to go to weekly fairs, and pretty soon the fairs were held more than once a week. Then those peasants who came into town to sell their onions and cheeses got to like the towns so much, they didn't want to go home. Think of it. People bustling around, buying, selling, talking. Who wanted to go back to some wilderness hut? The fairs turned into streets of shops open all week long, except for the Sunday closing bylaw. More peasants came into town and they just hung around until they found something gainful to do, and the next thing you knew, the town had more inhabitants. Then hardly anybody wanted to stay on the farm after seeing gay Paree, and they had to invent tractors and combines just to do the work that all those peasants had left behind. Of course business was too slow on rainy days, so you got indoor malls. I mean, that gallery in Milan was built more than a century ago. So then you had shopping malls and people needed cars to get to them, so the factories obliged and built the cars."

"And the cars polluted the air and here we are, frying in the greenhouse," said Lionel.

"Give me a break," said Odds, scratching his cheek. "I was just giving you an overview. Sure it's more complicated than what I said, but the gist is that things are not winding down. We're just going through a restructuring. Maybe we have to slim down a bit, get back to corporations like mine."

"Tell that to the Moroccans," said Lionel. Everybody knew there were no Moroccans left, at least not in Morocco.

"This is getting too morbid for me," said Dianne, and she stood up and stretched.

"Wait a second," said Butler.

He did not want Dianne to go to bed. He felt, without knowing why, that anyone who went beyond the light of the fire might never come back. They all had to be held there, in their contentment after the party.

"We should play a game of some kind."

Nobody picked up on that idea. Charades did not seem appropriate, and Dianne did not sit down. Teresa was the only one who kept looking at him.

"Butler's got the right idea," said Margaret. She was nursing her seventh gin and tonic and was having a good time. It was far too early to go to bed. "I've got a story to tell. In fact, I've got dozens of stories to tell," and she laughed into her drink and winked at Simon, who blushed and looked at his wife.

"I could tell you about my last husband. He was a bathtub maker with the cleanest body and the dirtiest mind I ever knew. When he

met me, he asked me what colour my labia were, and when I told him
I didn't know, he found out for himself."

Dianne smiled and sat down. Just as she did, something bumped
beyond the circle of light around the fire. Margaret stopped talking,
and Stan reached for his rifle. Maybe the bear had had a mate.

"I've got a flashlight in the car," said Andy, but he did not stand
up to get it. Alice Waver pulled her children closer to her, and Mike
pulled a burning stick out of the fire and held it up high.

"Who's out there?" he called.

In the unnatural silence that followed, all ears strained to hear
what they could. First there came a long sigh, and then a rattle that
sounded as if a pile of branches were being lifted. It was hard to tell
if the sigh had been human or animal or a mixture of both.

Strange things had been happening for the last few years, and
they would have been terrified but not surprised if an overheated
abominable snowman had walked into the circle of light. Stan cocked
his rifle. The loud sigh repeated, and a strange sound of sticks on
earth, of something being dragged, came at them from out of the
darkness. This time the sound did not stop, but drew closer.

A man stepped into the circle of light around the fire.

He was dragging a litter behind him, a roughshod affair with thin
branches badly tied and knotted around thicker ones. The load,
whatever it was, was heavy and hidden from view by dried ferns
draped across the top. The man had short, neatly cut hair with a sharp
part along the left side. He wore eyeglasses with thin steel frames and
had a windbreaker zipped up to his neck. His pants were off-white
cotton with razor creases down the front and his shoes a dusty pair
of brown Oxfords.

He looked like a man more comfortable behind a desk than
walking on the grass, the kind of man who enjoyed the feeling of a
starched collar around his neck. Even in the firelight, the lines that
went down his nose and around his mouth were very pronounced,
as were the concentration wrinkles around his forehead. His teeth
were probably flat from being ground together throughout the night.

Butler wondered what he had on his litter.

"Why didn't you say anything when I called you?" Stan asked.

"Didn't want to waste my breath. I'd get here soon enough."

"You might have gotten yourself killed."

"All the same to me, in the long run."

The man set down the handles of his litter, took a clean handkerchief from his pocket and dusted off his hands. He paid attention to the webbing between his fingers. His actions were slow and deliberate, and he eyed each of the people by the fire carefully, assessing them. Butler felt a chill come over him when the man's eyes passed over him quickly and dismissively.

"Any water I could use to wash my hands?" the litter-bearer asked, and Dianne pointed to a bucket of water that had been brought from the spring.

Silently, the litter-bearer walked to the bucket and rinsed off his hands. He was about to wipe them off with his handkerchief when Dianne said there was a bar of soap if he wanted it.

"No soap." He said it angrily - too angrily, and yet his voice was not loud.

"Soap has phosphates in it. It's part of the problem. Something we should have given up a long time ago. Isn't that so, Dianne?"

Dianne shivered.

"How do you know my name?"

"The acoustics are very strange tonight. I've been getting closer to you for hours, and I've heard everything you said by the fire. Very amusing," and this time he smiled at Margaret. She looked straight back at him and took another sip from her gin and tonic.

"My name's Victor."

"Sit down, Victor," said Simon. Stan shot Simon a poisonous look, but Simon only shrugged. The man had introduced himself, and it would have been bad manners to leave him standing. The litter-bearer sat down on a stone a little apart from the others. He made them uncomfortable, but there was no way anybody could stand up and leave. Not just yet, anyway.

"Have a little bear meat?" Dianne asked.

"Why not? Probably the last polar bear in the whole world. It'd be a shame not to eat some of it." But he made it sound as if it *was* a shame to eat the bear. When Dianne gave him a plate, he picked at the meat as if he was eating something from a display case at a museum.

Margaret was the only one who looked unfazed by Victor. She spit on the fire and poured herself another gin and tonic.

"What are you carrying in that litter?" she asked.

Victor thought about the question for a while. He put his plate down on the ground beside him.

"Garbage."

Mike laughed, but it sounded bad.

"That's right. Garbage." He got up and walked to his litter. He lifted the handles and pulled it closer to the fire, and then set it down carefully again. He took some of the ferns off the top. Butler thought it looked like he was carrying supplies.

"See this?" he lifted a can of rose-scented air freshener and depressed the button on top. A brief spurt of the chemical shot out before the nozzle sputtered. It was empty. Still, the faintest scent of rose persisted in the air, and it reminded Butler of shaggy pink toilet covers and floor mats in his aunt Grace's bathroom.

"This can was in somebody's toilet," said Victor. "Maybe the owner used it when he had guests over. One of them took a shit, and then instead of opening the window and letting the room air out, he sprayed some of this stuff to cover his stink. Innocent, eh? But the perfume in this can is propelled by CFC gas, and a little bit of the gas eventually worked its way into the ozone layer and punched a tiny hole into it. And see this?" He took out a piece of polyurethane foam that was formed into a box-like shape. "Somebody's ghetto-blaster was packed in this stuff. Take out the radio and chuck the foam. It was made with CFC gases too." He tossed the foam back onto the litter and took out a twisted piece of metal tubing. "Part of a refrigerator cooling system. You remember fridges? A lot of people just used the freezer to make ice cubes for gin and tonic. CFC gases in the cooling system. One more right hook to the ozone layer."

Butler looked at his drink. Thank God the ice cubes in it had melted.

"Look at this," and Victor took out a plastic holder that had been used around a six-pack of soft drink cans. "I found this on the seashore in Maryland. The oceans are full of this shit, and it never breaks down. It floats up on the shores of Caribbean islands and wraps itself around the beaks of birds. But I'm not even worried about that right now. I'm thinking of the factory that made this piece of junk. A little factory with a little smokestack pouring carbon dioxide and sulphur particles into the air. Doing its little bit to heat up the atmosphere. Here's a gas container. Somebody ran out of gas on his way to a poker game and used this to add to his tank. A bit more carbon dioxide. Here's a marshmallow bag. Some guy figured he'd have a camp fire with the kids and chuck some more garbage into the air."

"Okay, okay," said Margaret, "you don't have to unpack your dirty laundry in front of us. What's the point of all this?"

"The point is that the world is coming to an end. This is it, my friends. Siberia will be a bread basket for a while, but then it's going to overheat too. You and I and all of our kind are going to go the way of the dinosaurs. We're soon going to follow in the footsteps of the Malaysians and Egyptians and Costa Ricans. We're on the way out. We're almost dead and gone, but nobody I meet wants to face up to it. Nobody seems to get the picture. There are people like you all over this country, marching north onto the formerly frozen tundra in search of the land of milk and honey. I've seen types that think of themselves as the new pioneers, station-wagon cowboys and Winnebago trail blazers. They're sitting around camp fires right now, burning up trees to make smoke and using insect repellant to keep off the bugs. But we're just fighting a rear-guard action against the bugs. The bugs are the ones who are going to inherit the earth. They're the ones who are going to increase and multiply, and we're going to offer them up our bones and rotten flesh to help them along the way. Why hell, we don't even have to wait for death to have our flesh rot away. Look at that woman," and he pointed to Teresa. "Nice tan you've got there. Awfully nice tan indeed. I can even make it out in this bad light. How is it that you're not thinking about skin cancer? I've seen people with that horrible disease. I've seen people so far away from cosmetic surgeons that their faces are rotting right off their skulls. Flesh is falling off them as if they were lepers. And here you are, people like you, catching a few rays as if this was Malibu Beach in 1952. Where's your sense gone to?"

"No harm in a bit of sun," said Mike.

"No harm," Victor echoed. "That's right, no harm. Everybody said that. No harm in a little underarm deodorant in a can. No harm in a few thousand disposable diapers. No harm in clearing a few trees to raise kiwi fruit for the tables of the sated Northern hemisphere. But all those transgressions added up. All those little sins got us where we are today, burning up with our skin rotting off. I'm not a religious man, but if I were, I'd say that we had brought the apocalypse down on our heads. We didn't have to worry about atomic bombs. Those were the big, flashy machines that everybody was too afraid to use anyway. They drew our attention from the little things, those tiny everyday actions that added up to the hellhole we've made for ourselves. It's the small things we should have watched out for. When I think of how I watched kids playing with firecrackers and never thought about the carbon dioxide they were adding to the atmosphere. When I think of the number of times people lit matches for no good, solid reasons, why, it makes me shudder. We should have known, because our own lives were so miserable, that the garbage from our lives was going to add to the misery of the world too."

"My life wasn't miserable," said Margaret.

"Oh yes it was," said Victor, as if he had lived that life himself. "Every life from the very beginning was miserable in its own way. All you have to do is work in an old-folks home, the way I did once, to see how unhappily, how horribly most people end their lives. Saliva dripping down chins and incontinence spoiling their clothes. And even the ones with halfway decent bodies were grim about their lives. What had they been for, anyway, if not to add a little more garbage to the world to help bring it all to an end? Maybe that was really the secret mission of our race, to destroy itself with its own shit. Let's ignore the obvious examples of human folly for a minute. Let's pretend that we can ignore the holocaust, the Armenians. I'm not even talking about the gas chambers and the ovens, the electrodes on the nipple or the penis. Those horrors speak for themselves. I'm saying that every life was, is, and continues to be unhappy. Even this miserable dinner of yours. You've just had a meal over the body of a newly extinct species."

"What's the point of all this?" Alice Waver asked when one of her children cried out in its sleep. She calmed the child and brushed its hair gently with the palm of her hand. But she was afraid and it showed.

"The point is that I am going to drag this detritus of human civilization as far north as I can. And when I get the feeling that the world is really about to end, that the final scene is imminent, I'll build a cairn. It'll be a good cairn too, made with heavy stones. And inside that cairn I'm going to lay down all this garbage along with my body, which is on its way to becoming another piece of garbage too. I'm going to build a memorial to a stupid, selfish, mean and unhappy world. It's going to be a memorial to a world that burned itself up because it loved garbage."

Victor held up a crinkled ball of Saran Wrap, and the plastic film caught the light from the fire and reflected it like a tiny chandelier.

"The man's speaking sense," Lionel whispered. Margaret snorted.

"Victor's so full of shit that it reeks. Any man who tells me that my life hasn't been happy doesn't know a pair of round breasts from a bunch of coconuts."

"Tell us a story, Margaret," Butler asked. He wanted to hear something from her, if only to wipe Victor's words from his mind. He wanted to hear Margaret tell it, so that the gin in his mouth would taste good again. He wanted, at that moment, to think carnal thoughts. He wanted to breathe, and not think of carbon dioxide, but only of air. Margaret obliged him.

"Sit down Mr. Victor Bad News, and I'll tell you a story. That's right, Victor, put down that ball of Saran Wrap or throw it into the fire. You can tell a story later on if you want, but first you listen to mine. Alice, those kids of your asleep? This is a story for adult ears."

Alice nodded.

"It's a story about sex, and about a man who tried to turn it around and make it not as wonderful as it ought to be. It's got nothing to do with CFC gases, and it's got everything to do with living. That's right, Victor. Sit down and listen to this."

REVENGE OF THE PRINCESS
Margaret's Story

This all happened a long time ago, before rubbers became mandatory equipment for a night on the town. In those days, if the woman was on the pill or a man had a vasectomy, that was considered good enough. They even had oral sex then, because nobody had to fear the gremlins in a man's come or a woman's lube. Oh sure, VD was around, and some unlucky people got it, but all it took was a shot of penicillin and you were back on your feet, or on your back, in no time at all.

I know it's hard to picture a world like that now. It sounds like a golden age. So why weren't people hopping in and out of each other's beds? Well, they were and they weren't. Some people were doing it, but others were afraid. Tradition was against it for one thing. You could get a divorce for "sexual infidelity" in those days. It sounds pretty mild when you compare it to the price you pay for fooling around unprotected these days.

What some of you young folk might find harder to believe is that in those days some people took vacations in hot places. The only thing that kept people from going crazy most of the year was the thought of a vacation in November or March, those awful months when it wasn't quite winter yet, or when Spring was supposed to be around the corner, but it felt like it was a lifetime away.

Thelonius was a man who lived for his vacations. For forty-eight weeks of the year he lived on the cheap in Buffalo, but for the four other weeks he and his wife Monique lived like royalty in hot climates. Life in Buffalo chilled them to the bone. Like Sam McGee, they wanted to climb into a furnace, but they wanted to do it in style. Bathing suits had a lot to do with the attraction to hot places. Thelonius loved to see women in bathing suits, preferably topless suits like the ones they wore in Europe. Even better, he liked to see those young girls playing paddle ball on the beach or coming out of the cool water. Tight little tits bouncing and nipples erect.

Monique could look like an ice queen when she walked into the casino in Monaco wearing a low-cut, formal dress. Thelonius held her arm tightly then and wore ascots, which he could only get away with on the continent. He liked the awe in other men's eyes when they looked at his wife. To tell you the truth, it stiffened his cock when other women looked at her. Monique was fond of the attention too, and sometimes she would brush her hand over his ass as he stood beside the gaming table. But she always kept that cool look on her face all the while.

Thelonius loved untouchable women. On the nudist beaches, he always approached the ones who looked stand-offish, and he worked intensely to cajole them up to the sand dunes for quickies or back to the hotel room for longer sessions of sex.

In the early years of their marriage, Monique had been as venturesome as Thelonius, and more than once they had argued in front of their hotel room door as to which of them was going to have use of the room for the afternoon. Monique had even taken part in the various combinations Thelonius had created at the beaches and spas. But Monique tired of these games after a few years, and while she and he agreed that each could do as he pleased, Monique insisted that good taste be preserved in public. She herself was not opposed to the occasional fling, but she was no longer interested in short, passionate embraces in alleyways. Her tastes had become more refined.

Through all their sexual adventures, they continued to love one another. They had carnations on their breakfast table while they drank their *cafe au lait*, and roses and good wine with dinner in the evenings. Often, when they talked, they would bring their heads together as if they were sharing a secret, and Thelonius and Monique seemed to people all around them like new lovers wrapped up in each other and oblivious to the world. They danced each dance as if it were their first, and they looked like travellers while all others looked like tourists.

Life would have been perfect if Thelonius hadn't started to like his "morsels", his young pussy too much. By the time Thelonius was in his late forties, he preferred younger girls with hardly any experience at all.

Thelonius tried to turn his age to his advantage by impressing the young girls with his money, his *savoir faire*, and his expensive hotels. And as he became more aggressive and eager with the young girls, Thelonius slipped lower on Monique's scale of esteem. Broken-hearted girls who banged on their hotel room door lowered Thelonius even further down the scale. He was using girls too young to understand the rules he played by.

Things came to a head one summer when they were staying in the Negresco in Nice. They chose the place because it reminded them of another, more elegant time. Of course the city had not stood still, and it was mostly an amusement park for the young, but some of the old dowager hotels still stood and the Negresco was one of them. They strolled down the Promenade des Anglais as if Britannia still ruled the waves and they were heirs to the empire. Flags fluttered along the beach wall, Kir Royale flowed in the cafes among the palm trees, and they dressed for dinner every night. In the evenings, teenagers settled into sleeping bags on the pebble beach. To Monique they belonged to another, more recent and less elegant era.

They belonged to another era all right, and Thelonius wanted to be a part of it.

Monique observed but did not comment as Thelonius headed out to the pebble beach every morning around eleven. It was already getting too hot by then, but the students were rarely awake much earlier. Girls from Germany, Sweden, and America, all with large knapsacks, were the ones that attracted Thelonius now. Whenever he talked about them in front of Monique, he referred to them as "children".

Thelonius had managed to retain the rarest of commodities in men his age or older. He had a flat stomach to match his graying hair. This, to certain girls, made him look distinguished and sufficiently youthful at the same time. It helped when he said he was a journalist. The profession carried a certain panache for some girls. They imagined him as the foreign correspondent during the six o'clock news, or investigating government skullduggery.

To Thelonius's credit, he never claimed to be single, but to his shame, he hinted that his wife was a problem. He said Monique was a frigid matron who rarely left her room. For Margaret, a freckle-faced nineteen-year-old, this added to Thelonius's allure. She watched him sympathetically as he stared mournfully out to sea when the fishing boats returned for the night. She imagined him torn with anguish over his infidelity to his wife. Margaret bought the whole story when Thelonius talked about how much he admired the fishermen's honest way of life. She covered him gently with a sheet when he fell asleep after making love in her hotel room.

It was wonderful for Margaret, at nineteen years of age, to be the centre of this older man's world. As for Thelonius, it was charming to have a woman so thrilled to be beside him. At least, it was charming for a while. When it ceased to be charming, Thelonius sat Margaret down in a cafe and looked mournfully into her eyes.

"I can't see you any more," he said.

It was a shock to her. She was too young to have seen all the warning signs, the moments of indifference, and the sharp bursts of bad humour. As soon as he said it, she could hear all the cars whizzing by her on the promenade, and she realized she had not been hearing them for all her time with Thelonius. Margaret had her first real vision of impermanence at that moment, and she didn't like it.

"Is it because of your wife?"

He nodded.

"You've got to leave her," Margaret said intensely, and she put her hand on his. It was like putting her hand on a stone.

"She's not well," he said quietly.

"Not well?"

But he did not explain further. He let it be understood that he had an obligation to Monique.

Thelonius planned to lie low for a couple of days. He could always take Monique on a little trip to Italy or St. Paul de Vence. By the time they returned to Nice, Margaret would be gone. None of the backpackers stayed in one place very long.

But Margaret was a little more determined than Thelonius had bargained for. She did not return to her own hotel or pack her bags broken heartedly. She went instead to Monique's hotel room.

"Your husband doesn't love you," Margaret said when Monique opened the door. Monique had been writing a letter on the terrace and the French doors were open. Sheer white curtains fluttered in the sea breeze and a vase of fresh flowers stood on her table.

"Let's not talk in the hall," said Monique. "Come in."

Margaret took the offered seat and waited as Monique phoned down to room service to have some coffee and biscuits brought to the room. Monique's calmness worried Margaret. The elegance and presence of mind made Margaret feel as if she were thirteen years old.

As for Monique, Margaret was the last straw on the back of her patience. The women talked for a while. The conversation went from hot to cold to hot again, but in the end they came to an agreement.

Margaret left the hotel room, and Monique took up Thelonius's suggestion of a two-day trip to St. Paul de Vence.

When Monique and Thelonius returned to Nice, Thelonius scanned the beach and was relieved to find that Margaret had gone. One of her friends said that she had left to visit the Scandinavian countries. Thelonius did a few sit-ups to keep his stomach flat, and headed out to the beach again to find new prey. What he found took his breath away.

Two new women had appeared on the shore, and together they formed a terrible, alluring symmetry. One was dark, with short, almost mannish hair, and the other was blonde and wistful as a late summer's day. Rumour had it that the blonde was a princess, the heir to a lost East European throne, and the dark-haired companion a half sister by illegitimate liaison. They were young, perhaps twenty-one or -two, but they carried themselves with the grace and assurance of women ten years their senior. What were women such as these doing on a public beach?

The royal and the rich were known to exist on the expensive outcroppings of rock that formed exclusive retreats along the Cote d'Azur. But these retreats were behind walls, and the angels of charm and grace who lived behind them never came out except to appear, rarely, at the casinos or finer restaurants. And yet here they were, on towels draped over the pebble beach at Nice, among backpackers and American tourists.

Maybe they were slumming. But if so, why did they never slip off their tops with the other women? The two kept perfectly to themselves, as if the rest of the world did not exist, and requests for lights for cigarettes went unheeded, as did all other attempts to strike up conversation. It was as if no one else existed on the entire shore.

This odd combination of availability and untouchability, their very presence on a public beach, excited Thelonius more than he had ever been excited before. The women carried the combined allure of Monique and the younger girls Thelonius lusted after.

He let himself be seen at a distance. He carried heavy books to the beach to prove that he was a serious type, but he also swam far out to sea to show that he could be physical as well. He kept to himself, rebuffing comments by former friends on the beach, and so he established himself in their eyes as the exclusive type, a kind of mirror image of the twin goddesses. Twice, he felt the princess look at him, and he shuddered with pleasure at the knowledge.

One day the princess came down to the beach alone. Thelonius leaped, gracefully, at the opportunity. When he felt himself being watched, he turned and nodded to her. She smiled the only smile that anyone had ever seen come from her on that shore. As Thelonius approached the princess, half the men on the beach rolled onto their stomachs to hide their erections and regretted that the beach was covered with pebbles. A collective gasp arose when he gathered up both his beach towel and hers, and carried them up to the Promenade with her. He was triumphant, like a man bearing the carcass of a slain deer.

Inside the hotel room, the princess moved with incredible slowness. It teased Thelonius to the point of agony and pleased him at the same time. Here was a woman accustomed to moving with royal grace, and he savoured her charm. He kissed her gently, and she kissed him back. Then she bit his lip lightly, and he liked that as well. When the princess took four soft, silken ropes from a drawer, Thelonius willingly submitted to being undressed and having his wrists and ankles tied to the bed-posts.

"Now for the best part," the princess whispered.

Out from the bathroom came her dark-haired companion, naked and lithe and shining with oil. The companion kissed the princess and undressed her, and the two of them lay down on the bed beside Thelonius. He craned his neck to watch as they licked and sighed and shuddered, and his cock stood straight up like a straining flagpole. The princess and her companion finished their lovemaking and turned to Thelonius with smiles. He tried to restrain his eagerness, but a small "please" escaped from between his lips.

The princess kissed his mouth and the dark-haired beauty wrapped her lips around his cock. Thelonius wondered, briefly, if he was old enough to have a heart attack as the princess teased his tongue out of his mouth and into hers. He felt as if he was falling, and then he felt as if he was floating.

They must have exchanged signals that he was too excited to notice. With simultaneous short, sharp actions, the princess bit his tongue and her companion bit his foreskin.

Thelonius roared and tried to raise himself up, but the ropes were too strong and the knots sure. The princess stuffed a sock into his mouth to quiet him. The two women dressed quickly, took packed suitcases from the closet and left the room without looking back.

Thelonius writhed and raged and tried to see what kind of damage had been done to his cock. He could feel the blood dampening the sheet beneath him. He strained and pushed and eventually managed to get the sock out of his mouth, and then he shouted loudly until a maid and a house detective opened the door with a pass key. Both the maid and the detective had worked in the hotel for many years, and there was nothing they had not seen. Just another sexual game gone sour. They were not even interested. Thelonius's tongue had begun to swell and he was losing his ability to talk. He dressed as quickly as he could, wincing as he pulled his bathing suit over his bleeding cock. He raced out of the hotel room, swearing to kill the women if he found them.

But they were gone.

It seemed to Thelonius that Monique took it all with exaggerated calm. He would have appreciated a little sympathy, even anger, and he was troubled by her indifference. He had barely been able to speak with his swollen tongue, and she seemed more indifferent than it was possible for a woman to be. Thelonius lay silent on his bed for two full days, unable to speak and unable to move because he had refused to take stitches in his foreskin and threw the doctor out when he suggested circumcision as the simplest remedy.

Monique eventually dragged him to a cafe. They were sitting under the palm trees drinking Suze on ice when Margaret appeared and walked over to their table. Thelonius was mortified, but he reasoned that his silence would soon make her leave. He grew even more uneasy when Monique and Margaret greeted each other as if they were old friends.

Margaret asked for news and Monique proceeded to tell the entire story of how Thelonius had had both tongue and cock nipped. Thelonius kept his eyes off the women and stared at the traffic on the road. He felt like shrinking to the floor when they started to laugh. Monique tried to brush her hand over his crotch in the old discreet and familiar way, but it made him wince and jump.

"What's the matter?" Margaret asked, "pussy got your tongue?"

Chapter 2

Butler smiled. He had had a strange anxiety about the night and the dissolution of the company, but now it was going to be all right. They were going to stay by the fire for a while longer.

"That was you in the story," Dianne said to Margaret. "You're the one who planned it all with Monique."

Margaret shrugged her shoulders. "Dear, this story took place decades ago. How old do you think I am?"

Mike was unconsciously rubbing the crotch of his jeans as if he had a wound that was stinging.

They were deep into the night now, thought Butler, as he made his way to his four-wheel drive to get a pen and a notebook to write the stories down. There would be more of them, he was sure, and he did not want to lose any of the words being spoken around the fire. They had to be written down and weighed somehow. Maybe Odds had a scale that measured the weight of words, and if he put Margaret's story onto one side of the balance, it would compensate for the heat from the overblown sun.

"Hey Butler."

He was at the side of his jeep, fumbling with his keys to open the door.

"Wait a second, will you?"

It was Teresa's voice. He could barely make out her figure in the dark. She walked towards him unsteadily, and his heart began to beat a little more quickly.

"What's your first name?" she asked. She had come very close to him, as close as only someone drunk could. Butler had been drinking as well, but even he could smell the gin on her breath as she peered at him, only inches away from his face. Behind the gin there was a feminine scent, not a perfume, but some kind of essence of woman. He had not been this close to a woman for a long time, and her face and her smell brought back memories of Elaine.

"Alban," Butler answered.

And he felt then a great rush in himself, a great desire to take Teresa in his arms and to hold her. She too, seemed to sense what was going on in him, and she turned her head slightly to one side, quizzically, waiting to see what he would do. If only he could be sure, Butler thought, that if he put his arms around her then, she would not pull away or worse, laugh at him. There was always the risk, and as he had gotten older, he had become less and less willing to take any sort of risk. He had become more and more afraid, and as the memory of Elaine welled up in him again, it added to his fear.

Teresa was still very close to him. Waiting. He could feel her breath on his cheek.

Elaine. There was more than the fear of Teresa's pushing him away. Elaine had disappeared through the ice many years before, but he wanted to remain faithful to her. In his fear, Butler grasped at the memory of Elaine as if he were the one who was falling through the ice.

Teresa turned away. With her back to him, she straightened out her hair to go back to the fireside. If he acted quickly then, he might still lay his hands on her shoulders, but he would have to be fast about it.

"Let's go listen some more," Teresa said, and she walked back to the fireside.

Butler watched her disappear into the darkness. A few moments later, her silhouette appeared at the camp fire. Butler followed her sadly.

"Very amusing story," Victor was saying when Butler returned, but Victor's smile looked more like a grimace. "But it veers away from the dark side of things. A story like yours, Margaret, is like a man hitting the remote control of the TV whenever he sees bad news coming on. Much safer to switch to the situation comedies. But this is no comedy we are living through. This end of all things is a time of darkness, and the irony is that the sun is bringing the darkness upon us. Tell me a darker story, Margaret. Tell me about how things really turn out in this miserable world of ours."

"Some fun you are," Margaret began, but Eve interrupted her.

"I think I know what he means," she said. Eve was a quiet woman, Lionel's wife, and the two of them rarely spoke with the others. They were vegetarians, and sometimes they brought sweet bulbs that they had found on the shores of Hudson Bay and they made large stews that they shared with Simon and Alice's children. Eve showed them where the wild thyme grew, and she carried a large stock of Jerusalem artichokes that she planted in the earth around the spring. Jerusalem artichokes did not need much care, she explained to Butler once, and they would grow fast as weeds as long as they had enough water. Food was already a problem, and it was going to get worse. Eve intended to plant Jerusalem artichokes across the North so there would be some source of food when all the others, the people in the South, started their migration. Water was the problem and even though the earth was mucky with the melted permafrost, and any old place looked wet enough at present, she still searched out areas for her plantings that would stay wet even after the earth had dried out in the sun. Places that were near underground sources of water.

And yet for all her freelance gardening, she did not look like a happy woman. Neither she nor Lionel had any hope, it seemed, and they sowed their wilderness gardens in the sure knowledge that within a few years there might be few people left to harvest their crop.

"The women were the winners in your story, Margaret, and much as I like to hear about a man who gets what's coming to him,

it hardly ever turns out that way. Men will kill women and be sainted
for it. I'll tell you a story about a saint. It's typical, too. He was sainted
because he killed a woman. Listen to this."

Butler flipped open his stenographer's book to a blank page, and
got ready to write down Eve's story.

THE HEN AND THE COCK
Eve's Story

This happened a thousand years ago on the pilgrimage route to
Santiago de Compostella in Spain. Compostella was once more
important than Canterbury as a pilgrimage destination. It was
ranked with Rome and Jerusalem and the pilgrims walked down the
Jacobean route from Paris into the North-West of Spain.

Two pilgrims, husband and wife, were walking to Compostella
with their son, a boy who must have been fifteen or sixteen at the time
because he showed the kind of piety that boys that age sometimes
have. He showed the kind of egotism that all men have as well. The
family had been walking for hundreds of kilometres over the past
weeks, and they were weary. They stopped one night at an inn at a
town called Santo Domingo, and there the innkeeper's daughter fell
in love with the boy. She watched him as the family ate dinner, and
brought him soft bread that she had secretly kissed before handing
it over in the hope the boy would fall in love with her too. She tried
to catch his eye whenever she could, and brushed his hand more than
once. But the holiness of the pilgrimage to Compostella and the boy's
piety had blinded him, and he went to his prayers and to bed without
so much as looking twice at the girl.

But her attraction to him was so great that she crept up to his bed
while he was sleeping and began to murmur in his ear. The boy
smiled in his sleep, and then he seemed to awaken, and the girl
climbed into his bed and embraced him. Suddenly he was really
awake, and he cried out against the woman who had come to steal
his holy chastity. The girl caressed him, begging him to take her, but
his accusations grew so loud that she became afraid and fled the room,
conscious of the snickers she heard in the hall, aware of the crude
obscenities whispered after her by guests less fastidious than the boy.

She hid, in her shame, among the barrels of wine in the cellar, both fists held tightly against her mouth to prevent herself from crying out with anguish. But as she sat there, hour after hour, the anguish turned to anger, and she came to hate the boy who had turned her out of his bed. In the very early hours, well before dawn, she went to her room and took from its hiding place a gold coin she had had for a long time. Her father knew of this coin, but he did not know where she kept it. Then, before anyone had awakened, she crept back into the boy's room and hid the coin in the bottom of his sack.

In the morning, the boy said nothing, but wore an air of disdain and superiority about him. The little egotist had proved himself so pious. The girl averted her eyes from his and even stared at the floor, as if in shame. These painful moments did not last long because there were still hundreds of kilometres to go to Compostella, and the family hurried on its way.

Think how surprised they were when, a few hours later, they were overtaken by armed men on horseback who explained nothing, but tore off their sacks and began to search them. The soldiers found the coin and accused the boy of being a thief. The entire family was dragged back to the town where public opinion was strongly against them. Among the so-called pilgrims, there were always thieves and cheats, and the townspeople were satisfied at finally catching one of them. No protestations of innocence did any good. The boy was quickly tried and hanged.

The parents mourned the death of their son and could not bear to look at his body swinging from the gibbet. They may even have been unaware that it was the girl who had hidden the coin in their son's sack, for the boy, in his self-righteousness, had not even accused her. She, in turn, was not happy. How could she be? But the lack of happiness was filled by a sense of satisfaction and of wrong well-punished.

The parents went on to Compostella, sad and broken. There they prayed for the boy's soul. At least they could be sure he was in heaven. They dreaded their return to Santo Domingo, but they had to see that their son's burial had been properly taken care of. Now imagine their surprise when, on arrival, they learned that the boy's body was still hanging from the gibbet weeks later. It was painful to go there, but they went nevertheless, to pray at what they expected to be the rotting remains of their son. But no sooner were they on their knees than they heard the boy speak. "Mother and father," he said, "My faith and Santiago's intervention with God have saved me. Go to the mayor and have him cut me down that I might walk among men again."

Their joy was blunted by fear and shock. How could they be sure that the body had not been taken over by some demon that was taunting them? But the boy spoke again, soothed their fears, and filled them with happiness. The parents hurried to the house of the mayor, clamored at his door and rushed in over the startled servants to find the mayor sitting at his dinner table. He was a big, fat, reasonable man who liked food and wine and peace. He had on his table a roast hen and a roast cock, and beside them two pitchers of fine wine from the Oja vineyards. And now, here he was, confronted by this hysterical, barely coherent couple. The servants were gathered at the door, and he could hear the noise of an assembling crowd beneath his window. When the parents told their story, he pretended to believe it, if only to be left alone for a while to start his dinner. But when they demanded that he come immediately and cut down their son, he became impatient. "Your son," he said, "is no more alive than this hen and this cock on my table."

The mayor was looking at the parents when he said this, but a gasp from the servants made him look down. The roast hen and roast cock stood up from their plates, and then flew around the room once and out the window. The crowd below the window could be heard crying out in awe as the birds flew slowly away.

A great assembly of people rushed to the gibbet, a ladder was raised, and the soldier who held the sword said later that a great numbness came over his arm as he cut the rope. The boy fell to the ground, and then raised himself to his knees, loosened the noose around his neck, and prayed in thanksgiving. The people around him fell to their knees too as word of what was happening was whispered back through the crowd.

And there the official story ends. To this day, in Santo Domingo there is a glass-front coop at the back of the church where a hen and a cock are kept, and these birds cackle and crow even during mass.

I say it's the end of the official story, but I know there had to be more. There's no mention of the innkeeper's daughter after that, but I can guess what happened. I can see the boy finally rising to his feet after his prayers, the cut end of the rope still around his neck. He points out the girl hiding among the others in the crowd. She dreads the inevitable moment. The boy tells the story of her treachery in a voice hoarse from the pressure of the rope around his neck; the townspeople turn on her; the girl tries to escape, but someone grasps her by the hair and drags her in front of the multitude.

Now the people want her blood. They feel self-righteous and eager to show their desire to fulfil God's will, all the moreso because in their hearts they remember how joyfully they sent the boy to the gibbet forty days before. The remains of the rope on the gibbet are re-knotted, and when the mayor sees that the crowd wants blood, he quickly pronounces the girl guilty. It is she who now climbs the ladder, and it is she who is pushed off, and it is her body that swings from the rope. The boy, his family, and the townspeople return to the town to celebrate, and the mayor can't help but rejoice at the miracle his town has been blessed with. He knows word of it will spread throughout Europe, and rich clerics and nobles will flock to the town, their purses filled with gold.

You see, it's the girl who excites my sympathy. For this story to have happened at all, she had to exist and become the tool of the legend and its ultimate victim. I suppose you could say that God steered her hand when she hid the coin in the boy's sack, much as God kept the boy alive at the end of the rope.

Chapter 3

"Now that's my kind of story," said Victor. He had dragged the litter closer to the fire, and he kept a hand on one of the arms as if it were a particularly important piece of baggage, and he did not want a thief to steal it. The firelight was playing games with his features, darkening his eye sockets and exaggerating his cheekbones until his face looked like that on an elongated demon. "That story has more truth in it than the first, more power. Misery my friends, the world is full of misery."

"You make me want to puke," said Margaret, and she stood up to give Victor a dressing-down. Her desire was promptly fulfilled. She had been drinking gin and tonic steadily for over six hours and had consumed a large amount of nearly indigestible bear meat as well. Even her iron stomach could not take all this abuse. She did puke. Copiously, and with great abandon, turning from left to right and terrifying her fireside companions who scrambled away. Victor received a fine spray across his eyeglasses. When she had finished one long volley, her eyes rolled up in her head and she fell back onto the earth unconscious. The ground shook as if a wooly mammoth had just been felled.

"It's disgusting!" said Eve,

But Alice Waver just sighed. "Puke doesn't scare me. Once you have kids, puke and shit become as common as air and water. Simon, you haul Margaret over to that stone and make sure her mouth's pointing down so if she pukes again it won't go back down her throat. Wipe her face and cover her with a blanket. I'll take care of the rest." Alice brought a shovel from somewhere and cleared the ground around them as best she could, and then heaped some earth on the damp spots so the place looked clean again. Barely a hint of gastric juices wafted over the company as they settled back into their places.

"What are you doing?" Teresa asked Butler as he made a few notes on the last story.

"Writing down the stories."

"Going to publish them in the New Yorker?" Leopold asked, and some of them laughed grimly. The *New Yorker* had disappeared along with New York, except for the tallest buildings, whose upper storeys still poked above the waves.

Butler chuckled with the others and closed his notebook. Notes tended to make speakers nervous, and that was the last thing he wanted to do.

"How about your story?" Teresa asked.

"I don't have a story," Butler protested. "I just write down what the others say."

"Sure you have a story," said Teresa. "Everybody has a story."

And Butler sensed then that she was punishing him. He should have taken her in his arms when they were standing beside the car, but now it was too late. She was angry with him for being so stupid. And yet, perhaps if he told her about Elaine, she might understand. He hesitated because there were so many strangers by the fire, and he was not sure he wanted to talk in front of them. But he wanted another chance with Teresa, and this might be his only opportunity.

OUT OF THE GARDEN
Butler's Story

I was halfway through my studies in the seminary when I brought Elaine to the weekend retreat at the Jesu Cristu Gardens in Western Ontario. We had developed an almost perfect platonic relationship

over the last few weeks, and I thought that the imperfections could
be straightened out over that weekend. You see, I really wanted to be
a priest, but I really wanted Elaine as well. I had this fantasy that she
might want to become a nun, and we could be a kind of religious
teaching team. I really believed it could work, if only she stopped
saying "fucking this" and "fucking that."

The Gardens were on an old farm in Grey County, and they were
surrounded by a lot of abandoned farms that had been sheer misery
to their owners for three or four generations after they were cut out
of the forest. The poor earth was terrible. Cobblestones rose up out
of the ground every spring and chipped or broke the toughest steel
on the toughest plow. But not at the Jesu Cristu Gardens. The land
there was an oasis of rich earth that the Jesu Cristu Brothers had
covered with flowers. Only the tulips were up then, because it was
early spring, but the beds were planted all over that quarter section,
among the woods and down by the river. There were paths that
wound about the garden, the kinds of paths that were supposed to
encourage reflection. And at the centre of it all stood the centre itself,
two long strips, like motels, that had been laid across one another to
form a cross. The residence rooms were in the four wings and the
meeting rooms were in the centre, where the wings met.

Elaine almost got us into trouble the first hour she was there.

"Come into my room," she said, "I want to show you something."

"Not the women's wing, Elaine, and not in your room," I said.
"We're supposed to be getting away from that sort of thing."

"This is innocent. I fucking promise you."

I followed her into the women's wing feeling a little nervous. It
was not that men were not allowed there, but it made me feel as if
I had to be more careful, as if the floor was made of very thin glass.
I followed her into her room, which was small and simple, with only
a single bed, a closet and a writing table. The walls were painted
cinder blocks.

"Now close the door," she said.

"Absolutely not."

"There's a card on the back of the door that I want to show you."

"You can tear it off and show it to me without closing the door.
What's that?" I asked, pointing to her desk and trying to divert her
attention.

"My ghetto blaster."

"You don't bring one of those to a retreat."

"Why not?"

"It's just not in spirit of things."

"I've got some great gospel music."

"Well play it quietly. Couldn't you just have brought a Walkman?"

Instead of answering my question, she swung the door shut and leaned against it.

"Jesus Christ Elaine, open that door or we'll both be in trouble."

"I thought priests didn't swear. Relax, will you? I just want you to read what it says on the plaque, and then I'll open the door again."

"These walls are like paper. I bet your neighbours can hear every word I'm saying."

"Sister Mary-Arthur is seventy-eight years old. She's my neighbour. Deaf as a post. Just look at the plaque, will you, and then you'll be free."

I read the plaque.

SILENCE
Silence is the great healer
Silence calms the soul and prepares the way for the Holy Spirit
Silence is a gift from God
Silence will make your retreat meaningful
Silence is the right of your neighbours--respect it
God's voice can only be heard in silence.
Go quietly amid the noise and haste

"What about it?" I asked.

"It's kitsch. I hate kitsch."

"Catholicism is fifty percent kitsch. We wouldn't be Catholics if we didn't have statues and plaques. You should know all that by now. Didn't you have a glow-in-the-dark rosary when you were a little kid?" I was still facing the door and she slipped her arms around my waist. I could hear movement in the next room, so I was not about to move suddenly or say anything too loud.

"Elaine."

"Hmm?" She was nuzzling my back.

"Elaine, there's a window behind you, and if anyone is looking through it, I'm finished."

"How come priests can't get married?"

"We can talk about it another time. Just get your hands off me."

"Oh Albee, forgive me, for I know not what I do," and with that, her arms, which had been around my waist, began to drop slightly, and her hands, which had been around my stomach, started to drop as well.

There was a knock at the door.

"Who is it?" Elaine called out.

No one answered, and the knock was repeated.

"Quick, into the closet," Elaine whispered, and she opened her closet door.

"I'm not going in there!" I whispered back furiously.

Elaine shrugged. "Okay, I'll just open the door to the hall then."

I slipped into the closet and shut the door behind me. It was filled with her clothes and smelled of her perfume. I heard Elaine open the door. It was sister Mary Arthur.

"Yes Sister... I was getting dressed... No sister... I wouldn't dream of bringing a man in and closing the door..." And then more quietly, so I'm sure that Sister Mary Arthur did not hear a word. "You must have ESP, you old virgin."

I heard her close the door, but my blood froze when Elaine called out again. "Hello Father Abelard! Going for a walk? Yes, I just saw you through my window. Want to see some of my new lingerie?" I heard her pull the curtains shut.

"Just kidding," she said when she opened the closet door.

The weekend was not turning out as I had planned. Father Abelard was reading a book in the meeting hall as I passed through it on the way to my room.

"Using a new cologne?" he asked.

"Same old stuff. Why?"

"Better change brands," he said, looking at me over the eyeglasses that he had let slip down on his hawk's nose. He could smell human failings at twenty paces. "You smell like a woman, Butler. We don't want our priests smelling like pansies. Think of yourself as a soldier for God and buy your cologne accordingly. What kind of impression do you think that would make in a confessional?"

There were about sixty of us who met in the meeting-hall that night. A few priests and nuns and several seminarians. Mostly, though, it was middle-aged women with a sprinkling of men. Two young couples, pious pairs who were newlyweds, and Elaine. I did not sit beside her. My folding chair was against the wall and hers was in the middle. Father Abelard was going to be the first of three speakers that night, and he sat on a couch with a coffee table in front of him. Father Abelard did not go in for casual meetings, and I think he would have preferred a lectern. The rest of the priests were in civies, but Father Abelard wore an old-fashioned soutane.

"I was asked to speak first tonight," he began, "so the ones who followed me could make my words more palatable."

People looked at one another uneasily, and a rustle moved through the small crowd.

"The purpose of this retreat is to make you more comfortable with your belief. That's what Father Jimmy reminded me of just before we began. I'm not going to do that. It seems to me that this whole culture of ours is bent on making us so comfortable that our backsides are becoming our strongest muscles. Before the others talk to you tonight, I want to tone up our spiritual muscles. It's time for a little moral workout.

"The walls of hell are three thousand miles thick. So begins one of the homilies in a famous writer's book. This is the kind of statement that makes modern man laugh, and yet maybe we should think about it for a moment. What does it mean to say that the walls of hell are three thousand miles thick? Why simply this, that there is no escape from hell. It is permanent."

Father Abelard used no notes. He stared hard at his audience. Sometimes he let his gaze rest for a long while on some poor soul whose sins seemed to grow in magnitude the longer Father Abelard stared.

"Hell is not a popular subject any more. It makes us uneasy. We wonder if God would really consign us to perpetual suffering for deeds that seem so insignificant in the larger scale of things. I am thinking of lust, for example. The modern man claims that lust is an animal instinct over which he has no control, or even worse, that lust is somehow 'natural', and giving in to it is a normal extension of our animal natures. Modern man finds it hard to believe that an all-loving God would make him burn in hell, fry until his skin turned into pustulent blisters and the blisters broke and the fires made them form again. Modern man cannot believe that his heart would be pierced by thousands of thin, cold needles while the heart continued to beat in perpetual agony. Modern man finds it hard to believe that his fingernails would be torn from his hands, only to grow back and be torn out again. Modern man asks, *Would God really do that to me?*

"The bible tells us the answer. You bet He would."

The fires of hell made Father Abelard warm to his subject.

"And the reason He would do all this is because he sees the true nature of the sins which we want to gloss over and make inconsequential. He sees the moral rot, the evil ..."

My neighbour nudged me and passed me a note. The whole row of listeners was looking at me as I opened it up. It was from Elaine.

"This guy's been watching too many horror movies."

I just stared at the note and nodded my head as if she was sending me her view on an epistle to the Corinthians. By now Father Abelard had noticed everyone was looking at me, and he looked as well, but he did not stop talking. He had digressed from lust to sloth, which was his minor subject, but now he returned to his major.

"Of all the sins that our modern man is guilty of, and there are many of them, certainly lust must be the most prevalent, the most fashionable at this time. Films, and television, and advertising are built around the iconography of sex. Breasts sell beer and rumps sell jeans, and no one pauses to think of the absurdity of this situation. Breasts and rumps and all the other modern false gods are no more than body parts. Think for a moment, of using feet to sell cars, noses to sell ice cream or elbows to sell bicycles. The very concept is absurd, it is laughable. And yet Modern Man has allowed himself to be seduced by body parts that are usually covered, and whose baring has become somehow exciting."

Somebody in the audience laughed, but Father Abelard gave him a hard look. Father Abelard meant absurd, not funny, and he did not like it when any of his audience missed the point.

"And I insist on the term body parts, because our iconography of sex has eliminated the human being. We are asked not to be attracted to another human, but to a part of that human, a breast, a shoulder. Could you imagine falling in love with someone because of particularly beautiful finger?"

Elaine snorted back a lewd laugh.

"And this sin of lust, this absurd desire for body parts, will be punished severely, as much because it is a failure of the intellect as anything else. God loves simplicity, but he hates stupidity, and this love of body parts is the vilest form of stupidity possible. And this brings me back to the idea of hell again, which, you will remember, has walls three thousand miles thick. How many of you have ever burned yourselves? Surely everyone has done so at some time in his life, but the human mind wants to forget pain, so few of us can remember exactly what the pain was like. Let me remind you of it a little."

Father Abelard took a lighter from its place on the coffee table. It was one of those disposable jobs that you can pick up at any corner store. He lit the lighter, held it up and asked,

"Who will volunteer to put his finger in the flame?"

No one stirred.

"I promise you a foretaste of the pain. Does no one want to know a little of what hell will be like?"

Everybody was looking at the small flame that leaped up when he illuminated the lighter, but nobody was going to volunteer to put his finger in it. The audience watched the tiny flame and it fascinated them, as if it were a snake that the old priest had charmed. Father Abelard thrust his own finger into the flame.

"Already it is very painful and every nerve in my body is begging me to pull my finger out. But I can not. I am in hell now, and I can not remove my finger, nor the rest of my body from the flame."

He was sweating suddenly, and the beads showed up on his forehead. I wanted to reach forward and pull his finger out of that flame, and I'm sure the others felt the same way.

"My finger is beginning to blister. Imagine this, that I am burning because I was seduced by a body part. I am letting my finger burn, you see, and you ask yourselves why I am letting this happen. God too, must wonder why the lustful thrust themselves so happily into the flames."

He put out the flame.

"Have I made my point?"

He certainly had, but he continued to talk for another half hour at least, and the gesture had concentrated our minds enormously.

There was a glass of water on the coffee table in case any of the speakers needed a drink. Father Abelard kept his finger submerged in the water for the remainder of his talk.

The second speaker was Father Jimmy himself, the organizer of the retreat. He was dressed in a green polo shirt that had tiny crossed golf clubs sewn onto the left breast. He was in his early fifties, with thinning blonde hair and gold-rimmed eyeglasses and a pleasant face.

"Father Abelard is certainly a hard act to follow, and I'm sure he has given us a picture of hell that will stay in our minds for some time. I might remind you though, that the demonstration he put on for you should not be repeated in your own homes. It's not the kind of thing that we like to encourage. Use sackcloth and ashes if you must do mortification."

This got a titter from the crowd, and Father Jimmy smiled to show he approved.

"Much as Father Abelard's Modern Man has his faults, we sometimes have to use the images of modernity to express our ideas. And what could be more modern than the car? Now I'd like to put it to you this way. Most of us these days like to think of ourselves as drivers. We get behind the wheel of our automobile and drive off. But we know that Jesus is with us. He is always with us, yet he is usually in the back seat. As we drive through our lives, he gives advice about the sharper turns, sometimes tells us when it's unwise to pass, and always lets us know when the pavement is wet. This is fine, but all of us get annoyed with backseat drivers, and I put it to you, that after a while we tend to ignore the advice coming from the back seat. We begin to think that we can handle those sharp turns on our own.

"What's the solution? Do we stop and ask Jesus to get out?

"I'd like to offer a better solution. I'd like to suggest that we change places. Why not let Jesus do the driving for a while? Why can't you just sit down in the back and relax? Jesus knows the route to go and he never gets that white line fever."

"But is Jesus covered by insurance?" Elaine called out. A couple of people laughed and a few looked shocked, but Father Jimmy did not bat an eyelid. He just smiled his smile.

"Jesus is insured by God the Father and God the Holy Spirit. They specialize in covering all risks."

The crowd laughed then. Father Jimmy was a card, and he went on being a card for another half hour.

Sister Cecily was the last speaker that night, one of those modern nuns with an upbeat smile whose only sign of her order was a gold cross around her neck. That was not much of a sign, because gold crosses were as popular in singles' bars as they were in the convent. She wore a loose blue skirt and a matching blouse and she was ageless. She could have been thirty or fifty, and the only lines on her face were from smiling. I wondered whether Elaine couldn't be like her. Sister Cecily talked about love, one of her favorite themes, but the best she could ever do was make you think of your sister or mother. I mean she talked about that kind of love.

When the meeting started to break up, I slipped outside for a little reflection before Elaine could corner me. I needed some time on my own, to think. The paths had gas lamps at hundred foot intervals, and I followed one of the lighted ways to a rock garden where I sat down on a bench. It was a warm spring night and there must have been a funny microclimate in the garden, because the lilacs were in bloom already when everywhere else it was still only tulips. The lilacs gave the garden a heady, rich odour that it made it hard for me to concentrate. I kept getting distracted by the smell.

I was trying to imagine what I could do to earn a living if I didn't become a priest. I would have to do something. That was the frightening part. While I was in the seminary, my entire future was planned out for me. I could see myself at thirty and I could see myself at sixty, and the knowledge of my future was somehow comforting. I knew it would not be easy to be a priest, but I also knew that the entire way of life had appealed to me. Had appealed. Now I was not so sure.

"You're looking kind of sad," she said, and I did not even move aside as she sat down close. What was the point? I had no more need of propriety.

"Got a light?" she asked.

"I thought you quit smoking."

"I did. I just thought I might fry my finger for the sake of my soul."

I didn't laugh. There was something about Father Abelard's strangeness that I wanted to defend. It was as if, now that I had a premonition I would be leaving the priesthood, I had to defend all priests more than before. While I was one of them, I could take the criticism, but now that I was leaving them, they had to be protected.

"He's a good man," I said.

"He's a fucking weirdo."

"Jesus Christ Elaine, your dirty mouth is inappropriate here."

"I'm inappropriate here," she answered mournfully, and the tone set me back. She was supposed to be upbeat as usual. I was the one who was supposed to be depressed.

"Well the crack about insurance didn't go over that well," I said.

"I can't help it Albee. I'm just not cut out for this stuff. This whole weekend kind of takes the zip out of me, you know? If I had to cook a meal for this crowd, I'd make it potato pancakes and sour cream. Heavy. No imagination. Bland."

"I like potato pancakes," I said.

"So do I, but I couldn't live on them. Anyway, if this is what you've gotten yourself into, then I guess I'll have to leave it to you. I can't go this way with you."

"You're right," I said. In retrospect, I guess she thought I meant I intended to stay in the priesthood, but I'd meant the opposite. I could hear Elaine sniff. "Fucking lilacs give me a runny nose. Got a Kleenex?"

"Yeah," and I reached for the inside breast pocket of my windbreaker, but the zipper caught at the sleeve once I had my hand inside, and I couldn't get it out.

"You stuck?" she asked.

"I can't get the sleeve loose."

"Here, let me give it a try." But nothing she could do made any difference. She pulled and tugged, but the sleeve would not come out. I felt like a man with one arm in a strait jacket.

"I'll try it from the inside," she said, and she knelt down in front of me and put one hand up the front of my jacket and tried to pull down the zipper. This was the position Father Abelard found us in.

"I knew it would come to this," he said, "as soon as I saw both of you were gone. Let me knock some sense into your head, Butler," and he punched me in the jaw. The blow knocked me over the backless bench, and onto the ground, but Elaine was still stuck in my jacket. We were all tangled, and Elaine was on one side and Father Abelard on the other. He opened his arms wide and boxed both Elaine's ears.

"You whore of a misguided women. You serpent!"

"Fuck off, Father," she shouted, and she raised her free arm to fend off, imperfectly, another box on the ears.

"Father Abelard," I pleaded. "It's not how it looks!" and for my protestations I got another rock-hard punch across the jaw, and the force of it made my jacket zipper break and released me and and Elaine.

"This is tough love, Butler. I'm driving her out for your own good."

"You're not driving her anywhere, you crazy old man," and I pushed him aside when he tried to box Elaine's ears again.

"You dare strike an officer?" Father Abelard raged. He'd been an army chaplain once, and the past must have been returning to him. He looked around desperately, and finally pulled up a stake that the gardeners had attached to a sapling. He raised it over his head and wielded it like a fiery sword.

"Out! both of you, away from this seat of God!"

"It's only a fucking bench," Elaine protested, but Father Abelard was swinging his stake like a wild man, and the two of us began to back off. But that wasn't good enough for him. He kept coming at us, and when we finally turned and ran hand in hand, he came after us. I never thought the old coot had enough wind in him to walk up a flight of steps, but he charged after us like an enraged bull, and we tore across a field.

He wouldn't let up. Elaine and I ran to a fence on the edge of the property, and stumbled across the top of it into an abandoned neighbouring field. I was ready to run another mile if we had to, but the fence seemed to stop the old man.

"Go into the wilderness!" he shouted, "and never come back in here again."

"What about my clothes?" Elaine said.

By this time, all the effort had caught up with him, and Father Abelard leaned against his stake and puffed hard until he caught his breath.

"I never liked you Butler. I could smell the sensuality in you from day one. I'll pack all your things. You can pick them up at the seminary after you speak to Father Abelle. Now go!"

And he stood there like a guard to the gates of paradise. There would be no way around him, no way to get to Father Jimmy.

"Come on Albee," said Elaine. "Let's leave this Looney Tune behind."

"But how'll we get back to town?"

"We'll hitch a ride." And she took my hand and lead me into the field.

"No point trying to hitch hike until morning," Elaine said after we'd gone a hundred yards.

"So what'll we do?"

"Wait here until morning," she said, and she sat down on a stone.

"Simple as that?" I asked.

"Don't see any other choice."

I sat beside her for a while, thinking mostly about how my reputation was going to be mud. Not that it mattered much any more. Elaine was strangely quiet, which was unusual for her.

And it was funny, because after I while I stopped feeling bad and began to feel good. A kind of hilarity was coming over me, an exhilaration. I wished for a while that Elaine would put her arm around me, or sidle up to me. And then I understood that there was no reason for me to be passive about it any more. I put my arm over her shoulders.

"About fucking time," she said.

"You keep using that word."

"Fucking?"

"Yeah."

"Instead of just talking about it, why don't we do it for once?"

I wasn't quite ready for it then, but in addition to experience, Elaine had a wealth of patience.

Chapter 4

"I don't get it," said Mike. "I can understand you wanting the girl - that's normal. But what took you so long to go for her?"

Butler's face was burning. He had never told the story to anyone before, but there was something about the night that was bringing out secrets. The warm glow of the flame was making them tell their stories.

"But how did it end?" Victor asked.

"What do you mean, how did it end?" Butler said. "I told you how it ended."

"Where's Elaine?" Victor asked.

"That's his business," Margaret shot back. She was leaning up on one elbow underneath the blanket that Alice had laid on her. Margaret had drunk enough gin to knock over a bull, but it had only laid her low for half an hour.

"But it's not a story if it doesn't have an ending," Dianne complained.

"The woman's right," said Victor. "Where is Elaine?"

"In the heaven of former lovers," said Margaret forcefully before Butler could speak up. "She's gone into the photo album of his heart, you creeps. Let her stay there where she belongs, without the sordid ending. Nobody wants to hear about the loss of lovers." She giggled, but the laugh was husky. "I want to hear about how you find them, not how you lose them, so leave Elaine's ghost in peace."

"Where is Elaine?" Victor insisted.

Butler did not want to tell them, those faces around the fire, but he felt as if he owed it to the circle to bring the story to its end.

"Gone," Butler said.

"We know she's gone," Victor shot back. "If she wasn't gone, she'd be sitting beside you now. Did she end up in someone else's bed, or did you? Did she get bored with your spiritual hairsplitting, or did her dirty mouth lose its appeal? Did she finish up in housecoat and slippers watching daytime TV beside an overflowing ashtray? What happened to her?"

Where did Victor get his authority, Butler wondered. How could this new addition to the fireside make such pressing demands? He did not know, but he gave in anyway.

"She's gone."

Victor snorted. "We all know that. Where did she go?"

"Through the ice," said Butler.

"I left the seminary. We married. She kept on studying and I went to work as a fishing writer. It was a funny job for an ex-seminarian, but it was all right for us. I took Elaine with me on most of my fishing trips, when she wasn't in the middle of exams, and she'd take her books with her. She could read over the hum of a boat motor when I was trolling, and she brought along a folding chair to keep at riverside when I had to wade. She would have done better to stay at home the way things turned out.

"I was doing a story on ice-fishing. Funny, when I think of it now, because it was the last year enough ice formed on Lake Simcoe to hold a snowmobile's weight. Five years later, the Lake wasn't even freezing over at all any more. The story I was doing was going to be history faster than I had ever imagined, like a story on the last buffalo hunt. And Elaine came with me.

"Simcoe's a big lake, about fifty miles north of Toronto. It had a lot of cottages around it and marinas, so it wasn't exactly wilderness fishing, unless you counted the lake itself as a kind of self-contained wilderness. It was big, you see, so big that once you got out onto the water or the ice, you soon lost sight of the shore. It might as well have been a freshwater ocean in the summer, and the high arctic in the winter time. Treacherous as the arctic too, and that's what worried Freddy Macgregor when Elaine and I showed up.

Freddy ran an ice-fishing business, or at least he was trying to. He had fifty huts on the ice and in better times he had each of them filled with four fishermen at forty dollars a head. At those rates he'd been bringing in seven thousand five hundred every twelve hours. But to make the business go, he needed two things - fish and solid ice. Both were giving out. Just to add a little extra agony, the weather was getting unpredictable as well. Forecasts weren't much good any more, and a thaw could come in that made the ice unsafe in twelve hours. Freak snowstorms blew for days at a time, and when they did, he couldn't let his workers head onto the ice. If he had guests on those kinds of days, they just had to sit tight in their ice huts for twenty-four or forty-eight hours until the snow blew away. Freddy had food and lots of fuel for the oil stoves in the huts, so nobody froze or starved, but two or three days on the ice were more than most fishermen could take. They weren't coming back in the numbers they had before. The fish were getting more mysterious too. The year before, not a single lake-trout had been caught at Freddy's, and word about bad fishing gets out pretty fast.

Freddy was glum when he met Elaine and me at the shore.

"It's getting ready to blow," he said, and sure enough the snow-clouds were hanging heavy over the lake.

"Then you'd better get us out there fast," I told him. "My deadline is three days away and I don't have time to make alternate plans."

"You could get stranded out there."

"We're ready for it," Elaine said. She had half a dozen books to read and a big picnic hamper full of food. Smoked eel, tacos, "oeufs en gelee". Freddy took us out on the ice himself. He wasn't letting any other fishermen out that day, so he had plenty of time. He used the big covered snowmobile, and he talked over the roar of the engine as he took us far out onto the lake.

"The fishing's been lousy," Freddy said, "so I've moved the huts a few times. If you don't get a bite after an hour or two, move to another hut, fire up the stove and try it there. Watch out for the old fishing holes though, because the ice hasn't frozen up hard over them yet. I stuck poles in the snow by the old holes so you don't go tumbling in. Not that you'd have to worry about fitting in one," he said, and he nudged me in the side. My belly had started to grow after all the good food Elaine was giving me.

The snow started to come down just as we reached the first hut in a string of fifty set thirty yards apart in a wide semi-circle. We tossed our equipment onto the ice and Freddy shouted a few last words above the roar of the snowmobile engine.

"If the snow comes up heavy, stay in one hut and don't move except to relieve yourself. If you start wandering on this lake in the snow, you'll get lost and freeze to death. There's enough fuel to keep you going for at least two days. There's a shovel inside, and you've got to dig out the snow every hour or so or you'll get trapped inside when a snow bank builds up against the door. Gotta run." He slammed shut his plastic door, flipped the latch, and headed back the three miles to shore. Elaine and I watched him until the machine disappeared into the white. We heard the roar of the machine for a while after that, but then the snow swallowed it up and we were in the silence.

We didn't move for a bit. The flakes were coming down thick, but leisurely, and they settled on Elaine's long lashes. She looked pretty. I wish I could remember more about the look on her face then, but all I remember is the prettiness.

Freddy had prepared a big six-man fishing hut for us because business wasn't exactly roaring and the big huts were more comfortable. Each of the benches was long, and you could lie down for a snooze on the foam cushion if you got tired. I liked it in the ice huts. There was the smell of stove oil from the tiny metal box that burned your hand if you touched it. But the light was best of all. Ice huts didn't have big windows in them, so it was usually dim inside, and the main source of light seemed to come from the holes in the ice between the two benches. Fishermen would sit facing each other, you see, like men in a waiting room, but there were about six feet between them, and the floor was cut out. The ice was usually a couple of feet thick, and a strange blue light came out of the cut sides and cast a glow on the interior. It was like being in a diving bell and sinking into a bottomless electric blue. You couldn't see the lake bed when you looked down because it was far too deep, over a hundred feet, but you couldn't help peering down into that colour as if it were some kind of crystal ball.

I have gone over the scene hundreds of times in my mind, but I can't seem to find the detail that would explain what happened later. Elaine and I had only been married a few years, and we still lived in a kind of glow. Sure we fought, who doesn't? But I had no sense of anything wrong, I mean deeply wrong, between us. And she always seemed so tough. I thought she'd be much tougher than me if we ever got into a tight spot.

I set up a couple of balances that held the lines and tipped up whenever a fish struck. That left my hands free and I could help Elaine put out the food. It was warm inside the hut, so we opened the door and watched the snow coming down as we ate. And we talked about where we were going to live when Elaine finished her studies. I travelled for my job anyway, but she was going to look for a teaching job eventually, and we would have to move to whatever place offered her one. Our horizons seemed so vast then. Elaine toyed with leaving the continent altogether and going some place exotic. She worried that it might cost me my job, because although I could live anywhere in North America, I couldn't very well write a monthly column out of Dusseldorf or Sienna. I didn't care. Our world was complete wherever the two of us were.

There was no wind. It seemed strange that a blizzard should have no wind. If the temperature had been a little higher, we would have had rain, but as it was, the thick wet flakes kept falling and piling up higher and higher on our doorstep. It became oppressive, somehow, and I closed the door eventually and watched my lines as Elaine read her books by the weak light of the small window. We hadn't turned on the Coleman lamp because we didn't like the loud hiss it made, so we sat together in that blue light as the world outside was undergoing its strange transformation. Only about three miles away there were cottages standing shoulder to shoulder on hundred thousand dollar lots. People watched TV and kids made snowmen on the front yards, but we were in our small world of two in that miniature wilderness on the frozen lake.

My lines began to twitch and I started to pull up freshwater herring no more than eight inches long. Elaine looked over her book and laughed at me, because I was hauling them up like mad and tossing them outside to freeze on the ice. I had to move fast to keep my lines baited, you see. There is no story in freshwater herring because the fish are too small, but sometimes whitefish or the really big lakers come after the shoals of herring, so I had to keep my line down to get a big fish that would make the right kind of ending to a good story.

"Why don't you just write a twenty-pound laker into the story even if you don't catch one?" Elaine asked.

"That would be new journalism. It's not for fishing writers," I said. I was short-tempered, made uneasy by the snow falling outside and desperate to get a really big fish.

"I'm going out for a pee," Elaine said.

"Don't wander away," I told her as I pulled up another line. "Get lost and you'll freeze out there."

"I promise I'll keep my backside pressed against the side of the hut," she said. "You'll be able to hear me."

She left the door open as she stepped outside into the snow. I didn't even see her go, because just then my other balance tipped up, and when I began to haul in the line, I knew that I had something good on the end. There weren't many lakers left by that time, and this one was going to be big. I let him pull the line out slowly to tire himself, and he did it. I slipped on a glove because I might get the line twisted around my hand and I didn't want a burn or a dislocated finger. I played him for a long time, hauling him up higher when he grew weak, and letting him take off when he was stronger. It was the kind of moment that every fisherman dreams of, and I tried to second-guess the fish's every move. Fish are such simple animals, but you can't tell what they are going to do. What hope is there of ever understanding people?

Maybe fifteen minutes passed. Time is such a hard thing to understand in those kinds of situations. I never looked at my watch, but when it finally struck me that Elaine had been gone a long time, I looked out the door and there was no longer any sign of her passing. The thick flakes had already filled any footprints she had made. I was angry at being worried, so I called her name a few times as I played the fish. No answer. I became afraid, but even then I laughed at myself for my own fear. Perhaps if I had started to look then, things might have turned out differently. As it was, I waited about five minutes before I twisted the line around a bench leg and stepped outside to look for her.

So quiet. I remember the snow as enveloping all sound. I stopped for a second to listen for the crunch of snow under her boot, but I did not hear anything besides my own breathing. I walked around the hut, but she was not there. I called her name frantically and walked a few yards forward, but by then I had almost lost sight of the hut. She was lost on the ice.

I was in a panic, but I did not want to wander away and lose myself as well, so I returned to the hut and took a roll of fishing line from my sack. It was heavy line and long, about seven hundred yards, and I tied one end securely to the door handle of the hut, and then let the line run out off the spool between my fingers as I started my first slow circle at about ten yards out. Nothing. I let out another ten yards, and began to circle the hut again. By then I could no longer see anything, and I imagined I would bump right into her as I shouted her name. I continued to let out the line and make wider and wider circles around the ice hut. It frightened me that my only guide back to safety was the thin thread of nylon between my fingers.

On my fourth round, at about forty yards out, I ran into the side wall of the next ice hut. Perhaps she had found it as well. I worked my way around to the door and flung it open, but all I could see inside was the deep blue light.

And then I felt the tug between my fingers, and the roll of fishing line fell onto the snow. I couldn't understand it at first, but then I realized that Elaine must be out wandering in the snow, and that she must have crossed my stretched line somewhere.

I was afraid to tug at it. Either the line was still one length, and Elaine would follow it to me, or else she had broken it. Even if it had broken, she might have understood what it was. She might be digging through the snow around her to find the broken end that would lead her to me. I began to follow the line out, carefully, not tugging at it in case she was searching for the broken end. I was cold by then, and frightened as I had never been before, but I gingerly held the line between my fingers as I followed it back.

The line was broken all right, and there was no one at the severed end. I could see some marks in the snow that could have been boot prints. I called her madly then, as loudly as my voice would let me, but the snow ate my words.

I tried to follow the boot prints, but the snow was falling fast and the indentations soon became ambiguous. I walked and I walked, calling her name, and by now I had lost my lifeline as well and we were both doomed on the ice unless we found shelter. Why had she wandered away? I asked myself this again and again as I searched for her in that desert of white. My own boots were wet now, and I shook with fright and the cold, but I could not stop. Neither would the snow.

How much time passed? An hour. Two. I don't know. I just know that I kept moving, and that while I was moving I stepped into one of Freddy's old fishing holes. One leg went down as far as the thigh before I understood what was happening, and I grappled my way back up onto the edge of the ice. The hole was bigger than any Freddy should have made, and I cursed him for not putting a stick up beside the hole to signal its presence. But the pole was there all right, on the other side that I had come from. The thick snow had just made it harder to see.

And then I looked down into the hole that I had just stepped in, and saw that the ghostly blue light of ice and water was entirely uncovered by snow. It was impossible. The holes Freddy drilled were big and long, you see, maybe three feet wide by six long, and I'd only stepped through one corner. The rest of the hole should have been snowed over by now, unless it was my own step that had broken the cover. But no, the cover had been broken before. I looked around the hole and sure enough, there were traces of boot prints. There was more. I found Elaine's glove under two inches of snow.

My mind went numb. Elaine had gone through the ice.

I suppose that I was too numb with cold and fear to fully appreciate what had happened. I stared down into the hole, and then as if in a dream, I took off my own jacket, rolled up my sleeve, and reached into the water. It was bitingly cold. And what had I expected?

If only it had been a dream, I might have felt her hand grasp mine, and I might have pulled her back up.

But it wasn't a dream. I felt nothing.

I found my way back to the hut, I don't know how, and when I saw the fishing line that I'd left hooked on the bench leg, I was filled with a kind of horrible desperation. I pulled on the line, waiting for her brown curls to rise up through the ghostly blue water. Instead, I pulled up a lake trout that looked at me through dead, glassy eyes.

* * *

An awkward silence descended on the camp fire after Butler had finished speaking. No one knew him well enough to console him. Maybe he did not even need consolation. After all, the story had happened years before. Teresa was sitting nearby, and she looked at him--a drunk in reverie.

"What a sad, sad story," said Victor. Nobody said anything else.

"They all end like that," Victor continued.

It was quiet for a while. "You're such an asshole," said Margaret finally, and Butler guessed she meant Victor. He shivered. Cold had been banished from the earth, but he could still shiver.

This was not what he had in mind when he wanted them to stay by the fire to tell their stories. How was it that the stories had turned into confessions?

"Every love story is a sad story if you stick around long enough," said Gary. "As far as I'm concerned, they should all end at the marriage. Listen, here's a story that a friend of mine told me. I ran into him late one night in the building where I worked. This is what he said."

ORAL SEX
Antanas

Crushed in the winepress of passion, I hunger for the woman behind the library desk. She is there even now, one of the few who remains, for no one stays in this airless building longer than he has to. The memory of her presence across the counter lingers, and if I dared, I would go into the library again. I could pass near the counter to catch the fragrance of her perfume, I would devour her scent. Today she wore a black cotton sweater with a long row of mother-of-pearl snaps on the front. The first two snaps were undone, and the remaining twenty-eight were a series of possibilities. Her stockings were black as well. I could see them when she went back to the reserve shelf to check for my book. No such librarian ever existed when I was a child. No other such librarian can exist anywhere; the delicious combination of bookish intellect and feminine charm turns my head and distracts me from the job at hand.

My marking, my marking. Student papers where venial sins begin with split infinitives that need to quickly be crushed. If only they would break the rules with passion, but instead they are passive in the dullness of their prose.

I am trapped, fluttering, in a web of words.

Butchery students in tall hats, floraculture students with their blank eyes and smiling mouths, double dirty dozens of tech boys, mute business students, and all the others, forced to walk my straight and narrow of grammatical correctness and paragraph coherence.

Pity them. Pity me.

As the codes of morality shift, so the rules of grammar are fluid, and they change with the centuries - even the decades - but what rules there are must still be enforced, and I am the enforcer. I am the prison guard. Hunting down dangling participial phrases and fragments. There is no exit for those who do not learn to manipulate words.

Ted's words were simple enough when he called.

"I need to talk to you. Will you be home for a while?"

My son, Jonathan, was watching TV in the living-room, and we were both waiting for my wife Margaret, so we could leave before the rush-hour and go up to the cottage. There was no good in pointing out to him that I had *some* time, but only a *limited* time. Ted did not have an ear for that kind of distinction.

I made two gin and tonics, and took them out to the patio in the back to wait. I wanted it to look congenial, but I packed the rest of the gin into the trunk of the car. I was halfway through mine and the ice cubes in his were almost melted when he came around the back of the house.

I should have guessed it then, but I am not an expert in the effects of chemical substances. Ted's centre of balance was off and he leaned to one side. But unlike a drunk, he did not sway. He looked as if he could hold himself that way as long as the tower of Pisa. He eyed me wordlessly, and then scanned the windows of the apartment building that overlook my back yard.

"Not here," he said. "We have to go inside."

Ted was like that - direct - a man of action. He always made me feel fussy. He was a big, hairy man, and it looked like he had been stuffed with only modest success into a polo shirt and short pants. Arms stuck out of the short sleeve cuffs like pinched sausages.

"Make sure your kid doesn't come in here."

He had me off balance. I should have said something then, but I stuck my head into the living-room and yelled to Jonathan that he was on no account to come into the kitchen. Jonathan is seven years old, and he watches TV the way a young man might watch a woman undress for the first time. Normally, Jonathan did not hear a word I said to him, but this time, uncharacteristically, he was listening.

"Why not?"

"Just don't come in. I'm telling you."

"I want a glass of water."

"Get a drink from the bathroom."

I came back into the kitchen and shut the door behind me.

"Does the kid listen to you?" Ted asked.

"Almost never."

"Let's hope he does this time."

Ted took a plastic bag out of his polo shirt pocket. Using a small pocket knife, he laid out two neat lines of cocaine on the kitchen counter.

"First we'll do a line each and then we'll talk."

"No thanks. I've been drinking," and I showed him the drink.

What I should have told him was to go to hell, but the words run out on you just when you need them most. Ted didn't try to force me. He sniffed up the two lines and blinked.

I sat down by the kitchen table, and Ted brought a chair around to the same side of the table as mine and he sat as close as he could, with his hairy legs open and my two between his. We were both in shorts, and the hairs on our legs were almost touching.

I didn't like the proximity. Ted is eager and bright-eyed most of the time anyway, but the cocaine took him so far in the same direction that there was nothing left to him but raw eagerness.

He lit a cigarette.

"I want to talk to you. I mean *talk*. I feel like we haven't had the chance to bond the way I'd like us to. I want to talk about marriage."

I gritted my teeth instinctively, and then had to think about it to make my mouth relax. I no longer disapprove out loud about new words in the language such as "hopefully" and "parent" in its verb form. I am nevertheless silently and secretly appalled whenever I hear about "bonding" and the like. It's a kind of instinctive linguistic conservatism that no one else seems able to access.

On the other hand, I was annoyed by more than the words. He was not even my friend, but the husband of my wife's best friend. A friend-in-law.

I sipped at the melted ice in my drink and waited for him to go on.

"Tina's a great woman - she saved my life. I was going out of control before I met her, and now, except for the odd line of this stuff, I'm straight most of the time. We've got a house and my life is on track."

On track indeed. Ted was a reformed man. He'd lived the first twenty years of his adult life, as he once told me, for sex, drugs, and rock and roll. It had sounded attractive, in a way, especially for Tina. Just about everyone I know has a friend like Tina. She ironed socks and underwear.

Back to the man in my kitchen.

"But," I said to him.

"What?"

"But something."

"I don't know what you're talking about."

"Your life is on track, but..." I encouraged. I felt like I was back in school, helping one of the kids with an essay.

"I still don't get it."

"Never mind. Go on."

My students never knew what I was talking about either. For them, language is an awkward tool, a great axe that they wield to hack out approximations of meaning. My job is to try to make whittlers out of them.

"Tina's brought me stability, and pride in what I'm doing. I was hoping I could bring a little bit of the wild side to her life by way of exchange."

He was leaning closer and closer to me as he spoke, and his leg was actually touching mine. I pulled back.

"But she's so damn organized. If I start playing footsie with her under the dinner table, and I say we should go for a tumble on the floor, she's game. She's game, but first she undresses and then folds her clothing into neat piles on the chair. By the time she's done, we're both standing there naked, and I'm so turned off, all I can think of is the food on the plates is getting cold and the sauce is going to congeal and I'll never be able to wash it off. So there we are, standing naked on the broadloom, and she's waiting for me to make the first move, because I'm supposed to be the crazy one in this relationship, and suddenly I don't feel like it any more. But I do it anyway, and then I feel like I'm being a bad actor and it drives me crazy."

"So you're telling me your relationship is in trouble?"

"Not yet. Want to do a line?"

"No."

"You sound like a schoolteacher."

"That's what I am."

"Sometimes I think you should have married Tina."

He made an uncharacteristically long pause, and I heard a scratching sound at the door.

"Meow."

It was Jonathan.

"Get a drink of water from the bathroom," I shouted to him.

I heard him walk away.

"I'm talking sex," said Ted.

"What about it?"

"I'm saying that I want to open up my marriage. I've been faithful all along. I mean I've kept from slipping all these three years. Three years! Do you know what that means? That's the longest I've ever not slept around. And I want to keep it that way."

"So what's the issue?"

"The issue is that I need a little excitement. That's where you come in. I mean, I wouldn't want you to do anything you didn't want to do, but maybe you'd like a switch, or something, everybody in the know. You're more suited to Tina than I am anyway."

There was a second part to that comparison, but he didn't say it. If Ted had always made me uncomfortable before, he'd just taken a quantum leap in his ability to raise my anxiety. I could have stopped the whole thing by saying no right at that moment, and yet if I did, I knew that in some strange way, I wasn't "going the distance with" him again. This doesn't mean I intended to say yes, just that I was constrained.

"Or if that's too much for you, then maybe we could get Tina and Margaret to do a few lines and then go down on each other and the two of us could watch."

All I could think of was Jonathan in the hall. He might have been standing outside the door for all I knew. Then I thought about vocabulary acquisition. Would a boy of seven know the meaning of "go down on"? It was an interesting kind of verb anyway, a phrasal verb with two prepositions after the verb proper.

"Now remember," said Ted, "I'm the one taking a risk here. I'm being honest with you. I want no holds barred - I want to be completely honest."

The word terrified me.

"The problem with being honest is it's hard to do," I said.

"It's not so hard. I'm doing it right now."

"You think you're being honest, but how can you know yourself that well?"

Ted looked puzzled for a moment.

"This is not a lesson. I know I want your wife to go down on mine and I'm telling you that. What I want is your answer."

The kitchen door opened and Margaret walked in with two armfuls of groceries for the cottage.

"Hello Ted! Jonathan told me he couldn't come in here, and I thought William was having an affair in the kitchen."

It was not the kind of tone I would have chosen her to use, but she liked Ted. I could never understand that. Margaret is an addict of the well-turned phrase and the neatly reasoned argument, but she claims that Ted has an appealing earthiness.

Jonathan was right behind her, curious.

"Hey kid," said Ted, "come here."

Jonathan walked up to Ted and then crawled onto his lap. This was extraordinary. The boy usually stayed mum in the presence of strangers, and Ted was not really around that much.

"I was just telling Ted that I have to shower and we're off to the cottage."

"You go ahead and shower. I'll talk to him and we can go when you're done."

I wanted to tell her that he was stoned and that he might pull out the sack of coke again. But Jonathan was on Ted's lap, acting like a kid badly in need of a big brother.

In the bathroom, I was generating enough steam without turning on the water. But I thought it was time to show control - no need to panic. I wish I'd had time to give Margaret some kind of signal, but then perhaps she could take care of it on her own.

The bottle of gin was on the table when I returned to the kitchen. Margaret had gone to the trunk of the car and brought it back.

"Time to get moving," I said.

"Why don't you finish packing the car and get Johnny ready," said Margaret.

I hated it when she called him Johnny, but the only alternative was to sit down with them, and so I did as she asked. Even when I'd finished, Ted wasn't ready to go, but I was jangling my car keys and he had no choice. He stood on my driveway as we backed out, as if he owned the house and we'd come to visit him. He kept talking through my open window as I backed out.

"I want us to be friends," he said, and then he shouted more as I pulled away, "We have to see more of each other. You never come over to visit us. Maybe we can go out together."

I left him behind.

I let Jonathan play with his Gameboy in the back seat to keep him quiet. The traffic was already bad, and we inched along the three lanes that took us out of the city. I opened the window a bit to let in some noise, and the volume on Jonathan's video game was so high I thought he wouldn't hear.

"I was trying to get rid of him when you walked in," I said.

"I know."

"Then why didn't you help me?"

"You never liked him much. I wanted him to feel welcome."

"You make me feel like an ogre."

"Sometimes you are. You're not that way to me or Jonathan, but I just wish you'd relax."

I could feel the tightness in my jaw, which meant that I was gritting my teeth again. The dentist said I'd worn a perfectly good set of molars flat by doing that.

"You don't know what he said."

"I do."

I didn't want to start comparing notes with Jonathan in the car, but I couldn't believe she would be so calm if she'd heard the same things I had.

"He did two lines off the kitchen counter," I said.

"What does that mean?"

"C-O-C-A-I-N-E," I spelled it out quickly so Jonathan wouldn't follow if he was listening.

"Poor, poor Ted."

This sympathy was one of the things that had attracted me to Margaret in the first place, but after a number of years of marriage, it started to grate.

At the cottage, I unpacked the car, and Margaret put the food away in the fridge while Jonathan pumped up his floating toys, changed, and waited by the screen door complaining about the length of time it took us to get ready for the beach.

"You shouldn't get so upset by all this," Margaret said as she folded the towels up to take to the beach, "Look at the bright side."

I was squeezing a bottle of suntan lotion when she said it, and I ended up spraying the rug with white greasy spots.

"Isn't it the kind of fantasy men are supposed to have? And if all he wants is a switch, there's no deception involved. Isn't it what you've been wanting recently, I mean deep in your heart?"

The sun was low by the time we made it to the lake, and it was that odd time when the early evening strollers have already come out in their jackets, while some of the bathers still linger in the strange orange light. We have been going to this cottage since I was a child, and so there are many hellos that need to be said. An unsaid greeting can be taken the wrong way at the beach, as a sign of uppitiness, and there is still enough of a Scottish Presbyterian atmosphere left that no greater sin can be imagined. Ukrainians, and Italians and Portuguese probably constitute the majority at the beach now, and yet the old ethic prevails.

What I wanted in my heart indeed. On the one hand, I was appalled that she could think me so crass, and on the other I was terrified that he could see into me so well.

After the swim, Jonathan was excited and happy, and putting him into bed was like trying to force a jack-in-the box with a very strong spring back into its home. I had lost my taste for gin and tonic, so I poured a couple of glasses of Madeira and waited for Margaret to finish up in the kitchen. She seemed to take a very long time.

"What did Ted say to you?" I asked her as she set herself into an easy chair.

"Jonathan's still awake. We can talk later."

"We can speak in French."

"What's your rush? Let's watch the news."

I began to wonder if there was something I didn't know. Tina and Margaret met for dinners or movies together once every several weeks, and they had to talk about something. I'd never thought about this before. What did these women talk about?

Margaret and I have been married for ten years. This is a long time, especially when most of our friends are either divorced or on their second marriages. I think we're looked on as the old-fashioned type, although you can never be sure what your friends are saying about you.

At the end of it, I went to make sure Jonathan was asleep. When he finally did succumb, he looked like a soldier that had been shot in the field. He lay on his back with his mouth slightly open and his arms splayed apart widely.

"All right," I said when I got back, "why the long silence?"

"Because I was mad at you."

"With me?"

"You never liked Ted. You don't give him a chance."

"I don't give him a chance? He comes to my house and blows a pound of coke up his nose while my kid is locked out in the hall, and then he tells me he wants you to go down on his wife. Why should I give him a chance?"

"Go down on Tina?"

"That's what he said."

"You men have such funny fantasies."

"How come I get lumped with the guy who's just driven me crazy?"

"Because you know you want the same thing."

"I do not."

"What do you talk about whenever we make love?"

I had heard the expression about one's face going hot, but I had never experienced it before that moment. It felt as if my cheeks were being fried.

"I think that words spoken on the marriage bed should be exempt from evidence."

"Pompous ass."

I could not believe my ears.

"And I suppose you think that a little swap would do us good."

"It might."

I retired to the bedroom with a sense of wounded dignity. It was late August, and the nights were getting cool, so I put on my pyjamas and lay down with a history of the English language that I'd been reading on and off for the last three summers.

After ten years of marriage, even our arguments follow a pattern. We tend to fall into a deep silence, but since both of us like to talk, neither can keep it up for very long. "This time," I swore to myself, "I'm never going to talk to her again." I could hear her in the bathroom getting ready for bed, and for a while, I thought about turning out the light. But no, far better to be seen reading and unconcerned. She came into the bedroom, a tiny room, and yet managed not to look at me at all as she undressed. I tried to do the same, but even after ten years, I still like to look at her when she has her clothes off. There is something appealing to me about the stolen looks I take when she is in the shower, or changing, or getting ready to sleep. She slipped her nightgown over her head. Since the room is so small and I sleep on the outside edge of the bed, she had to crawl over me. The unintended physical contact softened my resolve, but I managed to keep my back to her and my eyes on the page of the book, even if I was reading no words.

"Good book?"

"Fair."

"Open to suggestions?" I felt her finger tracing a line on my neck.

"First we've got to talk."

"Talk, talk, talk. That's what I get for marrying an English teacher."

"And now you regret it?"

"Oh no. Talk is a kind of foreplay."

"Is that what you were doing with Ted while I was in the shower?"

"Ouch."

"What did he say to you?"

"He said he wanted a menage a quatre."

"And what did you say?"

"That I wasn't really interested. Imagine, Tina and I went to elementary school together. I'd start laughing if I ever saw you kissing her."

I thought about that for a while.

"I know what you mean. Seeing you and Ted together would be like beauty and the beast."

"You're being unfair to him again."

"Well he drives me crazy. He's always got to lead the way when we're together, as if he's some kind of trailblazer and I'm his sidekick."

"He's more of a man's man."

I thought about that for a while too. If I were a woman's man, in the sense that I appealed to them more, then that was all right. On the other hand, if she meant I was more womanly than Ted, I was not so ready to be pleased.

We were facing each other now, both turned in to the centre of the bed, and there was a pleasant smell of cedar from the walls and of flannel and bodies.

"What do you like so much about Ted?" I asked.

"He's game for just about anything."

"And I'm not?"

"You're an aesthete and he's a gourmand."

"You mean I breathe rarified air?"

"There are things he'd do that I think you wouldn't." When she saw my look, she added, "Say a food-fight."

"Say swapping partners?"

"That's right."

"Don't be so sure."

"Oh come on."

"I'm serious. I could see myself performing all sorts of indecent acts with Tina. She's so thorough, it'd be like a good work-out."

"How boring."

"Please, my fantasy need appeal only to me."

"Not quite. In a swap, the fantasy has to appeal to both partners."

"So could you see yourself in bed with Ted?"

She just smiled at me, and it was enough to make me sick with envy.

"You haven't answered my question," I said.

"I'm not so sure I'd want to sleep with him, but I would like him to see me as a bad girl instead of goody-two-shoes. Sometimes I feel like you and I are still being good students, even though the teacher's been out of the room for twenty years."

"You can't have it both ways," I said.

"I wonder."

Our hands had begun to wander long before this. Flannel is supposed to be a child-like material that makes you think of Teddy bears, but there is something appealing about a woman's body in a flannel nightgown. The superficial innocence makes the underlying desire so much more appealing. Give me flannel over black garters any time.

There is no need for me to repeat here what I said to Margaret as we made love that night. Nor do I think it appropriate to rate lovemaking the way one rates gymnastics at the olympics.

We must have been very close to 9.

After it was over, I could not sleep. That was a luxury reserved for Margaret.

I tossed and I turned the whole night, half-dreaming and half-imagining Margaret in bed with Ted. In the dream, I walked down the front path of our house to the street, where Tina was waiting for me in a car. She was naked in the driver's seat, and she started to undo my shirt with her free hand. But dreams are perverse, and just as I was about to slip out of my pants, I became aware that Jonathan was in the back seat. There was nothing in the car I could cover Tina with, so I started throwing Kleenexes at her while pretending to Jonathan that nothing was out of the ordinary.

It was windy the next day, so most of the other families set themselves up in the dunes a hundred yards back from the lake. Margaret doesn't mind the wind, and Jonathan wanted to dig in the compacted sand on the shore, so we set up our folding chairs close to the water. I wore sunglasses to keep the wind and blown sand out of my eyes. Seagulls hung like kites against the breeze.

"I've worked it all out," said Margaret when Jonathan had waded far enough into the water to be out of earshot. "I'll buy myself some frilly underwear, and we'll invite Ted and Tina out for drinks. Get your mother to take care of Jonathan. We'll do a round of the strip clubs, and then we'll get ourselves invited back to their place. Maybe a few pornographic films, and a little cocaine and then we can do it. It's important to be at their place so we can leave when we want, and we'll make the rules very strict. Watching is ok, but no touching of the other couple."

Jonathan was wading at chest level.

"That's cold-blooded!" I said.

"I'm just sketching out what you've said a hundred times in bed."

So much for the sanctity of pillow talk.

"To say it is one thing, but to mean it is another."

"I think you do mean it. I think you're like all men in some ways. You've built yourself this happy home and soon you'll be forty and you'll begin to think you need a little adventure. Then you're going to blame Jonathan and me for tying you down and you'll want an affair or to go off to East Timor or something. I'm just giving you a safe outlet."

"This isn't safe! This is dangerous."

"So live dangerously for a change."

I would have argued with her more, except that I really had been getting a little restless lately. I had not thought of East Timor, but the Amazon jungle was beginning to sound more and more interesting, especially since no one knew how much longer it was going to last. I had taken out a subscription to National Geographic.

Jonathan was at neck-level in the water, and it looked like he was going to wade all the way across to the American side of the lake. I had to go out to prevent him from drowning himself.

"We need to talk about this some more," I said when I'd towelled down Jonathan and set him up with some buckets on the sand just outside of hearing range.

"We can talk here. Jonathan can't hear us."

"Maybe we should slip back into the dunes."

She smiled at me. The dunes had been well-used by us the summer before we were married and we were spending a week at the cottage with my parents and an aunt.

The secret that Margaret and I now shared both terrified and excited me. For the rest of the day, I kept trying to engineer a way for us to get away together, but there was no place I could send Jonathan. Even if he'd gone over to a friend's, I was no longer sure that Margaret would be willing to come to bed with me. She had become so mysterious, so full of unexamined possibilities, that I thought she might turn me down as soon as take me up on the offer of sex.

When we got back to the city on Sunday, all nine lights on the answering machine were blinking, and I sat down with a pencil and a notebook while Margaret put the dirty clothes in the hamper and refolded the clean and put them back in our dressers. Jonathan glued himself to Doctor Who, which he had recorded on the VCR while we were gone.

"Hi, this is Tina. It's Friday night and I'm looking for Ted. He said he was stopping by at your place on the way home. If you're there, pick up the phone."

"Tina again. Still looking for Ted. If he calls you, tell him to phone me."

All the rest of the calls were from her, and they were all the same, except for the last, which was time-stamped early that Sunday morning.

"I'm calling from the Addiction Rehab. Centre. I'm kind of glad you're not home yet, because this is easier to say to a machine than it is to you. Ted finally called me last night - he was wired and over the edge. He'd been blowing the stuff up his nose for two days with his old buddies when he phoned for help. I drove him straight to the rehab centre, but on the way there he told me what he said to you. I'm so embarrassed. It's just disgusting, and I want to apologize to you. He was stoned. Okay? He didn't mean what he was saying. It as just one of those male fantasies gone ...."

The tape had run out. I called in Margaret and played it back with her.

We left Jonathan in front of the TV and went into the kitchen for cups of coffee.

"I guess that's the end of it," said Margaret, and there was something mournful about her words, as if the rest of her lifetime with me was a kind of prison sentence.

"Maybe we could think of something else."

"Like what?"

We talked about other friends we knew, or about advertising in one of those strange magazines, but our hearts weren't in it.

"It's all for the best," I said. "There's nothing wrong with fidelity. It's an old idea that we should cherish more anyway."

Margaret looked at me the way my students do sometimes when I begin to talk about the beauty of this language we share. A kind of silence descended on us in the kitchen, and then Margaret went to do the laundry because the work week was beginning for her the next day and she needed to prepare her clothes.

Successive layers of silence have descended on our conversation since that time. Pillow talk has stopped for both of us, and we now make mute love. I think, after all, that although there may be a time to speak, there are far more times when silence is appropriate. So strange, when you think that words are really nothing but bends in sound waves. In my own mind, I have turned the whole incident into nothing more than a series of unpleasant sounds. I do not know what Margaret thinks.

The summer has long since passed, and now it is early December, and it has been dark outside for hours. A light rain falls on my office window, and it may turn to ice before I finish with these papers. Soon the cleaners will come by, and even the library will close. I could give up my grammatical policing and still make it back to the library to speak to that woman again. She knows me by sight, and we have chatted from time to time. We might trade quotes for fun, something from "To His Coy Mistress". Then I would help her to close up the library. Perhaps, if the spark were bright and hot enough, we could lock ourselves into the temple of words, and then we might go to one of the study rooms, embracing already on the steps, and then rushing to close the study-room door behind us as double security against prowling night watchmen.

But all of these are only words. Words and nothing else. The rain on my window is already beginning to freeze, and the tear-covered glass is the only opening upon this room.

If only it were spring.

Chapter 5

"You see!" said Victor. "All the relationships end unhappily."

"That's unfair!" said Margaret.

"He's got a point," said Ned. "Things get hard over time. Sometimes they get impossible. I've got another story."

Ned was an old-fashioned looking man, a Valentino, a gigolo. He had slicked back hair and he smoked cigarettes one after another like people used to do before they knew better. And he looked startled all the time, as if he belonged in a tango from the 1920's and had been yanked into the future and was still trying to get his bearings. He had appeared with John, a much younger man who smoked as much as Ned did. They were usually quiet men.

SHIP ON A REEF
Ned's Story

Up at the poolside bar, the saxophone in the marengo band kept squeaking as if the player had never mastered his instrument properly. Holmes couldn't believe it was the kind of sound anyone would want to make voluntarily. The four men in the band wore sandals, straw hats, and colourless shirts and pants. Local people, apparently, brought in to play at the poolside bar at "happy hour" every afternoon. It was happy for most. Four o'clock was a good time to start drinking, but Holmes had started far earlier.

"How deep is the water out there?" Holmes asked the young couple on the beach chairs a few feet away. Rows of bathers sat beneath the rows of coconut palms that spread from end to end of the hotel's private beach. Although the marengo band was a good fifty feet away at the bar, the squeaking saxophone still annoyed Holmes.

The couple he had spoken to exchanged concerned looks. Actually, the man looked more annoyed than concerned. He was a dark, sullen type, who wore a bathing suit much too small.

"About six feet as far out as the reef. Drops off after that."

"Still deep enough for a man to drown in," Holmes said, and he saw that funny look from them again. The woman seemed very young to him, almost a child, yet he had seen her expression on the faces of nurses and doctors. For all he knew, she might even be a nurse on holiday.

Holmes panicked, but was careful not to show it. He sipped on the melted ice in his glass and tried to remember. Damn his fading memory. Maybe he had already asked the same question once or twice before. Maybe they'd never spoken at all, and his sudden question was misplaced intimacy. Yet it seemed to him that they had been talking to one another.

Better to shut up. Much better to shut up.

"I'm going back up to the bar for another round," the man said after a few minutes. "My turn to buy. Are you having the same?" Holmes was so relieved he just nodded.

So they had been talking to one another before. Maybe he'd just dozed off or something. That must have been the reason for his sense of dislocation. He looked out to sea so he wouldn't have to talk to the girl.

It was hard to tell just how far out the reef really was. Maybe half a mile, maybe three quarters. There was a line of white spray where the choppy outer sea broke against the reef; inside, the water was flat and green. A pleasant green, and safe too. No sharks could make it through the reef unless they wended their way through a narrow channel that was marked out with buoys. No reason for them to bother. Altogether, the reef was a good thing, a providential thing that set one's mind at ease. At least from the perspective of the bathers. Sailors might think otherwise.

There was a broken ship on the reef. It loomed unnaturally high, as if it were much larger than any wooden ship had a right to be. It seemed to be the bow of a ship, with the rear end probably battered away by years of heavy waves. It was the only landmark on the water, except for the line of spray, and any time Holmes came down to the beach, the ship distracted him from the otherwise perfect view. It annoyed him, the way the squeaking saxophone music did. Nobody seemed to be able to tell him if marengo music was supposed to have a squeak, nor how the bow of a ship came to be sitting on the reef. The desk clerks spoke English, but they didn't know, and the waiters and maids only spoke enough to sell drinks or take simple instructions. Holmes did not speak Spanish.

The man came back and gave Holmes a pina colada. Holmes did not like pina colada. In fact, he hated it, but he did not say anything. The man might have made a mistake at the bar, or Holmes might have been drinking the foul sweet muck all afternoon. He thought he had started with gin and tonic, a good traditional drink, but how could he be sure? The empty glass. Of course. If he looked at the empty glass in the sand by his side, he would be able to see if there was a twist of lime in it. A crushed twist, because Holmes always dug the lime out of his drink with his fingers and then squeezed a few more drops into the gin and tonic. "My vitamin C for the day," he used to say. It had been funny to him once, but vitamins weren't funny to him any more.

"Describe the food you eat on a typical day," the doctor had said. He was a young doctor, but cut from an older mold. The doctor knew what was best.

"Mostly liquid diet," said Holmes, trying to be breezy about it. He did not feel breezy. He felt much older than his forty-nine years. It was important to remember details like his age when he was talking to this doctor.

The doctor's frown deepened and his eyes remained cold and humourless.

"That's what I thought," the doctor said. He leaned back in his chair. "Ever hear of Korsakoff's syndrome?"

Holmes wondered briefly if it was a trick question to check his memory.

"No."

"It's caused by heavy drinking and poor diet. Over years, usually. The combination causes a vitamin deficiency and leads to brain damage."

Holmes was horrified. It was a nightmare.

"Sufferers get befuddled and start to lose short-term memory. You can dry out the drinker but you can't bring back the damaged cells. People with this condition are usually institutionalized."

The nightmare was getting worse.

"How can one be sure one has it?" Holmes asked nervously. He wanted proof and he wanted a lawyer. But who could bring a lawyer into a doctor's office? There was no jury to impress.

"You can't be sure, unless you do an autopsy. That might be premature."

Was there the flicker of a smile that passed over the doctor's face? Monster.

"We did do a brain scan."

"Yes, of course." Holmes tried to look calm, but he could remember none of it.

"I'm surprised you have any recollection of it. When you first came in, you were in no shape..."

"Yes, yes," Holmes said. He did not want to talk about what he had been like when his brother brought him into the hospital. Holmes's sister-in-law had already described his mental and physical deterioration all too well. Especially his attempts to place calls to his wife.

His wife.

"The scan showed a small section of damaged tissue in your brain. Now there's no guarantee that it was brought about by Korsakoff's syndrome. As I said, we'd need an autopsy for that. Anything you want to say about how the damage might have occurred? Any childhood accidents? Concussions? Unusual diseases?"

What was the correct social etiquette for a situation like this, wondered Holmes. Was he supposed to lean back in his chair and reflect? Was he supposed to admit that he had willfully pickled his own brain? Anyway, it did not bear thinking about. He felt enough of a zombie already. The man with half a brain. It was enough to make you laugh if you weren't crying. Why couldn't they have dried him out and sent him on his way instead of putting him into the psychiatric wing?

"Do you think I'm being rough on you?" the doctor asked.

"You have a shitty bedside manner."

It made Holmes feel better to say it. He would have felt better still if the doctor hadn't smiled as if he were getting a conditioned response.

"I'm being rough for a reason. Lots of people walk around with damage of one kind or another. Maybe the majority of people. I'm not convinced that your alcoholism brought on the memory loss, at least not directly."

What an asshole, thought Holmes. Then the doctor started grilling him with questions. Holmes had expected it, and he was ready for it.

"What's the date today?"

"Valentine's Day."

"I said the date."

"February the fourteenth."

"Which way is North?"

Holmes pointed.

"Wrong."

"Then put a window in your wall so I can get my bearings."

"How old are you?"

"Forty-nine."

"Where were you born?"

"Kingston, Ontario."

"Mother's name?"

"Lola."

"That's not what the record says."

"She slept around a lot. That's what her boyfriends called her."

Count to a hundred by eights, count backwards by sevens, who is the current Prime Minister? How long have you been in the hospital? What is your occupation? Where are we? What is my name? How long have we been in this room? What is the date today?

Holmes gave cocky answers whenever he could think of them. It made him feel better to do it and he knew that most doctors believed that scrappers were the ones who survived. Brain damage. Best not to think of brain damage or it might interfere with the answers. He was doing fine, just fine. He was beating the pants off the doctor and having a good time at it.

"Why can't you phone your wife?"

"She's dead."

It came out faster than he had intended it to. He hadn't wanted to say it at all. He hadn't wanted to think about it and he wasn't going to.

"How long has she been dead?"

"Shut up doctor. She's dead. That's all that matters. I don't need to play games around the fact. Certainly not with you."

"This is a psychological examination, Mr. Holmes. I'm not asking out of a sense of curiosity."

"And I'm not answering because I've got a sense of propriety. She was mine when she was alive and now all I've got is the memory of her. I don't have to share that with you or anyone else."

"I think you do."

"Well keep your thoughts to yourself. I'll keep my memory of her."

"What *is* your memory of her?"

Holmes clammed up. Enough was enough.

The doctor had that faint smile on his face again. The bastards were supposed to stay poker-faced. Everyone knew that.

"For a while, we thought that you might even have the same condition your wife did, complicated by alcoholism." The doctor dangled the bait, but Holmes wouldn't take it.

"I'll assume it's obstinacy and not damaged cells," the doctor said, and he sat up and made a few notes on a pad on the desk in front of him. "You can go home."

The interview was over.

Palm trees, swimming pool, six bars, three restaurants, nightly cabaret show. Air conditioning, view of the beach, cable TV. When Holmes and Jane had holidayed at Acapulco, locals came by every ten minutes or so selling coconuts, or vases, or sandwiches. She was an easy mark, and knew it, and she always tried to explain to Holmes why she needed yet another clay vase or was still hungry after two sandwiches. Here the beach was private, with guards at either end. No locals on the beach. Jane would have found it too quiet. She would have wanted to get out for a while.

Stop it.

Holmes said goodbye to the couple on the beach and started back towards the bar. The Germans were playing the Canadians in water polo. There was lots of splashing, but all the players moved so slowly. They weren't used to running in the water. A poolside drinker got splashed and everyone laughed. Holmes returned two empty glasses to the mustachioed barman.

"Thanks Mr. Holmes."

Holmes couldn't remember talking to the man before, but he slipped him five dollars for services rendered and forgotten.

The main restaurant, another bar, the dance floor and reception were all under a thatch roof three stories high. He stopped by the desk to ask for messages.

"Nothing today, Mr. Holmes."

Did everyone in the place know him by name? There had to be five hundred guests at the resort, yet every receptionist, barman and maid seemed to know him by name.

Just as well there weren't any messages. His brother had already sent two telegrams reminding him to stay off booze. The telegrams arrived three days apart. He probably thought Holmes's memory wasn't good enough for much longer than that. At this rate, he would send three more telegrams before Holmes got home.

The air conditioning blasted him in the face when he opened the door to his room. He'd forgotten to turn it down. Holmes flicked the dial down two settings and opened the glass door to his balcony. He sat down to wait until the open window warmed the room a bit. Six rows of coconut palms and then the beach. The resort had once been a coconut plantation, and beyond the fences the plantation was still worked. It ran along the beach as far as his eye could see. Behind those six rows of palms and behind the resort, nothing but swamp and dense jungle growth.

A new beginning. That had been the intention of this trip. A little change of scenery before going back to Canada to start life all over again. But the thought of returning to his apartment, empty these three months, was not appealing. His sister-in-law had vacuumed the place and thrown out the food in the fridge, but Holmes knew the place would be stale with unwashed memories. Better to have given up the place, given the key to an estate buyer, taken the cash and started up somewhere else. Someplace without a past. It would be nice to walk into a new apartment with walls freshly painted an off shade of white. A bare place without any dirty corners or finger smudges by the light switches. In an end of town he didn't know, or even better, in a city he had never visited before.

He went back into the hotel room and shut the door behind him. By mid-afternoon of each day, he began to remember both too much and too little, and the only way to obliterate the confusion was with sleep.

Holmes awoke with a sour taste in his mouth and an atypical resolution to stop drinking. He went to the bathroom and flossed and brushed his teeth, showered and shaved and put on new pants and a white shirt. Down at the reception, he changed a hundred dollars into pesos and then walked down towards the pool. He ordered a coke and watched the girls sunbathing. It was six-thirty, but the sun was still strong enough to redden their thighs.

Boredom. That was what made him want to drink. It was too late to go out snorkelling or sailing, and there was nothing to do at the resort in the evening but drink and eat. He had to get away.

There were no more cars at the rental kiosk, but the man still had motorcycles. Holmes had never ridden a motorcycle before, so he rented a small Vespa because the gearshift was easy to operate.

"Any place interesting to visit around here?" Holmes asked the rental man.

"Beach road's nice. Runs beneath the palms for miles. There are villages too, but better not to stop there after dark."

Holmes did not ask why.

The Vespa felt too small beneath him. He was like a chimpanzee on a tricycle. The tiny Vespa moved with alarming speed, but he felt too ridiculously large on the machine to go slow. The guard at the gate motioned to Holmes.

"Make sure the light works. It will be dark soon and you do not want to run into a horse."

The light worked.

"Do you have your room key? The night guard does not speak English, and he has been told all guests must identify themselves. Freeloaders have been coming in at night and causing trouble."

Holmes showed him the key and the guard flashed a smile and raised the gate.

A group of women sat underneath the trees just beyond the gate. Hotel workers, waiting for the bus back to town. The women did not smile at Holmes. They were sullen and tired and sick of looking at tourists all day.

The beach road was a badly paved track that cut around through the swamp and circled back towards the sea. There it turned into a sand trap that hugged the coast and ran beneath the rows of palms. Holmes speeded up to keep from getting stuck in the sand. He laughed when the Vespa fishtailed where the sand was soft.

It was good to get out of the resort, out of the protected world and into the real one, where the palm fronds that fell onto the earth lay ungathered, or were strewn across the road for added support in the softer spots. An old man, shirtless and in a straw hat, stood up from his work in the palm grove and waved to Holmes. He had a machete in his other hand and a horse was tethered nearby.

In a few minutes, Holmes began to come upon the concrete block houses at the outskirts of the village. Not bad, he thought, but his opinion changed as the houses thickened. Closer to the centre of the village the houses became small, two-room huts slapped together out of weathered, rough-cut board. Some of the houses had Knorr soup signs nailed to them and children watched him from the doorways. Chickens walked across the sand road, and clucked in anxiety as he drove past them. He passed a small store with tables set up outside. Circles of men sat around bottles of rum.

Two women walking on the road waved him down. He stopped the Vespa.

"Un peso," the older woman said, holding up one finger to make sure he understood.

"Sure," said Holmes, reaching into his pocket. Poverty made him feel uncomfortable.

At the far end of the village there was another store, but this one had a large terrace with a thatch roof. Couples danced in the shade to music from a boom box. Holmes slowed down as he passed.

Beer, he thought. Beer was not the same as alcohol.

It was and it wasn't. He could use a beer to make sure he didn't get the shakes. On the other hand, he hadn't been on the island long enough to get heavily addicted again, and he didn't think he would get the shakes if he stayed dry. But maybe it was better to ease off the booze instead of trying to do it cold turkey. If he did get the shakes, he'd run to the nearest bottle of gin or rum and not slow down until it was empty. Better to stay under some kind of control.

A boy ran up and took the Vespa from him as soon as Holmes stopped in front of the terrace. Holmes let him do it. It was cool under the thatch, and he took a table of rough-cut wood to himself. The music changed to marengo, and Holmes heard the saxophone squeaking again. So it was supposed to squeak.

"Cerveza," said Holmes to the waiter. He knew the important words. The waiter brought him a quart bottle and a plastic glass.

Good to get out, thought Holmes. Good to get out into the real world. He could smell the salt off the sea. The music pounded in his ears, but it was not unpleasant. The boy was washing down his Vespa and Holmes watched him for a while. He drank the beer fast and tried to inspect the people around him without staring. He was a little unsure of himself, a little frightened. On other islands, natives were supposed to hate tourists, but this island was said to be different. These islanders were supposed to be noble.

There were a lot of machetes in the bar. Some were strapped onto men's belts and some lay on the tables. He drank the beer quickly and gave the boy a peso for washing down the Vespa. He continued on his way.

The quart of beer had given him some confidence. He raced along the road as fast as the machine would go, once spinning onto his side at a sharp turn in the sand road.

Jane hadn't liked to drive fast. She was more acutely aware that they were drinking more than they should, and she was careful because of it. To avoid fires, she always emptied all the ashtrays into a tin apple juice can before they went to bed. She didn't want the butts to smolder and catch fire in the waste basket. Car keys were given to hosts on arrival at a party, and the hosts' advice was always taken on the way home. Taxis if they said so, careful driving if they gave back the keys.

Her attempt at moderation did not save her.

The beach road was very close to the sea now. He could see where the reef made its final bend towards the beach and ended altogether. The beach beyond that was unprotected, and the surf larger.

Holmes had stopped, and now he turned off the engine. The roar of the surf and nothing else. No other sound. An unreasonable fear began to rise in him, a fear of being alone. The roar of the surf was horrible, a wordless thundering. Desperately, he tried to turn the Vespa on again, to get some more noise to give him comfort. The engine sputtered a few times before catching. His heart was beating furiously. Go back? No. He wasn't going to give into it. He drove the Vespa further along the road.

The coconut palms on his left gave way to jungle. Vines meshed with thin tree trunks to make a near-solid mass that grew in a vast shallow marsh of tepid water. His heart slowed down, and in celebration of this minor success over his anxiety, he decided to continue a little further. He rounded a promontory. The waves broke against the tail end of the reef, and beat in slow, curling rolls against the exposed, unprotected beach. That was the place he wanted - the beach beyond the reef. Intoxicated with his own courage, and going fast to keep from falling over in the sand, he took the Vespa down the steep embankment and rode along the beach proper. Holmes kept up the speed until he was well beyond the reef. Twice, he swerved to avoid large conch shells. Then he had gone far enough. He stopped, and turned off the ignition.

The sound of the waves was louder here. He wasn't going to give into it. What was there to be afraid of? And yet he felt so exposed on the beach.

He rolled the Vespa up to a fallen tree and leaned it against the trunk. Then he began to undress. There was no one to see him, unless some solitary worker in the coconut grove, but Holmes still had traces of shame. Shame before himself because of his white, puffy body. Too much booze and too little exercise.

He stripped off his clothes and the low sun felt warm against his back and buttocks. The beer had made him sweat and he wanted to clean himself. Holmes walked slowly towards the curling waves, and went in as far as his ankles. Even at that shallow depth, he could feel the strong pull of the water back towards the sea. The water receded and his feet began to sink into the wet sand. Another thinning lip of a wave washed his feet again. "Undertow", he thought, "sharks". It was good to have something real to be afraid of instead of the nebulous dread.

He walked out as deep as his knees, and suddenly felt the bottom give way beneath him. He floundered and gasped and beat his arms to stay afloat. A wave washed over his head and he floundered some more until he found his footing again. Once he was secure on his feet, he looked carefully at the sea bottom where he had fallen, and saw that the water was a different colour there. A kind of pit had been gouged out of the sand bottom. There were more of them, deep pools in the shallows. Too small for sharks, he thought to himself and laughed. Unless one got trapped there. He looked for dark, restless forms in the deep pools, but there weren't any. He waded out further.

The waves hit him hard. He could not stay on his feet, so he dove under a wave and started to swim, but the next curl caught him and washed him back to the beach. That was all right. He crawled back up the sand and sat there for a while to catch his breath. When he waded out again, he dove under the wave as each breaker came at him, until he let the last one catch him so he could surf back to the beach. He held his balls with one hand to keep them from being scraped by any conch that might be protruding from the sand.

He rested again and then swam out, ducking beneath the four succeeding waves until he was beyond the surf. Strange, conflicting currents pulled him one way and another. He watched the surface for a protruding fin and resisted the temptation to hold onto his balls. He needed both arms to swim. The sea was pulling him further out, but it was not an invincible tug. If he swam hard, he could make progress. He caught the first breaker and it helped carry him back to the beach.

Breathing hard, he crawled up on the sand and turned and sat to rest where the diminishing waves still washed over his feet and buttocks. It took him a long time to catch his breath, and at first he gulped air and listened to his heart beat hard against his chest. When the air came more easily, he walked to where his clothes were draped on the fallen tree beside the Vespa. He took a cigarette from his shirt pocket, lit it, and smoked.

A battered green frisbee lay among the plastic junk on the beach. Some kid must have thrown it into the ocean in Florida, and it had been washed all the way to the island beach. He could hear crabs scuttling over the fallen palm fronds in the grove behind him.

Better. The fear was better now. He could feel the hunger for a drink, but he wouldn't get the shakes. He could go back. Home. Or if not home, than at least back to the resort.

It took a long time to start the Vespa. He turned the key until the motor finally caught, and he walked the machine up the steep sand slope to the grove, twisting the throttle of the motorbike to get a little speed so the machine would climb up by itself.

It was already getting dim on the road beneath the palms, but not yet dark enough for the headlight to be of any use. He mounted the Vespa, and it stalled as he opened up the throttle. Damn. He turned the key until the battery was almost dead, and when the engine caught he mounted again. A hundred yards further on, the machine stalled one more time and then it would not start. He drained the battery trying to get the engine to catch.

How far was it to the resort? Six or seven miles, he guessed. Maybe four to the village where someone might be able to help him start the Vespa. He began to wheel it along the sand road, but the machine was low and he had to bend too far over to be comfortable. It kept losing traction in the soft sand, and then he had to bear down and push forward and his back started to hurt.

Getting dark, and as it did the noise from the bush on the other side of the road began to rise. Screeches and squawks that sounded as off-key as the squeaks of the saxophone in the marengo band. He pulled the Vespa up onto the shoulder of the road where some grass was growing and the machine did not get stuck in the sand traps. He tried the light switch and there was still enough power in the battery to give the lamp a weak glow.

It was still all right. It could have been worse.

He was sweating now. Crabs scuttled out of his way. They were vague shapes against the darkening earth, the darkening world. The sweat was taking the alcohol out of him. It made him feel cleaner, but he would have taken a beer if anyone had offered it to him. At the village. He could get a beer there.

Dark. Very dark. No starlight penetrated the coconut fronds above and the headlight of the Vespa was getting weaker. It was an erratic beam that shifted unexpectedly whenever he turned the Vespa slightly to avoid a log or a stone. Better off without it. He turned off the light and pushed on in the darkness, slipping onto the sand road sometimes, and having to push harder then until he found his way back up to the shoulder.

He was tired. He stopped for a smoke. He did not want to sit down because he could still hear the crabs moving about below, so he leaned up against a tree instead. Insects were attracted to the glow from his cigarette, and he slapped at mosquitos that landed on his neck.

How far could he have gone? A mile at most, with three more or so to go to the village. It was too much. He butted the cigarette and wheeled the Vespa close to the drop-off to the beach and lay it on the ground. It couldn't be seen from the road, but he put some palm fronds on top of it in case a car or truck passed by and the headlights caught the machine. Then Holmes tumbled down onto the beach proper where the starlight and weak luminosity of the night-time sea helped him to see where he was going. He had to walk close to the waterline where the sand was firmer underfoot.

Jane's headache had become unbearable while the two of them were picking strawberries in a U-pik patch. For three days before that she had been gulping aspirins, one after another, but the headache would not go away. They were on their knees between the rows of strawberry plants when she turned to him and said, "You don't know how bad it is," and started to cry. Kids were running around and their mothers looked up from beneath their straw hats as Jane cried loudly in the strawberry patch. She picked up a handful of strawberries from her basket and threw them at a couple of kids in the next row. Holmes took her to the hospital.

Holmes could not see any light further along the beach, and he could not remember how much the coastline curved in and out. Maybe the village was just around the bend, or maybe it was so far away its glow could not penetrate the night.

The local hospital thought that Jane had had a mild heart attack, but they still flew her out by air ambulance to the city. "I'm only fifty," Jane said over and over again. "Women don't have heart attacks. Not at my age," and she cried some more. Holmes held her hand all the way to the city. She would not let go, would grasp for it if he moved away.

The doctors in the city agreed that she had probably had a heart attack, and for three days they kept her on medication that did nothing to stop the headaches. The only times Jane fell asleep were when the combination of exhaustion and drugs was great enough to force her. Holmes would then rush home to shower and change in order to be with her when she awoke. What sleep he was getting came in the chair in her hospital room. The nurses said they disapproved of his staying there so much, but they did not complain convincingly. In their hearts, they hoped someone would sit with them when their turn came.

Holmes felt confused and powerless and he kept grilling the doctors about what could be wrong and why her headache would not go away. They didn't know. A body scan would tell the story. A lot of people were waiting for body scans, but they gave Jane priority. That scared Holmes more than it reassured him.

It was cooler walking on the beach than it had been on the road between the palms, but Holmes kept on sweating. Hard to keep on the thin line of firm sand, and he swerved sometimes onto the dry, softer sand, or into the water. His shoes were wet and the sand in them grated against his feet, so he slipped off both shoes and socks. Asking for it, he said to himself, thinking of broken rum bottles and shards of conch shells. His feet felt better without the shoes and socks, but the rest of him felt bad. Sick. He stopped for a second and held his hand out in front of him. It was too dark to see if there was a tremor.

The doctor said it would take a while to do the scan and a bit longer to analyze it. Holmes could go to the apartment and change and be back in plenty of time. But three days of fatigue caught up with him, and when he lay down on the couch for a minute, he fell asleep and stayed that way for seven hours. He woke up in a panic and drove straight to the hospital, but it was evening by then and Holmes could not find the doctor. The intern didn't know anything and neither did the nurses. Jane was sleeping quietly, though, and she slept right through the night.

"I'm better now," she said. Holmes awoke to see she was sitting up in her bed smoking a cigarette and looking at him wryly. So it really had been a nightmare, he thought. "They were giving me the wrong kind of medicine," she said. "After the scan, I got some new pills and the headache went away in an hour. I feel good." Holmes's relief was tempered by anger at the incompetence of the doctors and the hospital.

Jane was hungry, and around noon he went out to buy some Chinese food so she wouldn't have to eat the bland hospital lunch. The doctors were waiting for him when he got back. There were two of them: a tall, thin East Indian and an older man with white hair. They looked at him expectantly when he came through the door, and he set the bag of Chinese food down on a table. He had torn a small hole in the top of the paper bag and a whisp of steam came out like hot breath.

The two doctors were surgeons. Jane and Holmes looked at one another when they found that out. Holmes took her hand in his, but her touch could not bring back the morning's good mood.

Jane had a tumor. In her head. They were not to get too upset because nothing was conclusive yet. At least, it was conclusive that she had a tumor on her brain, but it was not conclusive that the tumor was malignant. There were two types of tumors: those that grew on the inside of the skull and could be removed easily, and those that grew within the brain itself. The latter were more problematic. In any case, it would be necessary to do exploratory surgery as soon as possible. Tomorrow or the next day. A small sample of the tumor would be taken and sent for a biopsy. That would clear matters up. For the time being, Jane would stay on medication that kept the swelling of the tumor down and held off the headaches.

The surgeons left, and Jane started to cry. Holmes tried to think of something to say to her, but he couldn't. He was crying too. The Chinese food steamed through the hole in the bag, but it smelled bad now, and after they had cried themselves out and the food was cold, Holmes gave it to the nurses at the station. When he got back to Jane's room, she asked him to call their lawyer. She wanted to arrange things.

Holmes saw the faint glow ahead of him. There was no electricity in the village, so the light was coming from the many oil lamps set outside on tables. From the distance, he could hear marengo music being played on someone's boom box. He would be there soon. He was very tired.

Jane wore a scarf around her head to hide her shaved skull. They waited three days to get the news on the biopsy. He took time off work and they played cards together and talked. Jane kept giving him advice all the time. Just household things at first; don't forget to water the flowers, empty the ashtrays into the tin before going to bed at night, pick up the goose she had ordered from the butcher but cancel the dinner party they had planned for the following Saturday night.

The nature of the advice began to change. She talked about how much they had drunk over the years. It had been far too much. Holmes had a few shots any time he went home to shower, and she could smell it on his breath when he came in. She had always drunk as much as he did, but now she told him not to buy any new bottles for a few weeks. They had always kept a big bar and the size of it weighed on her now. Better to finish off what he had and be done with it. Not stop. She wasn't talking about teetotalling, just cutting down. Cutting down a lot.

Her speech pattern was changing. She spoke as much as she always did. They had both been big talkers, social talkers, but they had been good listeners too. They had kept each other company well. But now she was talking differently. Holmes noticed that she was saying "this", "that", and "thing" all the time. She was forgetting the names of objects, their proper names. It was easy enough to understand what she meant when she said, "Give me that," and pointed to a cigarette, but sometimes it wasn't so easy when the antecedents either didn't exist at all, or when they were hundreds, maybe thousands of words back in what she had said. The "thises" and "thats" were becoming confusing.

They kept Jane in the hospital for two weeks after the biopsy came back just to give Holmes time to work out the details of home care. He had to find out which of their insurance policies covered twenty-four hour stay-at-home nurses. The paper work was complicated, but on top of that, Holmes found himself slowed by lethargy. He should have been able to do it much more quickly than he was managing, but he did not. He was afraid. Jane was changing, and he knew she would change more at home.

Jane wanted to go home right away, and she thought Holmes was dallying. She shouted at him for the first time in years, and then she cried. And it was true he was dallying. He was afraid to have her in the apartment, and he hated himself for being afraid. It took him fifteen days to get everything arranged.

The day and night nurses were regular, but the afternoon shift was hard to fill for some reason, and three nurses came and went before they got someone permanent. She was around thirty, divorced, with two kids at home. Holmes wondered who stayed with her kids while she was gone, but he didn't have the courage to ask her. She smoked too, and made good company, although she wouldn't take a drink. The other two nurses were all business and housekeeping. Alma became a friend.

Jane stayed in bed or a wheelchair most of the time. Her speech was deteriorating faster now, and sometime she got frustrated trying to talk. But she found the words to give the cancer volunteer hell. The volunteer was trying to explain how to cope with the disease, and the strategy was brutal honesty. The volunteer told Jane that right at the end they would take her back to the hospital and she would die there instead of in the apartment. Jane yelled at the volunteer, but her control of the language was bad by then. When the half-forgotten words finally did prove too hard to put into sentences, Jane hit the volunteer across the ass with a ladle. The volunteer didn't come back.

There wasn't any pain, or at least that was what Jane said, and their family doctor agreed. "No nerve endings in the brain," he said, "so there's no pain to feel."

"How about the heart?" Holmes asked. "Doesn't the heart have nerve endings?"

"Well of course, in a heart attack the situation is different," the doctor began, but he stopped when he got the point.

Holmes came upon the village from the beach. He had lost his socks somewhere behind him, so he slipped his shoes onto his bare feet and headed up to the terrace where he'd had a beer earlier that day.

The terrace was full of villagers, all dancing or drinking. The boom box held true to its name and blasted its music out of nine-inch speakers set up on a beam below the thatch roof. Oil lamps hung from the same beam, and they cast a weak glow on straw-hatted men and kerchiefed women. At a few of the tables, lone men sat with glasses and half-empty bottles of rum. Holmes was the only tourist among them all.

He had intended to ask for help to get the Vespa going, or at least for a lift out on someone's truck to pick up the machine and return it to the hotel. But he didn't speak enough Spanish to explain himself and he didn't know who to ask. There were no waiters, or at least none of them looked like waiters, so Holmes leaned against the wooden railing and waited to figure out how he was supposed to get a beer. It was awkward, staring at them the way he was doing. They must have felt like animals in a zoo, and Holmes would have left if he did not need a drink so badly. An old man at one of the tables beckoned to him. Holmes pretended not to notice, but the man beckoned again, and Holmes took the chair across from him.

He was a dry old man, wrinkled and white-headed, but his arms looked strong. Holmes could see the muscles even in the bad light. The old man said something slowly, but Holmes shook his head. "No hablo Espanol," he said, and then, in desperation, said one of the few words he knew. "Cerveza?" The old man pointed to the store beside the terrace. Holmes got up and went to it. It did not have much food for the only store in the village. Some Knorr soups, rolls, and canned food. There were a lot of candies, a cooler, and dozens of bottles of rum on three shelves across one wall. There was a sullen woman minding the counter, and Holmes got two quart bottles of beer from the cooler. Then he thought it might be a good idea to offer something to the old man. He bought a half bottle of rum and a can of Coke, and the woman gave him a glass. Awkwardly, Holmes carried everything back to the table.

I must look like a real American, Holmes thought, carrying too much stuff at once. He set the bottles on the table, opened the rum and offered a drink to the old man. The old man nodded. Holmes opened up a beer and tried to drink it fast without making it look fast. He had had lots of practise.

The old man pointed to the rum. He wanted Holmes to drink some. "I can't," Holmes explained. "I'm trying to get off the stuff. This beer is bad enough, but if I get started on rum, I'm a gonner." He hoped the idea would get through. It didn't. The old man insisted that Holmes drink with him, and the black hand poured three fingers of rum into Holmes's glass. The hand added a splash of Coke.

Holmes was drinking when someone patted him gently on the back. It was a young man in a red shirt and red pants. He had a machete strapped to his side. "Moto?" he asked. Holmes pointed down the road the way he had come and made motions of disgust. He had intended to ask for help, but the machete at the man's side dissuaded him. A group of men became interested in the fate of the Vespa. They gathered around and began to speak loudly. The smiling man wanted Holmes to go with him. Together, they would get the Vespa and bring it back. But they all wore machetes and Holmes felt uneasy, so he shook his head. "Manana", he said, "hotel", hoping they would understand that he would let the hotel do the job the next morning. This started another round of chattering and gestures. More people looked at Holmes and some of the couples stopped dancing.

Holmes drained his glass. Good people, he thought. Wonderful people. Maybe if he said it often enough, he would stop feeling uneasy. The rum had helped, and he drank some more beer. That helped too. He got up and went to the store again, where he bought two bottles of rum and some plastic glasses. Back on the terrace, he opened one bottle of rum and began to pour the liquor into the glasses and pass them to the men. It was hard to tell if the men were genuinely pleased with the drinks. Holmes hoped it did not look like he was trying to buy them off.

He passed the second bottle to one of the men and sat down at his table again. The old man was shaking his head. So it had been a mistake to buy drinks, Holmes thought. The old man split the remainder of the half bottle between them. "Rapido", he said, and drank the rum down. The instructions were clear enough, and Holmes followed suit. The rum burned his throat, and he chased it with more beer. So much for his resolutions. The rum would hit in a minute, and he braced himself for the blast. Think clearly, he told himself.

He would soon be abandoning thought altogether, so it was necessary to plan strategy. The old man did it for him. "Go home," he said in English. "Rapido."

Holmes tried to compose his face so it looked like it belonged to a dignified man. But he did not feel dignified. A sense of hilarity was rising in him, and he fought to keep it down. He shook hands with the old man and then rose from the table carefully, not wanting to knock his knee against the chair. Careful, he thought. Don't make a fool of yourself. He turned to wave at the people on the terrace. "Thanks everyone," he shouted, not too loudly, he hoped. "Thanks for everything and have a wonderful evening." What the hell, why not, "And may God bless."

Oil lamps glowed inside the open doors of shacks on either side of the road. Holmes thought about every step he took because he did not want to be seen as some typical drunken tourist. Men were playing cards at a table set up outside. At some doors there was no light at all, and only a cigarette end showed that someone was sitting in a chair and watching him pass. It was important to keep walking straight. Children were not as reserved as their parents, and one boy rushed forward and asked Holmes for a peso. Probably not a good idea to be handing out money, Holmes thought, but his hand was passing the child a bill even as his mind was thinking he shouldn't do it. The boy squealed in delight and then checked the number on the bill under a nearby lamp. Too much, thought Holmes. I must have given him ten.

He was out of the village now, or at least on the outskirts. This was where the concrete block houses stood. They were shuttered tight, and behind one of them Holmes could hear the unsteady beat of an electric generator that needed tuning. The sound of the suburbs, he thought.

It was safe to laugh now. He had been so funny on the terrace. Passing out booze like a missionary passing out rosaries. He was the emissary of alcoholism.

As Holmes laughed, he walked off the road and found himself among the coconut palms. Careful. Drunk. He was nearing the swamp and bush that surrounded the hotel grounds. A natural barrier. The road narrowed and he could feel it getting stony underfoot. Careful. There were pot holes there. He had almost driven into one of them with the Vespa. One wrong step and he'd break his ankle and have to crawl back to the hotel.

The bush on either side of the road closed in on him now. Not much room. He would have to move over to let pass the people coming up from behind him. He wondered why they were walking towards the hotel. Strict entry rules there. No question of grabbing a quick drink. They were wearing sandals. He could hear the flop of them against the road surface behind him. They must be in a rush. They were running.

He thought it was a joke when the arms grabbed him from behind. A full Nelson; he hadn't put anyone in a full Nelson since high school, when they'd tried to see if anyone could break out of it. Then other hands began to reach for his pockets. They were big, rough hands, and then he remembered the only way to get out of a full Nelson was to step on the holder's instep. Hard.

Holmes heard the crunch of breaking bones followed by a howl, and now he was really afraid. He had hurt the man. The arms dropped off his shoulders and he beat off the hands that were digging in his pockets and began to run. Only one way to go. The bush on either side of the road was too thick to cut into, so he'd have to run straight. How far to the gate? A mile? How fast could he run a mile? He would beat them to the gate. He was scared as hell and he could feel the wind whizing past his ears as he ran. Not even winded yet.

The slap of sandals against the road behind him. How many feet? Six? They couldn't run fast in sandals. That was sure. His legs were starting to ache. He had a stitch in his side, but he could not stop. He had to run. The slap of sandals on the road behind him.

Hands were reaching for his shirt. He lunged forward and the hands broke away. Dark. He would make it. He was scared and he could run faster than they could.

An arm curled around his throat and threw him back onto the road. No voices. They didn't say anything. The man with the broken foot could not have been among them, so they would not be angry. He thought of machetes. Could they have run that fast and still have been carrying machetes? Hands flipped him over so his face was pressed against the gritty pavement of the road. Two pairs of hands held him down as another pair went through his pockets and removed the contents. There was hushed talking. The voices sounded familiar. A conference? A judgement?

He got a kick in the side and he vomited immediately. Another kick caught him behind the ear and scraped his face against the pavement. Another kick in the side and something broke. "Bastante". Fast slap of sandals against the hard surface of the road. Receding. He vomited again.

Sit up. Move away from the filth and try to get some air in your lungs. Don't gulp air or you'll puke again. The booze was supposed to be a pain killer. It shouldn't have hurt the way it did. Bastards. His head was bleeding behind his right ear and his face felt as if a hundred tiny pebbles had driven into the skin. He felt his side, trying to see if anything was broken. Couldn't tell.

He tried to stand up, but he flopped back onto the road again. Breathe. Breathe slowly and deeply. Count a hundred breaths. He stood again and did not fall this time. He started to walk towards the hotel. His side hurt.

Was he walking the right way? Dark. Hard to tell. He did not want to end up in the village again. The one with the broken foot would be very angry. Holmes stopped and checked his pockets. Money gone. Key to his room too. He would have to get a new one at the front desk. Probably looked a mess. Everyone would see him if he went to the desk for a new key. Get the guard at the gate to get him a new key. Avoid the lobby at all costs.

He came out at the intersection of the road and the hotel driveway. He could see the lights at the gateman's post. Walk straight now. Mouth must smell of puke and rum. Don't get too close to the guard.

"Stop please."

Holmes tried to follow the command, but it took a long time to make his body stop, and when it did, he swayed forward and then fell onto the road. The guard did not come forward to help him. Holmes stood back up himself.

"Fuera."

"I'm a guest here," said Holmes.

"You're bleeding."

"I said I'm a guest here."

The light was shining behind the gateman's head and Homes could not make out his features.

"Show me your key."

"For Christ's sakes, I've been mugged. My money and my key were stolen. Are you going to let me bleed to death here on the road?"

"Como?"

"Sonofabitch, you heard what I said."

"You got a key?"

"My name is Holmes. Everybody here knows me. Ask the barman."

"You got a key?"

"Are you a parrot or something? What kind of assholes do they put at this gate anyway?"

"No key."

"Move aside."

The gate man held him. It didn't hurt, but Holmes couldn't move.

"Wait. I will call the desk."

"Let me pass."

He was pushed back. He stumbled and almost fell again.

"You wait."

"Fuck you. I'm not going to wait for anybody. I'll walk around to the beach and come in through there, you asshole."

"I will phone the beach guard and he will stop you. Wait until I phone the desk. Someone will come."

It was so reasonable. Holmes knew the gate man was being reasonable. Why couldn't he just wait and let the man do it?

"Fuck you. I'm going through."

The guard finally lost his patience.

"Okay you Club Med cocksucker. Go back there. We have our own drunks. Let the Club Med doctor sew up your head."

"I'll get in. Just watch me." Holmes turned around and walked out of the circle of light.

Stupid. He knew he was being stupid. But he wasn't going to sit down, meek and mild, and wait for some other guard to come and pick him up. He could not go back the way he had come. He turned the other way instead. The road cut through the swamp that way too, behind the resort and around to the beach on the far side. The beach was no good. The guards there had radios. He had seen them. He would cut straight through the bush that surrounded the resort and come in by the tennis courts. The trick was to figure out how far along the road he should go before he cut through the bush. Didn't want to go scrabbling through the jungle and end up at the gatepost again. The idiot would probably shoot.

Drunk. None of this had to happen, but I got drunk.

The road was very dark and narrow now. He guessed that he had gone far enough and the resort would be no more than a few hundreds yards away, on the other side of the narrow swath of jungle. He started searching for an opening in the bush. He wanted to sneak back into the hotel compound. Holmes found a place where he could walk in among the vines.

"Is there no therapy you can give her to help her with her speech?" Holmes asked the doctor.

"The tumor is affecting her brain. Exercises won't change that."

"Surely there must be something you can do."

"Holmes." The doctor put his hand on his shoulder. Holmes didn't want the hand there, but he didn't want to shake it off either. "She's dying. The only thing you can do for a dying woman is keep her happy and comfortable as possible."

But how could he keep a dying woman happy?

The nurses helped. Jane couldn't walk any more, and they showed him how to lift her into the wheelchair. She was losing the ability to use her hands. He made coffee and let it cool until it became lukewarm, and then put a straw in the cup and held it up to her mouth. She could still suck the coffee. That and inhale cigarette smoke. She didn't eat much. Once she tried to say something, and could only get out a few garbled sentences. She stopped talking altogether. If he knew Jane, it was because she heard herself saying nonsense and was too embarrassed to keep on. She didn't want to croak out strange sounds. Better not to speak at all.

"It's something she's going through, and you just do the best you can for her," said Alma, echoing the doctor's words. The other nurses said the same thing, but it sounded better coming from Alma. She was sitting at the kitchen table, reading the front section as he went through the sports pages. Her second cigarette was burning in the ashtray, keeping his second glass of whisky company. He bought the cheap brands now because he did not have guests any more and it seemed a waste of money to pay for fancy labels. If he could not cut down on the drinking, at least he could cut down on the expense.

"Who takes care of your kids?" Holmes asked impulsively over his newspaper. He only lowered the paper an inch, so if she gave him a short answer, he could raise it back up again.

"My mother-in-law."

"I thought you were divorced."

"I am, but I kept the apartment and she lives in the same building. Easier for the kids and their father that way. He kills two birds with one stone. Sees his mother and his kids at one stop, and I don't have to be there when he comes around."

"We never had any kids," said Holmes.

"Choice?"

"No. Jane had two miscarriages. We married late. Now I'm glad we don't have kids so they can't see what's happening."

"Kids can take a lot. They're tougher than you think. I only see mine weekends and mornings and we get along okay, all things considered."

"I don't feel very tough."

He hadn't wanted to say it, but it just came out. "Sometimes," he said, dropping his voice so Jane wouldn't overhear him, "I can hear her breath start to rasp, you know, when her lungs haven't been pumped yet, and I go into that room and it's like someone else is lying there. It's not Jane any more. It's some kind of monster that crawled into her body and I'm afraid to touch her, and then I'm sick because I know she's dying. I think maybe I should sleep beside her because she must get lonely at night, but I'm afraid to do it. I'd think of her reaching for me at night and I'd jump out of bed and run away from her. And she knows how I feel. I can see it in her eyes. At first she doesn't even recognize me when I come into the room, and then this kind of wisdom comes into her eyes. It's like she finally sees what I'm made of."

Holmes felt tears coming on. Alma dropped her newspaper and came over to his side of the kitchen table. She crouched down beside him and put her hand on his knee. He managed not to cry. That was something. At least he hadn't cried on her shoulder.

Holmes stepped into a deep puddle of warm water and then felt his feet sink into the muck at the bottom. Something with a hard, shelled back scuttled into the undergrowth away from his feet. Holmes lifted his foot, but it came slowly, making a slurping sound as if the mud underfoot were a mouth trying to suck him down. Mosquitos were feasting on his neck. "Drink my blood and you'll get drunk," said Holmes. He was sweating and pushing aside vines and he did not want to think about Jane. But it seemed as if he didn't have much choice. She was coming back to him whether he wanted her to or not.

Jane did not get out of bed much any more, not even to ride around in the wheelchair. Holmes ordered a hospital bed that could be cranked up so she wasn't always flat on her back, but fluid still accumulated in her lungs and it had to be pumped out with the machine that made gurgling sounds. Her hair started to grow back in, and the nurses stopped putting on the scarf Jane had worn to hide her baldness. Jane had always had black hair. Friends had laughed about it and called her the black-haired temptress who finally lured him into marriage. But the hair growing in was partially gray. Holmes did not even know how long she had been dying it. Maybe years. It hurt him that her secrets were being stripped away. He took all of the mirrors out of her room.

Alma held his hand. He knew he should have felt stupid about it, but she sat beside him on the couch watching TV and she held his hand. Alma wasn't so good about the housekeeping, and the night nurse complained about unwashed supper dishes. The night nurse always eyed Holmes as if he were a criminal.

Jane lost so much weight he didn't want to look at her any more. Skin hung down from her arms. Holmes no longer knew if she even recognized him. With her right hand, she started to reach up towards the spot on her head where the surgeons had made the cut for the exploratory surgery. She would reach up suddenly, as if she were checking to see if the wound were bleeding. It had healed a long time before. She explored the spot with her fingers and then let the hand drop. In a minute, she repeated the action.

"Does it hurt?" Holmes whispered to her, but she made no response of any kind. Maybe she didn't understand him any more or maybe she just couldn't be bothered. She was drifting away from him.

"It's been one hell of a day," said Alma when she came in that afternoon. She didn't even bother to look in on Jane, but sat right down at the kitchen table and lit up a smoke. "My ex came over while I was working yesterday afternoon. Drunk. Wrecked the place and scared his mother and kids half to death. She couldn't find my number to reach me and she was afraid the cops would lock him up if she dialled 911. Big deal. She's so worried about her son she lets him terrorize his kids and smash four hundred dollars worth of dishes that she gave us as a wedding present. I was up all night cleaning the place and calming down the kids. Today I phoned the police and lodged a complaint."

"Drink?" Holmes asked. He was on his fourth whisky of the afternoon.

"Got any vodka?" she asked. "The night nurse is a bitch. She's got a nose like a bloodhound. You pour it for me and I'll check on Jane. Lots of ice."

Holmes poured the drink.

"Not too good, eh?" Alma said when she came back.

"What do you mean?"

"I mean she's not doing too well. What's the last time the doctor came by?" Alma started to flip through the notes the day nurse had left. "Maybe you ought to take a look in on her," she said.

"Now?"

"Good a time as any."

Holmes started to walk down the hall from the kitchen. He had not been in to see her for two days. He could hear that her breathing was worse, heavy and laboured. The sound was like a sigh, and then it almost squeaked and whistled, and then it gurgled when she inhaled. It was dark in the hall, but he could hear the breathing all right. He made it as far as her door, but he could not look in.

When he came back to the kitchen, Alma had finished her drink.

"You look terrible, honey," and she poured another one for each of them. She'd been calling him honey for a while and he liked it. Once he'd worried that Jane might hear, but he had stopped worrying about that. "Come into the living room," and she led him by the hand and turned on the TV. They had another couple of drinks.

Holmes was lost. He stopped and wiped the sweat off his forehead. The blood from the wound behind his ear had dried and caked, but the mosquitoes seemed to be all the more attracted to it. If only that damn marengo band were playing, he could follow the sound of the sax back to the hotel.

Alma and Holmes moved closer and closer to one another on the couch until it only seemed natural that they should begin to undress one another. He had not been with a woman for so long that he had forgotten how much he wanted it. He came very fast, but Alma cooed in his ear and played with him until he was hard again and then they had done it one more time.

"You'll see honey," she said, "it'll make you feel better."

Holmes was not sure he felt better at all. He straightened out the cover on the sofa as Alma went to check on Jane.

"Can I use your shower?" she asked when she came back. Holmes looked at her and she must have seen the funny look.

"I've got to look good when the night nurse comes in," said Alma. "You make us some coffee and I'll only be a minute." She was fast, out of the shower before the coffee had finished percolating. She took a quick sip of her coffee. She stood close to Holmes and he could smell the toothpaste on her breath. He wondered whose brush she had used.

"Next comes supper," and Alma started to peel and dice onions. The smell was very strong and it made their eyes water. She added some garlic and hamburger meat and made a fast spaghetti sauce. It was strange. Alma didn't usually cook very much. He thought she was just being nice, but she looked preoccupied. She ate quickly.

"Bring me the glasses from the living-room, will you?" she asked Holmes, and then she washed the glasses and the dinner plates. Holmes was going to pour himself a drink after they ate, but she asked him to hold off. She turned on the radio.

Holmes walked down the hall to the bathroom. Alma had put everything neatly in place. His towel was wet, but there weren't even any stray drops of water on the floor. When he came out, he paused outside Jane's room.

No sound. He looked in the door. Jane lay very still; the raspy breathing had subsided. He waited to see Jane raise her hand to the side of her head in the reflex motion that had been going on for weeks. Nothing. He hurried back to the kitchen.

"Alma!"

But she was washing something else in the sink and she did not even turn around.

"She's dead," said Alma.

"Well, do something. Punch her heart. Get her breathing again."

"Holmes, she's dead. It's all finished." This still from the sink.

"But who do I call? The doctor?"

"No, the hospital. But not now. Vodka doesn't smell much, but it smells a bit. The onions and garlic should have covered it, but I'll have to wait a couple of hours to be sure."

"Why did it have to happen now?"

"You can't choose the time," said Alma.

"Go and eat some breath mints. I'm calling the hospital."

"Wait. Don't rush. It doesn't make a difference to her any more. I might lose my job."

The mosquitoes were a cloud around his head, buzzing and biting at all the exposed parts of his skin. It was so very dark among the vines and the trees. He put his hand in front to feel for a way to pass through the vegetation, but he could only feel solid plants. No way through. He began to feel further, and made a complete circle without finding a way out. It was impossible. He had come into the place somehow, and if there was a way in, there had to be a way out. He felt again, making the circle, and then he tried feeling lower, for he might have entered the circle through a low opening in the vegetation. There was no opening of any kind. He had walked into a closed circle.

"Help me Jane. I'm lost," he said.

Chapter 6

The story provoked silence. Even Paul, the jolliest of jolly men, the kind who was asked to play Santa Claus, dug moodily into the fire with a stick. He turned over a log and a shower of sparks flew into the air like short-lived fireflies. At Margaret's urging, Simon picked up a bottle of gin and started making the rounds, topping off people's glasses. Victor shook his head solemnly when Simon offered him a drink.

Teresa took half a glass, and when Simon had finished pouring, she rose from her place and walked over to where Butler was sitting. She sat down beside him.

"What are you scribbling?" she asked. Her hair looked wind-blown, even though there was no wind, and she had her sunglasses perched up on her head. Her sweater was tossed over her shoulders and the arms knotted above her breasts. Her hip, warm and insistent, was pressed against Butler's. Another chance, thought Butler. He was desperate for another chance.

"Just some notes on the story," he said, shutting the notebook to show that she meant more to him than the notebook did.

Victor had uncanny hearing ability. Everything that was said seemed to find its way to his ears.

"Not just notes, my quiet little scribe. You are recording the whole proceeding."

The others at the fire looked at Butler.

"Every time somebody tells a story, you dig through it to find hope for the future. You're keeping score, but I know the score already. The evidence is piling up in my favour, and it's going to pile up higher still."

This was the kind of talk the seminary had trained Butler to deal with, but the warmth of Teresa's hip against his own distracted him. She put her mouth close to his ear and cupped her hands.

"Do you think oral sex is too dangerous?" Teresa asked, and then smiled.

"Definitely not," Butler answered immediately. Victor was still looking at him, but Teresa's presence was more important. He could smell the gin and tonic on her breath. He liked gin and tonic, and he would have liked to taste the traces of it on her lips. For the first time in years, Butler's heart was beginning to stir. He could hear it beating in his chest and he felt short of breath. He was afraid it was a prelude to a coronary attack.

"I'll make you a bet," Victor boomed at Butler.

"I don't gamble," Butler answered. Her lips were so close and so soft. A strong prudishness had grown in him after Elaine disappeared through the ice. He had come to fear women somehow, first because another woman would have meant the betrayal of Elaine, and later out of habit. He was afraid, but he was willing to give up his fear and kiss her at fireside. He was ready to have the others laugh at him, or look away in embarrassment. It did not matter. Nothing mattered but her lips.

"I say I'll make you a bet anyway," Victor insisted.

Why couldn't the man leave him alone?

"All fishermen gamble. They gamble that they're going to catch something, and when they're not fishing, they're playing poker."

"Cliches," said Butler. He could still do it. He could still reach for Teresa.

"I'll make you an offer like one you've never had," Victor went on. "I'll give you the world if you win, and annihilation if you lose."

"You haven't got the means to offer either," Butler answered. Victor was distracting him. He pulled back from the proximity of Teresa's lips.

"I do. And I make my offer to all of you, not just Butler. This world is on its way out, but the closing scene drags on and on and I'm getting sick of it. There've been too many encores, too many reprieves. The whole story of the end of the world is beginning to bore me to tears. I say we speed the whole thing up. I think we should play sudden death."

Sudden death. The words had taken the coolness out of Victor's voice, and it became tense with repressed excitement and disgust. He was disgusted with all those at the fireside, with himself, and with the very earth under his feet.

"Listen, all of you. Butler here will keep a tally of the stories you tell. He'll be our score keeper. Anyone can tell a story. Until dawn. That will mark the end of the game. When the sun comes up, we'll check the score. Think about it, you can say anything you want. Spin fairy tales if you like. If you win, I'll let you keep your miserable world, such as it is. But if I win, well... if I win, I'll bring down the apocalypse."

Victor smiled.

"Think of it. The end of the world. I can hear the hoof-beats of the four horsemen coming over the horizon. All I have to do is give them my signal, and they'll be with us. I'm offering you the end of all existence. Peace. But you have the power to stop it if you want to. All of you here, with your little anecdotes, can stave off sudden death. If you can find enough good faith in this night, why, you can live on to drink gin until your livers shrivel into little figs."

"You're nuts," said Stan.

"Nuts. Sure. I'm crazy. Anything you like. I don't care what you call me. Just tell me if you're willing to take me up on my bet. Butler?"

All thought of Teresa fled. The man was probably crazy, but the intensity of his conviction was catching, and a slow wave of fear began to wash over Butler.

"You haven't got the means to offer destruction. So what's the point in betting with you?"

"But I am God," Victor insisted. "In this one way, I am God. Believe me, in my litter I've got the means to end it all right now. I'm dragging the end of the world with me. Why should I wait any longer? I'm getting tired. I'm as exhausted as the world, and both of us need to be put out of our misery."

Butler looked at the litter, and it seemed to confirm Victor's insanity. The thing was packed with garbage. Aerosol cans and candy wrappers. And yet Victor spoke with such assurance. He talked with the conviction of power of a man who held a gun in his hand. Everyone looked from the litter to Victor. Everyone but Teresa, who looked at Butler.

"I'm not exhausted," she said. "I still want to do everything. Sex is just one of the things I can't give up. I mean, I know that AIDS and syphilis and gonorrhea and cyclymata and herpes, and that new disease, CLOT, are all waiting to do me in. Not that I'd get into it with someone I didn't know and trust. I'm not *stupid*, you know, but I'm not willing to give up that bit of intimacy either. I'm willing to make a few compromises. Look, it's like deodorant. I know those spray cans are ruining the environment, so I try to get a pump container if I can. But sometimes, especially these days, I can't find any pump containers and the roll-ons and sticks are all sold out. So what if nobody used deodorant before the fifties? Somehow they lived without it, but I'm not part of that time. I can't give up deodorant any more than I can go into a convent the way they did in the middle ages. I'm a victim of consumerism, sure, but I'm also a woman of my time."

"What's the point?" Victor asked impatiently.

"I want to know if you're a virgin."

"What does that have to do with anything?"

"Well, you talk like someone who's never been laid."

Butler shifted his weight with alarm. Why was she talking to Victor about sex? Teresa should be talking to him about it.

"You trivialize. Just like a woman to oversimplify."

Teresa did not seem to be offended in the least.

"Misogynist, eh? Don't like women? That's okay. Have you ever been laid by a man?"

"The thought is repugnant."

"Well you just don't seem to like anybody. What's the matter, doesn't your dinky work?"

"Butler!" Victor shouted the name loudly to drown out Teresa. "Will you be the score keeper? Will you write the stories down?"

"I'll write them, but that doesn't mean I accept your gamble."

"How is he supposed to keep score?" Dianne asked. "Who's going to decide if the stories save the world or not?"

"You'll know," said Victor. "You'll know when the stories are done if you smell victory or if you've got that sick feeling in your gut. Ever quit smoking? Do you know the anxiety you feel when you wake up one morning and know that you can smoke no cigarettes that day? Not after coffee. Not after lunch. Never. You think maybe you're going to explode, or lose your mind. If you've got that feeling when this night is over, then you'll know the end has come. The end of the world at last."

No one stirred. Victor was standing now, beside his litter in the firelight, and there was something about his triumphant bearing that made him utterly convincing. And yet, how was it possible?

"Just silence at the end," said Victor. "Peace and silence. Why are you looking so depressed? The end is coming anyway. We are being fried in a slow oven. Why not help the end along? No more frustration. No more hunger. No more anger at the stupidity of the world at large. I'd look forward to it if I were you. And I am carrying the end of the world with me. The end of the world is waiting for us at dawn."

"Do you have any kids?" Alice Waver asked. Her two children were still asleep with their heads on her lap. She would have put them to bed long before, but Victor's presence at the fire made her uneasy and she wanted to keep them beside her.

"No."

"Of course you don't, or you wouldn't be talking the way you are now."

"I don't have any children, but it's not through any accident. I thought long and hard about children, and when my musings were over, I went to a doctor and had a vasectomy. Getting the vasectomy wasn't easy either. They wanted me to be a father with a brood of children before they'd let me have one, just in case I changed my mind later on. Nothing I said about the steadfastness of my resolution did any good. I'm sure it would have been much easier for me to get an abortion. But I did find someone, finally, to do the job for me, and I'm happy to say that I'll never bring children into this world, not even by accident."

"Nobody would fuck you anyway," said Teresa. "If your cock is as sour as your face, it'd sting when you slipped it up."

Alice too, was unimpressed by his argument.

"You wouldn't be looking forward to the end of the world if you had children."

"There will always be children, and some are bound to be caught in the apocalypse. It's just their bad luck, or the fault of their parents for bringing them into the world in the first place. I know I blame my father and mother for the sorry state of the universe as I found it. And as the universe is in a sorrier state now than when I was born, I expect my children would hate me all the more. And another thing. Everyone is always talking about living for their children. This has been going on for centuries, millenia! Why can't people work on improving their world instead of getting sidetracked by the little brats? If everyone is living for kids, who is living for himself? Would Aristotle have been a finer man for having spent half his life changing diapers? Would Nietzche have thought better thoughts if he'd spent every Saturday and Sunday afternoon watching his kids climb up the slide in the park?"

Alice Waver just shook her head as if Victor were an idiot, but Odds cut in.

"I'm kind of curious about this end of the world business you keep talking about. It's important to me, you see, because I've got a lot of goods on that wagon, and I'd be embarrassed if I got caught with so much stock on hand when the end came. So I'm thinking that even now I should be having a big sale of some kind if what you say is true."

"About children?" asked Victor.

"No, about the end of the world. You want to lay down all these rules and you want to make Butler a score keeper. But look at that man, will you? Teresa's all over him and I wouldn't be surprised if he was more interested in his pecker right now than he was in these stories we've been telling. No offence, Butler. So here you are, offering to end the world for all of us, but I'm not really sure you can do it. What are you planning, some kind of rain dance to bring on another flood? That wouldn't do any good, because I've got inflatable boats and MRE's enough to last way longer than forty days. Or are you carrying an atomic bomb in that litter of yours? One of the new kind, maybe, the small ones? But even that wouldn't mean the end of the world, because you'd only be able to blow *us* up, along with a few square klicks of the muskeg. That wouldn't really be the end of the *world*, now would it? The end of *our* world maybe, but not the end of the world at large. So if you're going to play this game of yours, and we haven't even said we agree to the rules yet, we've got to know whether or not you can deliver."

"I can deliver all right," said Victor. "I've got all I need right here in my litter. Just stretch out my hand and push, and the whole world ends."

"But what's your weapon, a Tootsie bar wrapper?"

"Better than that, my capitalist friend. I have the smallest weapon ever developed to bring about the end of mankind. Let me tell you how I got my hands on it."

"I think he's talking about his dinkey," said Margaret, but Victor ignored her.

"I started heading North a long time ago. I'm from Florida, but no one has lived there for the last eight years. I was one of the last ones to leave, one of the last ones to survive the reign of the giant alligators that spread as the air grew hotter and the salt marshes swelled. I had this idea for the litter even then. I've been pulling the scrap behind me for seven years now. I'm sure there's not one piece of the original left, because I've had to build and rebuild it as parts wore out. When I got the idea for the cairn, I had to be choosy. If I'd picked up all the garbage I found along the way, I'd have stalled long before I reached South Carolina. I'd have needed all the garbage trucks in America to haul the trash I found, so instead I decided to pick up only a few pieces. Representative pieces. I got an empty toilet paper roll to represent all toilet paper. A potato chip bag to represent all wrappings, and so on. But as I moved North, I found that I was missing one piece of representative trash. I wanted something military. I could have gone to a gun shop and bought a revolver. Even a bazooka. But I wanted something better than that. I wanted the ultimate piece of military equipment. I thought of those small atomic bombs you talked about, but even the smallest ones were too too heavy to drag very far. I needed something just as lethal. More lethal, if possible, but something I could take along with me.

"And I found it--at an army research base in upper New York State. The place was pretty well abandoned, and falling apart like everything else. But some people can never let go of what they have been doing. I have seen car repair garages where no automobile passed for months. And inside this research station, I found a man in a lab jacket still experimenting as if the Soviet Union still existed and still continued to be the biggest threat to our existence. He was a real pure science kind of fellow, the kind who did not give a thought to how his discoveries might be used. He was reticent, and hated to talk to me because I was interrupting his work, but I found out all I needed to know from a former guard who was the only other person who had not abandoned the base.

"What kept the guard there was the easy availability of alcohol. He was an alcoholic, and the worst kind at that. He was steady about it, the kind who drank throughout the day without ever lapsing into a binge. The kind who did his job, more or less, and was ignored as long as he got by. He stayed because there were forty-five gallon drums of alcohol all over the base. Almost pure, white, tasteless alcohol. The guard liked to add a little water to it. He said it was better than vodka.

"And like most drinkers, this guard liked to talk. Here I was, his first audience for weeks, even months, and he showed me around the base as if I was a visiting general.

" 'Here are the concrete bunkers where we keep the nerve gas,' he said, and he showed me how he kept the iron doors sealed all the time. He was proud of his guard duty, you see. He wanted to prove to me that even though he was an alcoholic, he could still get the job done. He finally opened the seals on the door and led me into a locked storage room. It was very impressive, with triple steel doors and airlocks that still worked.

"But the store room was largely empty. At least I thought it was. Shelves upon shelved lines the walls. But at the end of one was an ordinary-looking tin.

" 'Nerve gas', the drunk said proudly. So what? I asked him. I had expected to find even more evidence of human folly.

" 'Not just any nerve gas,' he said. 'It's the most powerful nerve gas ever developed. It's fail-safe nerve gas. One good, long spray, and most of the world gets wiped out in a few months. Maybe even the whole world. There's been no chance to try it out. If you spray it, you see, you're the first one to drop.

"The tin looked so ordinary, I didn't want to believe him. I thought the drinking had given him delusions. It was a king-size spray can with the kind of nozzle you see on disposable fire extinguishers. And there was no antidote.

"That was the weapon the scientist was working on. An antidote, or failing that, a better delivery system. He hasn't found the antidote yet, and the odds are he never will. You see, one long spray, and you drop. There's no time to reach for an antidote.

"Getting my hands on the tin was the easiest thing I've ever done. Shop-lifting is harder. I just reached up to the shelf, picked up the tin and slipped off the cap. What could the guard possibly do? Threaten me? I walked away with the most powerful weapon man has produced, and I put it in the litter with the rest of my garbage.

"So you see Odds, I do have what it takes. Look at this."

Victor dug into his litter and removed a tin. It looked like a family size can of Dreamwhip, except that the can was painted black. Victor flipped off the top and exposed the spray nozzle.

"One long spray and we're all dead. We, and eventually, everyone else on this continent. Maybe everyone else in the world once the wind and water carry the poison far enough.

Butler's eyes were on the aerosol can, so small in Victor's hand. It seemed impossible that the tin contained all of the world, all of the living and breathing animals and insects, to say nothing of people. If what he said was true, then a spray from the nozzle would mean the end of all living creatures on the earth, though perhaps not the plants. Victor had said nothing of the plants. The lichens and grasses and trees would cover the earth again, but the woods and the fields would be silent, empty of the chatter of monkeys, the whistle of birds, and the strange humming of cicadas. The thought of forests whose only sound would be the rustle of leaves in the wind was somehow both calming and horrifying, like a stage upon which no actor ever walked.

"Will you take my bet?" Victor asked.

"The man is so cocksure, I'm half tempted to do it," said Margaret. "We can say anything we want all night. We can tell dirty jokes until the sun comes up, and then be done with him."

"Man's probably out of his mind anyway," said Mike. "His story sounds like a lot of bullshit to me. Who ever heard of a spray can that could end the world? It's nuts. Engineers and weapons-makers don't think like that. They think in terms of big delivery systems. More money in it."

"Then let's just do it," said Victor.

"Wait," Butler said. "No one's agreed!"

"No one disagreed, so now it's too late," said Victor, and he settled himself on the earth at the fireside. He cradled the spray can in his lap, but he did not put the cap back on it. The poison, if it really was poison, was within easy reach.

"Who's going to talk first?" Victor asked.

The silence was long. Nobody wanted to open his mouth first, and for a time the only sound had been the crackle of flame as some new branches caught fire. Butler wondered what time it was, and whether there would be enough time to save the world from extinction. He laughed to himself. He wanted to remind himself that Victor was just a crackpot. He could neither save the world nor end it.

"Time is going to run out on you if nobody says anything," Victor finally said, and the words made the air taste bad.

"No way to have a party," said Paul. "No time to get blue. Everybody's just taking things too seriously."

Paul liked to say he was retired, but Butler had never been clear on what he had retired from. Few people had regular jobs to be retired from any more. Perhaps he was just a man who had retired from care. He had a broad face with so many lines and wrinkles on it that it looked like a topographical map. It looked like the kind of face that was easy to read, because all the wrinkles were made by a lifetime of laughter and smiling and conviviality.

Paul was a bit comical. You could see him living happily in a trailer park, fussing with the gas barbecue and offering beers to the neighbours. But you could also imagine the bottom falling out of his grocery bag and the ketchup and worcestershire sauce falling to the sidewalk with a splat. Paul would grin sheepishly when it happened. You expected him to run over the cord if he used an electric lawn-mower, and to be taken for a little extra cash by the plumber.

THE PARADE DOWN MAIN STREET
The Cross-Examination of Paul

"Come on gang, brighten up!" said Paul.

"What makes you so happy?" Victor asked.

"Just the way I am."

"I don't believe it."

"I'm a party man. Always was, always will be. It's the way I was raised and it's the way I'll be until the day I die. Parties and I go a long way back, all the way back before I was born."

"This sounds like the first story to me," said Victor, and he hunkered down with his shoulders low and his hands clutched together between his legs.

"Me? I'm not much of a story - just one party after another would sum my life up pretty well."

"Let's consider that life," Victor said, and his tone was friendly for a change. He sounded as if he wanted to chat about something as ordinary as a baseball game.

"I can tell you about it in a minute. What set the tone of my life was the way my mother and father met. People meet in all kinds of ways, but my mother and father's was special. It set a stamp on their whole lives, and mine too. They fell in love at a parade. You know, a no-holds-barred, swinging party. Why, I can see the majorettes tossing their batons and the brass band blasting out Yankee Doodle Dandy. There were floats too, lots of them. Big green papier maché frogs that rumbled over the streets. Clowns jumping around and tossing bucket-fulls of confetti onto the crowd. You know how clowns are. They might have picked somebody out of the crowd and hauled them into the parade to join the grand procession. And at the end of it all there was a big bonfire, the biggest, grandest bonfire you've ever seen."

Victor nodded as if he could see the picture in front of him.

"Are you an American?"

"Lived most of my life in Chatham, Ontario, but I was born in Europe."

"I don't see why a brass band in Europe should have been playing Yankee Doodle Dandy," Victor said.

"Well, you're right, of course," Paul admitted good-naturedly. "Must have been my imagination running away with me. My last name isn't really Josephson. That's just a rough translation of Juozapavicius, which was a name too big to fit into an American mouth. My father told me to be proud of that name, and I am, but he also told me we were living in Canada now, and there was no need to drag the old world along with us."

"So where was the parade?" Victor asked.

"In Vilnius. It's the capital of Lithuania."

"Go on."

"Yankee Doodle Dandy or not, there was something about that parade that must have set the tone for my parents' life and mine too. My father always liked a party and I'm the same way. The more people the better, and if there's music, it's better still. My old man threw parties the likes of which have never been seen since, mostly, I guess, because everybody who came was a Lithuanian, and those people knew how to have a good time. I can remember, even as a little kid, everyone coming to our house to celebrate my father's namesday. Uncles drove up from the States with bottles of duty-free Seagrams in the trunk; maiden aunts who usually kept to themselves came in their best clothes and friends from church were knocking on the door every minute. My father always laid on a big stock of ginger ale as mix, and it was heaven for all of us kids. We were kind of poor then, I guess, but that's not even right. It's just the way working-class people lived in the fifties. Soda pop was expensive and we didn't get it unless there was some kind of special occasion. Hell, the pop wasn't even bought for us. It was mix for the booze. Nobody thought of buying cream soda or black cherry for the kids. I tasted my first orange crush when I had my own money from a paper route.

"My mother had been cooking for two days and we kids always got yelled at for walking barefoot across the newly-waxed floor and leaving toe-prints that dried in the wax. We slipped across the shiny surface when we tried to walk across it in our stocking feet. And who wanted to drink from the water bottle in the fridge when there was pop in the house? My mother had to hide it or we would have drunk ourselves sick before the guests arrived.

"And when they arrived, the aunts brought herring with mushrooms and tomato sauce and one of them made a great big Napoleon cake, the kind that took two pounds of butter and two dozen eggs to make. Then about twenty adults crowded around the big dining-room table for pork sausages and roast beef and turkey and the kids ate on the coffee table or in the kitchen.

"The men talked about politics and about the war they were all expecting between America and Russia. But talk of war and bomb shelters didn't dampen anyone's spirits and it worked up a thirst and the men drank iced vodka to wash down the herring. Some of the women drank vodka too, just a little, and you could hear them laughing in the kitchen as they washed dishes between the fish and meat courses.

"One of the rules was that the bottles stayed on the table until they were empty or everyone had collapsed into bed. If someone brought a bottle, it was bad manners to put it away, as if you were saving it for later. No way. The bottles stayed on the table where everyone could see them and gauge how far the party had progressed. If they were lucky, there might be a few shots left over to have with beer at breakfast the next day. Oh, they used to drink then. My father drank like that right up to the age I am now. I have to be careful with alcohol or my head hurts for days on end, but those men got rid of hangovers with a shake of the head and a couple of beers. Hardly anyone drank wine then, unless someone brought a bottle of Mogen-David 'for the women.'

"The volume at those tables rose to a roar and relatives and friends shouted stories and opinions across the table and one of my uncles always told some kind of anecdote that made the women blush. They would tell him to hold his tongue and they would look at us to see if we understood. We listened as carefully as we could, but we could never understand the fuss about skirts and missing trousers.

"And by the time they hauled themselves to the living-room after dinner, everybody was stuffed and drunk and happy, and the evening was still young and there was dancing to do. We pulled out the coffee table and my father had to be helped to the couch because he wasn't too strong on his feet after the vodka and the rye, and he called out for his accordion. My mother hated the accordion because my father had no sense of volume control. The music just had to be loud and fast. The louder and faster, the better he liked it. Uncles and aunts always shouted my mother down and my aunt brought out the accordion and my father started to play.

"It was so loud that it hurt our ears, but everybody crowded into the living-room to dance polkas and waltzes and the younger aunts and uncles tried a tango. I could see the floor bend in an incredible arc at every downbeat, and I thought we'd all end up in the rec room when the beams gave. My older cousin from Montreal took me by the hands. She must have been around fifteen then, and she led me through an awkward rhumba. And even over the smell of sweat and booze and cigarette smoke, I could smell the sweet fragrance that came off her and made me want to be just a few years older.

"I fell asleep on the couch amid all the racket, and somebody lifted me into their arms. I woke, but I kept my eyes shut because I liked to be carried and someone took me up to my room and put me under the covers where a younger boy cousin was already sleeping. My girl cousin from Montreal was supposed to sleep on a mattress on the floor, but she was not there yet, and I desperately wanted to stay awake so I could hear her enter and then peek when she undressed. I listened to the music that always gave way to shouts as somebody got into an argument downstairs, like the time my aunt announced her engagement and my father said the ring was pretty but her finger was not. I waited, wrapped in a cover of longing for my girl cousin, but I could never wait long enough and sleep became stronger than my desire. I woke in the morning with the cloying taste of ginger ale still in my mouth and the searing smell of cigarette smoke in my nose. The house resounded with snores from all the rooms and the grunts of surprise at how vicious the hangovers could be. Only my mother was up and walking around in the kitchen, warming the breakfast ham and hiding some of the liquor left over from the night before so the men would not get drunk again too quickly.

"You see, my life revolved around parties from the first, so how could I help but keep on partying? So there's a reason for keeping us all alive, my friend. The joy of the party. And it was the joy of partying, of a parade, that started the whole thing for me."

Paul beamed at Victor, and the only sound was that of Butler scratching madly as he recorded the story on his note pad. But Victor did not look impressed.

"How old are you Paul?" he asked.

"War baby."

"So your parents met during the war too?"

"Right."

"What kind of parade could it have been if they met during the war?"

"Wars don't stop parades from happening."

"They don't stop them, but they make them different. I can't see how there could have been floats in a wartime parade."

"So maybe it was a military parade. Come to think of it, that's what it must have been. The military has its own bands and it has its own parades."

"But they don't have clowns throwing confetti out of buckets during a military parade. And if there is a war going on, then the parade is a show of might, to fill the spectators with confidence that they're going to win. Even so, it crosses the minds of the spectators that some of those marching men are not going to come home again."

"So maybe it *was* a serious parade. Maybe the look of love that my mother and father exchanged kind of stood out against the gravity of the situation, if you know what I mean. There was my father, a guy dressed like Humphrey Bogart. He had a new gray fedora and a trench coat, and when he looked at my mother a kind of spark shot out between them."

"What kind of man was he?"

"A man of his time, I guess. A good East European immigrant who came to Canada and lived happily ever after."

"Happily ever after?" Victor sounded dubious. "Those are words from a fairy tale. Fairy tales are never true."

"Sure he had problems. Who doesn't? Too much booze was one of them. He'd go into phases when he drank a bottle a day, and then my mother would have to come down heavy on him until he dried himself out. It was tough, and he was mean at times when he was weaning himself off the booze."

"And he was always weaning himself but he never managed to do it for one last time."

"He managed to quit for a while. He never stayed quit though."

"And he was always mean."

"No way. There were good times, really good times. When my mother was away sometimes, you know, at a baby shower or something, the old man would cook up one pan of loose-fried hamburger and another of potatoes, the only meal he knew how to make. Nobody thought of vegetables then. At least he didn't."

"What did you do after supper? Did he take you out to play baseball?"

"Hah! Are you crazy? You're talking WASP. My old man was a European. He thought baseball was for children and idiots."

"So what did he do after supper?"

"He went down to the basement and drank a quarter bottle of rye whisky. Then he tried to make sure he was in bed before my mother came home so she wouldn't be able to tell he'd been drinking. But the smell always gave him away. And sometimes he wouldn't go to bed at all. He'd sit in the living-room without bothering to turn the lights on, and he'd talk to himself. I'd be so embarrassed I'd stay in my room, but sometimes he'd come looking for me. I'd be in my room doing my homework, and he'd bang open the door and stand there staring at me, as if he'd forgotten what he came for. Then he'd blurt something out, like 'Do the dishes.' And when I told him I'd done them, he'd grunt and go back to the dark living-room. But he'd forget, you see. He'd be back up in five minutes. If I was in the toilet, he'd bang on the door and tell me to get out. 'Do the dishes--I've done them already. I told you before.' Back downstairs. He could do this all evening. He could say the same thing twenty or thirty times and I was angry with him but too afraid to say anything about it. But I don't want to give you the wrong picture. Those were the black times. He wasn't drunk all the time. He was off the booze a lot."

"And then what?" Victor asked. He was searching Paul's face all the time, like a nurse watching for a sudden gasp when the doctor probed a sensitive spot. But Victor was not interested in healing, and he did not stop probing.

"He gave me money to buy popcorn once."

"What's so special about that?"

"He didn't usually give me any money. He'd yell at me if he ever found out I took a case of empty pop bottles back to the store to get the deposit money."

The story had taken over. It was telling itself in spite of Paul's attempt to stop it from coming out. Victor was content to listen.

"I remember I was a little kid, maybe seven or eight, and it was just after school. My father had taken the day off because he was building a garage beside the house and he wanted to finish it while the weather held. It was autumn, you see. I was fooling around in the back yard when I heard the sound of a sustained whistle, and it got closer. It was the sound of a popcorn man. In those days, they wheeled their bicycle-driven carts throughout all parts of the city. The bikes had a glass box on the front and a steam whistle on the side by the compartment where they kept the tin of melted margarine to pour over the popcorn.

"My old man didn't believe in popcorn. It was as simple as that. He didn't believe in buying candies for kids either. Food, clothing and shelter was all he could understand and all he would spend his money on. Except for booze. That was his extravagance, and it was limited to himself. I knew this even then, and it seemed normal to me. Ordinarily, I would never have asked my father for money. But the lure of the popcorn whistle was too strong, and I actually went into the roofless garage that my father was building and asked him for a nickel for a bag of popcorn. He was sawing a board, and I couldn't believe my eyes when I saw him straighten out his back, lay down the saw and reach for his wallet. He pretended that it was empty.

" 'Hurry', I thought, because the whistle had already passed in front of our house and was moving on down the street. If the popcorn man mounted his bicycle and rode, I might never catch him at all. But I could never tell my father to hurry. The game had to be played his way or not at all. He dug through his wallet with painful slowness, and tried to offer me a penny first. When I laughed and told him it wasn't enough, he just shook his head as if he couldn't understand how popcorn could cost so much. When he finally gave me the nickel, he put his hand on my shoulder. "Let me go," I thought, "the whistle is getting farther away!" He told me to come back after I bought the popcorn and to show it to him.

"Like the wind. That's just how I ran, with the nickel in my hand and my side already aching from a stitch. The streets were empty. I don't know why that was. There were usually gangs of kids roaming around. But the entire baby boom left the street empty somehow, so there was just the popcorn man at one pole, my father at the other, and me in between. The popcorn man heard me coming. He stopped the cart and waited. He didn't even bother to turn around. I was too breathless to say what I wanted at first, and in that moment I was seduced. You see, the popcorn man sold candy apples too. Big red candy apples wrapped in cellophane at a nickel each. It must have been the colour. Everything else paled, but those bright red apples shone with a promise. I bought the candy apple instead."

Paul stopped.

"The end, Paul. Something happened. Tell me what happened when you came back with it."

"I went back to my father. I'd ripped off the cellophane, but I hadn't taken a single bite yet because I wanted to show it to him whole and round and shiny. He was sawing boards and he had his back turned to me. I tapped him on the shoulder. He was wearing a gray wool coat, an old one, and there were sawdust and wood chips stuck to it. It must have been the booze. I mean the withdrawal from it. He was edgy, you see. He was trying to wean himself from the booze, but it made him angry inside."

"What did he do?"

"He looked at me like I'd been brought home by a cop for shop-lifting. 'This house is full of apples. We have a bowl of apples on the dining room table. You're taking after your mother. You both waste my money,' he said. And he snatched the apple from my hands and flung it against the garage wall. The bit of colour smashed to pieces. My father went back to sawing his board."

"Paul," Dianne said, but Paul did not hear her. "Paul, my father was an asshole too. My father beat me up when I was a girl. But don't say any more. You don't have to tell your story to Victor."

But Paul and Victor were inseparable. They were tied in the marriage of narrator and listener, and the listener had rights. He had the right to hear the end of the story.

"What did the parade have to do with that?" Victor asked.

"So maybe it wasn't a nice parade after all. Maybe there were soldiers there, and some of the poison of war slipped into the look that my parents exchanged."

"What year was the parade?"

"Early forties. Forty-one, I think."

"Lithuanian troops?"

"No. The country was occupied. First there'd been the Soviets. They'd taken away my father's brother. I remember being told about that. My uncle was put on a cattle car and he died on the trip to Siberia. The car got shunted aside, you see, and the train authorities got mixed up or they didn't care. Just about everybody in the wagon starved to death or died of thirst. My uncle was one of them."

"Whose parade was it?"

"Not the Soviets'. The Nazis.' "

"So your mother and father fell in love as they watched the occupying forces march in."

"Yes. Sure. It was a sign of hope. You understand? As far as they were concerned, the Nazis were better than the Soviets. But they weren't exactly celebrating. The Nazis weren't liberators. That would become clear soon enough. They were on the brink of another wave of destruction, but my parents still fell in love. Love among the ruins. Isn't that a sign of hope?"

"They don't sound like hopeful people to me."

"Hope was the one thing that they did have. Listen, life wasn't easy, not for a lot of years. When the Soviets came back, my old man dragged the family West, right into Germany during the last days of the war. I was only three or four years old, but I remember it all right.

There were fires burning beyond the fields at the side of the road where some farm house had been torched by the Nazis, and my father kept driving the small horse that was so tired it was ready to die on its feet. He took me and my mother, and when he heard the sound of planes in the distance, he'd stop and listen carefully. He'd listen for the beat of the engines, and everyone else on the road, all the ragged civilians running away from the front, would look to him because his hearing was good. He could tell if the planes were German or Soviet. If they were Soviet, we had to move fast. The Nazis mixed themselves up with the refugees on the road, but the Soviets didn't give a damn about us. They strafed the whole road. 'Into the ditch,' my father would say, and everyone would scatter and the planes would start to shoot. The horse was too tired to rear and it was tied to the wagon so it couldn't bolt. I remember lifting my head from the grass where my mother had pressed it, and seeing the puffs of dust as the rounds from the plane kicked up the earth around the horse's feet. The horse just waited for all to be over. It was calm."

"What happened to the horse?"

"My old man thought the Italian prisoners of war must have stolen it. It was near the end of the trip, near Hamburg. He said they probably ate it."

"My parents had hope all right. That was the only thing that got them through those terrible times. My father was forty-five when he got to Canada. Pretty old to be starting a new career. If you can call house framing a career. He started to build a house for himself, but he ran out of cash before the winter came. So we all lived in the unfinished house, in the cellar. They had to have hope to keep living in that cellar. They had to have hope when the city inspector came and told them it was against the law to live like that, like rabbits in a burrow at the city limit. Hope was the only thing that kept them going. It kept all of us going."

"Hope and fights and booze. Too many fights and too much booze," said Victor. He seemed to have an intuition about the story. He seemed to know as much as Paul.

Paul nodded. "Too many fights and too much booze. Our neighbours were all WASPs and we were the immigrant family on the block. They despised us, but we confirmed them in their superiority.

When a lamp flew through the window, it made them kind of secure. It just proved that those funny people from Eastern Europe *were* primitive. Primitive and funny."

"But the parade wasn't funny," said Victor.

"No. Not funny. They fell in love at a parade, but it wasn't funny."

"Strange that the Nazis would have had a band with them. You don't usually have a band with you as you move in the shock troops."

Paul looked tired. His genial face began to sag, even though sixty years of smile lines tried to hold his face up.

"It was a forced march, not a parade," said Paul.

"Where did the music come from?"

"A fiddle. There was one fiddler at the front of the marching crowd, and they'd forced him to play a mazurka as the people marched through the street."

"Why did they have to force him if he was a soldier? You just give orders to a soldier."

"He wasn't a soldier."

"You mean they had a civilians leading a military march?"

"The military were there as guards. The only clowns were the Nazis who stood at the sides of the road."

"Who were the civilians?"

"Jews. The Jews had been rounded up and now they were being marched through the streets. The Nazis had a sadistic kind of humour. They forced one of the Jews to play his fiddle as the others were being led away. And everyone knew what was coming. The fires were already burning for the corpses that they were going to become. Somebody on the sidewalk, one of the people watching the march, couldn't stand it any more. He saw a doctor, the one who'd delivered his nephew, and he called out to him, 'Hey doctor, don't let these clown get the upper hand.' Saying it was suicide. One of the so-called clowns pulled him off the sidewalk and made him join the Jews on the street. It was death for him too. He was going to die because he'd opened his mouth and said the wrong thing at the wrong time."

"My mother was rushing home when all this was going on. She had some beef that she'd managed to buy through a friend, but she couldn't cross the street with her package. She was forced to wait until the procession marched by, so she watched. How do I know what was going through their minds? Were they afraid for the Jews or just for themselves? I would've been so proud to know that it was my old man who called out the line, but then I'd never have been born. Maybe they were just feeling lucky to be on the sidewalk instead of the street. But why did they have to stand there and watch? Why didn't they hurry away as soon as they saw that horrible spectacle? How could they stand there long enough to catch one another's eyes?

"My mother and father fell in love as the Jews were being marched away to the firing squads. How could they fall in love when heads were going to be shaved? How could they meet for coffee as the naked people stood in line? How could they bear to hear their own church bell tolling for their wedding when the distant loudspeakers shouted orders in the ghetto or the camp?

"Life goes on. Sure. Life goes on no matter what. But there was something about that parade that changed my life. It changed all our lives. It smudged the corners of family photos with soot. Sticky, smelly soot that can't be washed away. And I hate one thing to this day. That's the acrid smell of burning hair. It doesn't happen often, but it's the one thing about parties that I dread. All those people crowded together, you see? A woman stands too close to a candle or a cigarette brushes by someone's hair and a bit of it catches fire. Just for a second before someone snuffs it out. That acrid smell makes me want to gag. I don't know if I was even in the womb yet when the smell of burning hair covered the town where my parents fell in love and got married. But I know it makes me gag. It makes me sick for my past."

Victor looked about him at the faces around the camp fire. He was an attorney who rested his case.

Chapter 7

Butler was scribbling furiously. Teresa leaned away from him, lit a cigarette and poured herself another drink. Butler felt the slight distance grow between them, and it filled him with a sudden panic. He wanted to pull her back.

"I'll be finished in a second," he said.

"Then somebody else will tell a story and you'll be off again."

"What can I do? These are the rules of the game."

"You don't have to play. Walk away from it. It's such a male kind of thing to set up these rules and play by them. It kind of pisses me off."

Victor was playing with the nozzle of the aerosol can in an abstracted way, and he failed to notice, or chose to fail to notice, that most of the others were watching his finger with a fascination normally reserved for the erotic or obscene.

"I've got to pee," said Dianne, and she looked to Victor, who ignored her and kept playing with the nozzle.

"Will you stop fondling that thing as if it were your dick?" said Margaret. "My friend here has to take a pee."

"I'm not stopping her."

"Well you're holding us hostage here. We may not have our hands in the air, but you've got the weapon."

"My weapon is remarkable for its range. You could walk to the North Pole to fulfil your urinary desires and it wouldn't make any difference in the long run. One good spray from this aerosol can and the whole continent drops. Not immediately, of course. It would take a little time for the gas to spread. Perhaps even a few weeks before the wind and water absorbed enough of it to reach the extremities of the land mass. I'm not a scientist, you see, so I'm not sure of the details. I'm more a student of human nature, a kind of lay psychologist."

"For all you know," said Mike, "there may be nothing in there but underarm deodorant. Maybe Lysol spray."

Victor considered the proposition.

"There's always that chance, of course. It makes the whole game all the more interesting. Does he have it, or doesn't he? The guard at the army base was very convincing, so I probably do have the weapon he claimed. On the other hand, I admit he was an an alcoholic and he may have imagined the whole thing. We could find out the truth in a moment. If you're impatient for dawn, then I could give the air a good spray right now. But if the poison works, you'd be dead before you realized I was right, and that might be a waste."

"I guess that means I can pee," said Dianne, and she went outside the ring of light at the camp-fire.

"Crazy game when you don't even know how to add up the points," said Odds.

"Who takes the next story?" Victor asked.

"I think this is all a mistake," Leopold interrupted.

Leopold was usually quiet as a man with a name like that had to be. He was a thin and bushy-haired fifty-year-old. Leopold smelled of dust, the kind that you blew off the top of a book that had been on the shelf a long time. Occasionally, he smelled of the kind of dust you might blow off an old wine bottle, but this was rarer.

"What's the mistake?" Butler asked.

"Well as far as I'm concerned, you claim that people have brought the world to an end, or at least they're in the process of doing so. This whole notion of end is entirely a product of the short view of things. I'm not talking about geological time either, but about human interaction with the climate, the sea currents and the vegetation. The world has ended many times before, in a manner of speaking, yet here we are."

"I don't understand," said Victor.

"Then hear me out. The error you're making is to assume that human beings stand apart from an unchanging world, or one that would be unchanging if it wasn't for us. The fact of the matter is that people have always had a complex interaction with a changing world. Your error is not uncommon. Some Dark Ages thinkers perceived the world as a place of temptation and danger inhabited by man. Existentialists built a whole philosophy based on this idea of apartness. I find it a curious development, but traces of it have been around for a long time. When Adam and Eve were given dominion over the beasts and the plants, they were set apart from them."

"Have you got something to say, or are you talking for your own benefit?" Victor asked.

"Patience, my friend. We still have some time before dawn. Surely you have the time to listen to this."

"Make it quick."

"Our world has heated up to an intolerable level," said Leopold, "but this is not the first time something like this has happened. Take the long view. There have been hot periods and ice ages before. There have been famines and plagues, abundance and pestilence. It is interesting how human beings interact with these cycles of natural phenomena. Even more interesting and more germane to my argument is mankind's interaction not with the great cycles, but with the smaller ones.

"You see, the mistake most amateur historians make is looking for the grand effects that brought about the beginnings and ends of civilizations. It is always tempting to consider battles, heroes, and the march of armies as the bearers of civilization and its opposite. Even when people do consider the physical world's effect on history, they tend to stress dramatic events like ice ages and exploding comets. The rise and fall of peoples can more often be attributed to events that go unrecorded in narratives of the time.

"One colleague of mine claims that civilization was the subconscious gropings of primitive minds for scotch and water. This same colleague insists that our civilization will disappear when this drink falls into disfavour.

"Unorthodox as this view may seem, it is not far off the mark. I would substitute, say, bread for scotch and water. The history of bread has yet to be written, and it would be a shame, Victor, if you destroyed the world before that history had a chance to appear. It is not at all evident that seeds should be hulled, crushed, mixed with water and baked. And not just any seeds, but those of wheat or rye or corn. Wheat has the most gluten, which makes for a more elastic and therefore lighter dough. The Neanderthal who created the first loaf, probably more like a pizza without the toppings, opened the door for later developments such as sesame seed bagels, schinkenbrot, raisin bread, triple fudge layer cake and a host of other edibles; hosts should be included in this list, and the Neanderthal can therefore say he had a hand in the creation of Christianity.

"Bread did more for civilization, did more to shape us than you might think. Consider the saying that armies march on their stomachs. Loaves are relatively easy to hand out, and they are far more efficient to eat than handfuls of seeds. I suggest that it would take half an hour or more to consume a pound of seeds, and then only if the consumer had perfect teeth, which were not all that common in primitive times. A pound of bread, however, can be wolfed down in a few minutes and is far easier on the digestive system.

"Villages develop around bakeries and bakeries are attracted to villages. This symbiotic relationship provides a boost, a kind of leg-up towards the development of culture, or at least social organization. When nobles in the middle ages forbade the milling of grain on home mills, they were actually centralizing power. The peasants could no longer be quite as self-sufficient because they had to take their grain to an appointed miller and pay him a cut. Unjust as this was to the peasants, it helped to develop our complex society and its accompanying civilization.

"Bread then, or the lack of it, is one of the factors that led to the rise of Western civilization. Take away bread and you take away a building block of life.

"The destruction of a culture, on the other hand, can be caused by an ice age or a comet. But destruction is the wrong word unless every individual is annihilated. Societies are hardly ever destroyed. They just become something else. The Roman bureaucracy may have collapsed, but the members of the former empire did not cease to exist, at least not wholesale. Society just changed.

"Such a cool overview was probably not possible for the residents of Rome who watched their city being sacked. But Rome is a poor example for my point, which is that the world of material items interacts with people to make a society. The appearance of bread led to the growth of civilization, but the disappearance of, say, herring, led to the destruction of a way of life for thousands of Baltic fishermen, without actually destroying the people who had been fishermen. People are hardy creatures, and they will adapt.

"It is strange to think that we know so much more about herring than we do about bread. We even know that it was the Dutchman, William Beukelszoon, who discovered the methods of gutting herring and salting them right on the boat around 1350. I have eaten the odd Bismarck herring with a pint of beer, but I can't say that herring salad, bloaters, or kippers are important to my diet, although I have run across more than one red herring in my time.

"While herring are not particularly popular in fish and chip stores today, they were indispensable to the diet in the middle ages when there were 166 fast days on the calendar when meat, poultry, and eggs were forbidden for consumption. Only invalids were allowed to eat meat on those days, and they had to have a double certificate from both priest and doctor. This was well before the discovery of the Grand Banks off Newfoundland, and therefore well before the age of salt cod, the staple of the lenten diet.

"Most of the herring needed, at least for Northern Europe, came from the Baltic Sea. Imagine for a moment the complex systems that must have existed to bring the herring far inland. First there were the fishermen and their dependants, and then merchants, packers, carters, customs men, wholesalers and retailers hundreds of miles away from the Baltic Sea. This whole system of organization must have seemed permanent to them, as our former world seemed permanent to us.

"But the herring entirely disappeared from the Baltic Sea between the fifteenth and sixteenth centuries. Gone. As totally absent as the wine from last night's glass, and with equally devastating effect.

"Try to imagine the fishermen going out to sea when the spring season began, as they and their ancestors had done for decades, even centuries. At first they might have thought that the shoals of herring were just a little more elusive than before, but eventually they were reduced to living off the reserves of salt herring and rye flour. Moneylenders became nervous and first one and then another over-extended merchant went bankrupt. The carters had their livelihoods under them, and they merely rolled their primitive vehicles far enough away to find other work.

"Nothing one whole year. The next year, nothing again. Fishermen and their families either moved or died off and far inland some desperate man accepted mortal sin and ate meat because there was no fish to be had. The whole Baltic society, an entire mini-civilization and its economy collapsed, and all that remained were those who eked out a living catching eels. In effect, a world was destroyed.

"Given the situation we find ourselves in right now, I find some solace in the knowledge that an entire world was destroyed, and yet civilization marched, or rather staggered, limped and sidestepped forward. The world of the Baltic Coast was smaller than ours, but it was no less important to those who lived there. Hardly anyone knows this story of the Baltic herring, but I think it's something of a lesson to us all.

"Now Mr. Butler, in my own attempt to maintain the level of civilization we have reached, I am going to ask you for a gin and tonic, and beware refusing me or you will have the retardation of progress on your conscience."

"Just a minute," said Butler. "What happened to the herring? Where did they go?"

"No one knows, I'm afraid. The same thing happened in the last century with anchovies off the coast of Peru, and answers are as hard to come by now as they were all those centuries ago."

"Did they come back?" Alice Waver asked.

"The herring? Well, yes, they did. Almost a century later they reappeared in the Baltic and were fished again. But the old society on the seacoast was dead by then, and an entirely new one arose to take its place. There were fewer fast days by that time, so the trade in herring might have been less lucrative than it had been a century before."

"But the herring came back?" Alice Waver insisted.

"They certainly did."

"I get the point," said John

John was a man around forty with blow-dried hair (the dryer plugged into the car's cigarette lighter) and he wore cotton pants and a polo shirt. He looked like a golfer.

"You're telling me that the herring will come back. Well, sometimes they do and sometimes they don't. You can't be sure. I've got a story to tell. Listen up."

HOW I QUIT SMOKING
John's Story

I want to tell you how it was when the greenhouse effect just started to creep up on us. A few hot summers in a row at first. That's all, I thought. That's all anybody thought. Other things were more important to me, like my family. I wasn't one to go thinking a lot about climate. People usually think about people. It's natural, even if they only think of themselves.

There was this one day.

The neighbourhood kids had opened the fire hydrant and it was shooting a weak spray all over the sidewalk. Not enough pressure to make a proper fountain because hydrants were open all over the city. Kids were down to their underwear, screeching and racing in and out of the spray in their bare feet. I had to park a few spots down on the curb to keep out of the water. The car's air conditioning wheezed to a stop and I sat in the car for a minute before opening the door. I was expecting the heat, so that wasn't too bad, but the smell of the exhausts bothered me. Not much wind for weeks, it'd seemed, and the city smelled like a garage. On the street it felt like I was sucking on the tail-pipe of someone's car.

A cop was watching the kids run under the hydrant. It was funny. We knew about fire hydrants from old movies and stories about New York city. It was the kind of thing that kids from poor neighbourhoods were supposed to have done, but this was decades later and we didn't have neighbourhoods in Toronto that were as poor as the ones in New York. Not this neighbourhood anyway. Mostly single-family homes on tree-lined streets and pretty interlocking brickwork at the intersections to make the place look nicer.

People in Toronto obeyed the law. They didn't cross the street when the traffic light was red even if it was the middle of the night and a car hadn't passed for half an hour. A green hornet, one of those dead-beats who write tickets on illegally parked cars, once gave me a lecture about opening my car door from a street-side parking spot. Not safe, he said. I ought to check that no cyclists were passing by or one of them might run into the car door.

Toronto used to be an orderly city like that. Now there was this cop not doing anything about the hydrant. He didn't say a word. What was the use?

The air conditioner above the door in the Korean variety store was blowing hot air onto the sidewalk and dripping a steady stream of water. It was hard not to get wet. Inside, I picked up a newspaper from a stack on the floor and asked for a pack of Winstons. Only one pack because I was supposed to have quit and it would be bad enough being caught with one pack let alone two or three. Things were unsteady between us as it was, and I didn't want to aggravate my wife.

"No Winstons."

The clerk and I had never developed one of those relationships where you talk about the weather or enquire about one another's health. Each time we met it was as if it was for the first and last time. But we had nothing against one other.

"Sold out?" It was a pain because not all Canadian stores sold American cigarettes. You got to know who sold them and who didn't and then shopped at the same stores all the time.

"Not sold out. No more Winstons in Canada. Maybe no more in USA. Finished."

"What do you mean, finished?"

"Can't get them any more. The salesman says no more American cigarettes coming. Never."

It started to hit me then, I guess. Stupid, eh? There were a lot of other changes, but this was the one that got to me.

"Do you have any other American brands left?"

"Just Kools."

I hated menthol cigarettes.

"Give me three packs."

Back in the car I rolled down the window and turned on the air conditioning at the same time. I was cool where the vent was pointed at my chest, but the car couldn't get comfortable because the window was open. I didn't want the car to smell of cigarette smoke or else I'd have to make up some story about meeting a friend who smoked and giving him a lift someplace. The odds of that kind of thing being true were pretty small, and it wasn't the kind of story I could use more than once or twice a year without sounding suspicious.

I had three kids, the youngest six months and the oldest eight. I also had a cough in the mornings and I got winded too easily. With three kids in the house you get winded all the time. I'd promised my wife I'd quit smoking when we got married twelve years before, and I'd been quitting ever since. She put her foot down. She said it was bad for the kids and it was killing me too. Not that she wouldn't have been too sad, sometimes, to have me out of the way. If it had just been her, we might have fought it out one way or the other, but my oldest boy had asthma, and he coughed and wheezed any time he caught a whiff of tobacco smoke. So I smoked on the sly. Very sly. It was like being fourteen and smoking in the bathroom. Except now I was thirty-eight and knew you could smell smoke in the bathroom hours after the cigarette was flushed down the toilet.

It was stupid, but there you are. Changing is the hardest part. To make it worse, I was addicted not just to any cigarette, but to Winstons. Smellier than Canadian cigarettes and hard as hell to wash the stink off your hands and face. I drank a lot of coffees in McDonalds and Burger Kings before going home because they had strong soap in the bathrooms and plenty of it. The only problem was the dryers, which were hot air. I had to use toilet paper to dry my face and sometimes bits of paper got stuck to me.

I stopped at the bank on the way downtown but the place was closed. Air-conditioning broken down and nobody was selling freon any more. Funny to think how people got along without air conditioning in my parents' time. I even remember when I was a kid a lot of houses didn't have it. Families watched TV in the basement because it was cool down there, and they ordered food in because it was too hot to cook. Those days were long past. Maybe they were coming back. I got some cash from the bank machine and drove into the city.

I forgot to keep off the expressway and got stuck there for an hour and a half. Middle of the day and traffic not too heavy, but one overheated car slowed things down and then others started to overheat as they waited in line. Domino effect. I turned off my engine and stood outside where I could smoke a couple of cigarettes without worrying about stinking up the car. I got dirty looks because some of the drivers thought my car had overheated too. Sometimes you got beaten up for that. Nobody's fault, but everyone was edgy. Things happened. While I was smoking my second cigarette, I threw two of the unopened packs over the guard-rail of the expressway. I hated menthols, and if that's all there was going to be, then I might as well quit and be done with it. There used to be a boulevard beneath the expressway, but it was covered by water now. Water levels high all over the continent. I could see the cigarette packs floating among the swollen fish and a lot of plastic debris. I saved the pack I'd already opened.

I had to wait for a long time for a table once I got to the Rivoli, but I didn't have to wait outside. The Rivoli used to have an outdoor patio, but nobody wanted to sit outside, not even in the shade. I was the first in line, but I still had to wait for half an hour. A waiter finally walked up to a guy who was sitting alone in front of an empty glass.

"Lots of people waiting for an empty spot," the waiter said.

"I paid for my drink."

"That was an hour and a half ago."

"Then give me another one."

"Time to move on."

Like I said before, the town was changing.

The customer got up to go, but out of nowhere he started a wide, wild swing at the waiter. It wasn't going to be much of a fight because the customer was my age, running to fat a bit, and the waiter was about twenty-two. He was a gay body-builder type with reflexes as sharp as my boss's tongue. He had the customer pinned in a second. I figured he'd throw him out and that would be that, but the waiter held him close for a second and then gave him a couple of sharp raps on the chin. For the fun of it. Then he hustled him out.

The Rivoli is a cafe. You can get pretty good food there, trendy stuff but cooked right. Still, most people come just for drinks. Low lights and black booths make the place feel cooler than it really is. It's not that expensive a place, but it's artsy in an artsy neighbourhood and I'd never seen a fight there before.

The waiter wasn't fazed at all. Showed me to my seat and brought me a menu. I thought I'd better eat something. Ken was already late, but I chanced another cigarette before he got there. Ken was a reformed smoker and a blabbermouth. If he caught me with a cigarette, he'd tell my wife the first chance he got. He might even go out of his way to phone her. The waiter brought my gin and tonic without any ice in it.

"No ice cubes?"

"Fifty cents the half dozen."

I wasn't going to argue with him. I ordered a dish of ice cubes.

Then I remembered the Rivoli had a cigarette machine with Winstons in it. I got some change from the bar and went to the vestibule in front of the washrooms where the cigarette machine was. Winstons all right. I started feeding quarters into the machine and I was just a few shy when the lights went out. There was a groan from everyone in the restaurant. I kept feeding quarters, but when I pushed the button, nothing came out of the machine. It was dark and I thought I might have miscounted my money, so I tried a couple more quarters but nothing happened. I went back to the restaurant.

The electricity was out.

The waiter brought out candles and I finished off my drink, but didn't stick around much longer. Ken hadn't shown. It was already getting stuffy by the time I left.

The electricity was out everywhere. No stop lights working, so traffic was a mess. I could walk home or I could drive. Only a fool would try to walk half way across town in the afternoon. People collapsed trying to do things like that. I kept my door locked because the traffic was deadly slow and pedestrians had started a new trick. They came up to an idling car and got in. Nothing violent, you know, but they wouldn't get out until you came to their intersection. Then they got out of the car and tried the same trick on somebody else. It was a bit of a risk keeping the door locked because you might lose an antenna or a windshield wiper if you didn't give the lift, but my antenna was built into the windshield and the wipers I kept in the trunk anyway.

When I finally pulled into the driveway at home, I remembered that I'd forgotten to wash the smoke off my face. I was going to catch hell. No point in turning around and driving away now because she might have seen me pull in.

But nobody was home. It was hot and stuffy in the house. The electricity was still out and all the windows were shut. I opened them up and then took a shower to wash off the smell of smoke while I still had the chance. Soap and shampoo and a change of clothes and I smelled fresh again. Still nobody home when I got downstairs.

When you have three kids, you don't get much quiet in the house. I settled into a chair to read a magazine, but after half an hour I began to miss the noise. I checked the kitchen table and the fridge, but there weren't any notes. We only have one car, so I guessed they weren't too far away. Still, I felt kind of nervous about it. My wife had been edgy ever since the dog days had started, and we had a few more months of them to come.

It was still cool in the fridge, but I took out a couple of chickens and put them on the range to cook. Chicken spoils fast. Then the house really got too hot and I went out to the backyard. Sun sets pretty early in April, and soon it was too dark to read. I ate some of the chicken when it was cooked, and by then the nicotine level was low in my bloodstream again and I wanted another smoke.

Except something about it felt wrong. Not just that the whole family might show up as I was lighting up. I hadn't thrown away the pack of Kools yet. I took them from the closet where I'd hidden them, and put them on the shelf with the spices. You could see them perfectly there, or you could have if there'd been any light.

I scrounged around for candles but I only found two and I thought I'd better save those for when the kids got home. If they got home. Everything was changing, and it wasn't for the better. I went out to the back yard again.

Dark outside. Really dark. No street lights, no frames of light in the windows of other people's houses. I could hear some murmuring here and there as other people sat out in their back yards. But they felt far away. No airplanes flying overhead, no hum of machinery. Just quiet.

I started to feel nostalgic about the family then, but I cut it out. You should only feel nostalgic about things after they've been long gone.

"I quit smoking," I said out loud. I said it again. But it stayed quiet. No lights. All I could hear was the murmuring of half-articulated voices from other back yards. I wondered where my family was and when they were coming home.

Chapter 8

"Jesus Christ!" said Andy. "Tell him a few more stories like that one and we'll be dead for sure. I don't understand what everybody is being so morbid for, especially when there's so much at stake!"

Andy was wearing an apron. He said he always wore aprons at barbecues, and he said he was a specialist. He'd made a little sweet and sour sauce to dab on the bear meat they'd cooked, and it tasted all right. Dianne hadn't appreciated the interference, especially as she'd done most of the cooking. The apron he was wearing had a picture of Mr. Dithers, Dagwood's boss, with cigar in mouth and finger pointed in stern warning. The apron said, "Rule number one: the boss is always right. Rule number two: when in doubt, refer to rule number one."

"And as for you," Andy turned to face Victor, and Mr. Dithers' finger pointed at him, "I'm not pleased in the least with this system of judgement you have here. It's ludicrous!"

"I will not argue the rules," said Victor.

"Just listen to this for a minute, will you? Tolstoy or somebody said that happy families are all the same, but unhappy families have amazing range in their unhappiness. Unhappy families make good stories and happy ones don't. Did you ever see a soap opera where everyone lived happily ever after? Just listen to that expression. Happily ever after. It means it's the end of the story because there's nothing unhappy left to talk about. The wicked witch is dead, or the murderers have been caught and sent to prison. Finished. End of story. Unless there's a sequel. You see, if Tolstoy's right, then all the stories you're going to hear are going to be about unhappiness, one way or another. The happy moments just don't make for good tales, unless you pick victories of some kind. Look, who was the greatest victor? Alexander the Great. Right? Dies in his thirties of a cold after conquering half the known world. Even victors lose, and come to think of it Victor, maybe that'll apply to you.

"What I'm trying to tell you is that stories have nothing to do with reality, one way or another. Stories tend to work their own way. I mean, I've told quite a few of them myself, and I know that once the telling starts, then the reality falls away faster than money in your pocket. You start with a little exaggeration here or there to make the thing sound better, and the next thing you know you're off in some never-never land that the story is making you tell. My father was in the army, and after he died, I found out all his stories of combat were just great tales of bullshit. He'd spent his two years as a grease monkey and never left the USA, but he had stories about Vietnam that scared the pants off us when we were kids and made us admire him no end. I was upset when I found out the truth, but after I thought about it for a while, I couldn't blame him. The stories took over, you see. They have nothing to do with the real world.

"So what you're going to judge us on is not the way we lived our lives or anything. You're going to judge us on how well we can spin a tale. It just doesn't seem right. It seems arbitrary, as if you'd come up here and told us you'd save the world if we could do perfect back flips or something. You've set yourself up as a judge, you see, and now you're playing this God-thing with us."

"Don't accuse me of arbitrariness," Victor said. "You and all the others were arbitrary and God-like in your everyday lives. You played God when you used an aerosol spray and destroyed the ozone layer. You played God when you destroyed insects to keep your lawns green. What right did you have to impose your will on the rest of the earth? For so long we claimed to be the peak of the animal kingdom, and we slaughtered in the name of resource management. Well look around you. You see the results of your rule. You played God every time you went out for a nice dinner and some bloated-belly runt expired in its mother's arms because her tits didn't give milk any more. You played God every time you flushed the toilet and your shit ran out to the lakes and streams.

"My original offer still holds. Tell me some stories that will make the world worth saving for a while, and I will hold off from spraying the contents of this can."

Alice Waver's little boy sat up from her lap and peered into the sky.

"Is it getting light yet?" he asked. Butler felt himself begin to tremble, and everyone turned to look towards the East. There was a glow in the sky, but no hint of the red ball of morning. Victor was clutching his aerosol can.

"Well, I thought I was going to have to press the nozzle."

"Who says the stories have been all that depressing?" asked Andy.

"I do. I'm the editor and critic here. I spare you the necessity of making judgement. You don't have to read the book or think for yourselves. With a little help from Butler here, I'll decide if you have a best-seller or a flop that hits the remainder tray as soon as it comes out."

"Now that's another thing that bothers me," Andy went on. "What makes you so sure this greenhouse effect is going to destroy the world? Leopold here says that the world has changed before. Maybe this is just a dramatic shift in the whole pattern. Maybe we're actually on the way to a better life."

"Such ridiculous optimism. Look around you and you'll see we are burning up. The fire of the apocalypse is upon us, and it's all the more frightening for the slow way it is eating us up. We are frying with skin cancer, and although we are crispy on the outside, our insides, I mean our brains, are turning soft as mush. You can't touch the hood of a car most days because it will fry off your fingerprints. The lakes around the equator are evaporating away. So some of you turn on your air conditioners and those infernal machines produce

more heat that's spewed onto the street like a couple of extra tongues
of flame. You can't ward off the heat with a lightning rod or anything
else. It's enveloping everything and moving slowly North as surely
as the killer bees that must have crossed the Canadian border by now.
Haven't you seen the parakeets and monkeys? They are marching
North. The tsetse flies and green vine creepers are on the way, the
marshes and lizards and green slime muck of stagnant, tepid water.
The bamboo groves and coconut palms and breadfruits are coming
too, but don't think it's some kind of paradise they're bringing up
here. Those plants and animals are just running scared in front of the
forest fires that spew smoke into the sky and heat us up just a little
bit more. Those animals feel their tails being singed by the flames and
they hope to escape. But the fire is surrounding them all and they're
going to fry. They keep running because they are dumb animals, but
you around this camp-fire are supposed to be the pinnacle of the
mammalian tree, and yet you are running too. Just what did you
expect to find in this formerly great white North? Holiday Inns and
White Christmases? On some level I can even comprehend the long-
range stupidity of mankind. At the beginning, we didn't even know
the gases we farted out would cause such big problems. But what
about you? Where are your brains? What kind of redemption did you
expect to find up here, or are you just like those animals who think
only to keep the fires off their fur?"

"Calm down there Victor," said Andy. "Every time you talk
about the apocalypse, you sound like you're getting your rocks off or
something. As for us, why, we're just trying to do the best we can in
the only way we know how. No harm in heading up this way, is there?
It seems to me you've got yourself all mixed up. Let's talk about the
things that make people happy, and I don't mean stories. What about
sunsets?"

"Sunsets?" Victor was appalled. He looked at Andy as if he had
gone out of his mind.

"Don't block me out on this Victor. I'm just trying to tell you
that some of the simpler things make life worthwhile, and I mean
those brief moments, those seconds of well-being that don't last very
long. Like the moment when you taste the muffin dipped in tea and
your whole childhood comes rushing back. Yeah. I'm talking

sunsets, and even if they don't mean much to you now, don't you remember a time, say when you were an adolescent, that sunsets suddenly seemed incredible to you? I mean a moment when you looked around and you were just blown away by it all?

"Look, anything that's precious to me won't seem real to you. You've got your own moments, but one of mine was waking up on Saturday in the suburb where I lived and hearing the buzz of the neighbour's lawn-mower. I was maybe seventeen and the guy was cutting his lawn way too early for my taste, because in those days I could have slept all morning. But I remember too the smell that came in through the open window - the smell of freshly cut grass. And I was seventeen and the whole world was in front of me, and I'd lie in bed and stare at the ceiling and breathe in the smell of freshly-cut grass. That's enough for me. I mean to say, it's enough to know that there are a few moments in life like that for everyone, and what you propose to do is take them away. You intend to destroy the smell of freshly-cut grass for me, and God only knows what for others."

Victor did not answer. He seemed to be considering what Andy had said.

"Come on somebody," Andy appealed to the others at the fire. "Help me convince him. Somebody must have a story."

*   *   *

Butler scribbled and scribbled. He didn't know shorthand and it was hard to write everything down as it was said because he could never write as fast as the speaker spoke. And he could never be sure he was getting it down exactly as it was being said. He was exhausted, and every time he paused for a second to rest his fingers, he kept looking at the sky and hoping that there would still be time left, time for a few more stories. At least a few.

Would it really make any difference to Victor if he heard someone tell the story of a miracle? If only it could be proved to him that God had a sense of humour and reprimanded someone for, say, farting in an empty elevator, would Victor screw back the top of the aerosol can? Butler had been a melancholy man for years, ever since the death of Elaine, but he did not want the world to end in the morning. It wasn't time yet. It would never be time, he supposed, but it certainly wasn't time now. Not while Teresa hovered nearby.

Why couldn't someone tell a nice, sweet story or two and be done with it? Everybody knew that their future depended on it, yet everybody was telling stories that would make Thomas Aquinas himself slit his wrists.

Butler had to go to the bathroom. He had an hour or two of life left to live if things turned out badly, and he had to waste five minutes going into the darkness to take a leak. He would get another notebook while he was at the car.

It was still quite black outside, and that was a relief, except that he could not see very well after staring into the fire all that time. He had forgotten his flashlight in the pride of his night vision. He stumbled along until he found the edge of the rock all the rest of the cars were parked on. He stepped up on the edge of it, turned and undid his fly. It seemed like bad form to pee on the rock itself and leave a stain that the others would see in the morning. If any of them were alive to see anything at all in the morning.

Butler finished, and went to look for a new notebook in his car. He was trying to find the right key in the darkness when the howl began. It was an unearthly sound somewhere in the darkness, a sound of pain and terror. Butler tried each key methodically, in a manner that was far calmer than what he felt. He slipped the right one in, dove into the driver's seat, pulled the door shut and flipped the lock down behind him. Inside his car, he could still hear the howl.

He identified it in his mind as a howl, although it sounded closer to a moan--the kind of a moan that might have come from a woolly mammoth in pain. He thought about turning on his headlights to see what was out there in the muskeg, but he was not sure he wanted to see. He imagined creatures crawling out of Hudsons Bay, scaly things with teeth the size of carving knives. Something that got cooked up when atomic waste was dumped there half a century before. A cross between a shark and a lobster. Something that could breathe air when it wanted to. And hungry. It would be hungry.

Flashlights beamed out into the darkness as the people by the camp-fire searched for the origin of the sound. Somebody else went to a car and turned on the headlights. Then the car was backed off the rock and was driven around in a slow circle with the high beams on. The howling stopped, and Butler had seen nothing.

The rap at his car window made him dive across the front seat to the passenger side. The muffled voice came through the glass.

"We thought you were in something's jaws there for a while darling. All chewed up and digesting by now."

It was Teresa.

Butler opened the door and pulled her inside, and then crawled back over her to lock it again.

"Now this is more like it," said Teresa.

"I think we should stay here," said Butler. "It's safer this way."

Teresa kissed him on the lips. It was so unexpected he forgot to get nervous. And then he remembered how to kiss.

"Why weren't you doing this an hour ago?" Teresa asked.

"What's wrong with now?"

"They told me to get you. If I take too long, they'll come looking."

"To hell with them."

He kissed her again, and the sensation of her lips filled him with wonder. It was so simple, this pressure of lips on lips, but he had not done it for so many years. It was hard to remember why not.

Someone rapped at the window. Butler looked out, but could see nothing until a hand came up and rapped again. Whoever it was had to be on his knees. Butler rolled down the window and looked out. It was Odds.

"You coming back?"

"Later."

"Victor's pissed off, and that makes everybody nervous. Doesn't like his spotlight being stolen by the noise. Do us a favour, will you? Save it for later."

"What if there is no later?" Butler asked.

"Hey, be an optimist. We've got a few more punches left in us yet. Leopold wants to start a new story."

"That fart? We're doomed."

"He says it'll be okay. You coming?"

Teresa opened the door for them, and they both stepped out and all three of them began to return to the fire.

"Victor says it could have been miles away, whatever it was that made that noise. He claims he heard us from a couple of miles out, so it only makes sense we can hear that far too. Cow with a broken leg, maybe."

"That was no cow," said Butler.

"I don't think so either. More like a wounded rhino. Stan and Mike have got their guns out, so it's still safest by the fire."

Teresa was holding his hand and they entered the circle of light like two adolescents who had paired off on a camping trip.

"Ah, the chronicler has come back," said Victor. "Sharpen your pencil, my friend. It's time for a new story."

"You know what I thought when I heard the howl?" Teresa whispered in his ear.

"What?"

"I thought you'd gotten stuck in your fly while you were taking a leak."

Butler smiled.

THIRTY FRANCS
Leopold's Story

We were sitting in the upper room of Steve's triplex apartment in Paris, finishing off the champagne from the wedding celebration. About ten or twelve of us were left in the glass-topped penthouse and the rain was coming down so hard we could barely hear each other's words. It was a nice break after all the chit-chat during the dinner. Strange to be in that odd room with a glass ceiling--it reminded me of being in a tent during a rain storm. The rain was so close you could smell it. Rus was the groom, but he wasn't there. He'd collapsed downstairs after two bottles and an incoherent thank-you speech. The bride was sleeping, stretched out on a sofa in her wedding dress.

I'd come up from Spain for the wedding three days before, and now I was tired. I'd been nervous because Rus told me I was best man on the morning of the ceremony, and I didn't even have a decent jacket to wear in the church, and I'd had to ad lib all the toasts and introductions to the speeches. The reception had been held in an old horse barn in the Parc de la Bagatelle.

Now it was almost three a.m. and the gutters down in the streets below had long since run over the sidewalks. Paris was one great, shallow lake and my hotel was a fifteen-minute slosh away.

"How much will it cost to take a cab to the Bastille?" I asked Steve.

"Around thirty francs."

I'd used all my small bills and only had a five hundred franc note. Paris cabbies have a mean streak. If I passed a note that size, the cabbie would sigh at best and the dog on the front seat would raise its head and give a reproachful stare. At worst, he'd shout and drive to a cafe and make me get out in the rain to search for small bills. I needed to find change. Nobody in the room had any.

"Steve," I said, "lend me thirty francs." Steve was the groom's brother. I only saw the groom every few years, and Steve even less. He knew I wouldn't be able to pay him back for a long time.

Steve only half-heard me because he and a stunning Japanese third world aid consultant were making the moves on one another. The Japanese consultant looked at me as if I were a fly buzzing around her face. She was leaving early the next morning and she didn't have much time to consummate her attraction to Steve.

"Thirty francs?" Steve asked. "What's in it for me?" Steve was a businessman, and he liked to play hard-nosed.

"I'll make you famous," I said. It was the only thing I could think of.

"That's not a bad deal."

"It's a great deal."

"I'll hold you to it."

"Done."

He told me where to find the money in a change jar downstairs. I kissed the sleeping bride good-night and shook the limp hand of my friend, the groom, downstairs. He was still sleeping too, but I had to leave for Spain on the early train so I wanted to say goodbye. There was a cab right at the door downstairs, and it took me back to my hotel.

I haven't seen Steve since then, and it has been over twenty years. I owe him a debt. Maybe I can still make him famous, at least among us.

I'm not really sure how to go about this. If I say things just simple and straight, you might not understand why Steve deserves to be famous. If I highlight certain things about him, such as his weakness for falling in love, I'll only give part of the story. I suppose I could make a fiction out of it, but that would be a lie as well. Maybe it's best just to tell it straight.

There's something saintly about people like Steve. I don't mean in the way we're accustomed to thinking about saints, but in a new way for our post-post age. No niches for him in cathedrals - no tourist-attraction tombs. I suppose in his own eyes, Steve'd think of fame as making it into some local Who's Who, but even then he'd find it funny. He's an American, and like all the best Americans, he can never be totally serious about himself.

Steve was more American than anyone I'd ever met, and it stood out in relief because he lived in Europe. He wanted to be rich and he wanted to have a brilliant, beautiful and submissive wife. Most of all, he wanted to be a kid forever, and he'd pretty well succeeded. At forty-five, he was still skinny and lithe and his hair stood up in cowlicks. He hadn't been much different ten years earlier when I'd met him for the first time.

That was when Rus and I and an assortment of Americans, Dutch and Israelis were living aggressively literary lives in Paris. We read each other's work and got into fights about whose work was better, and denied loudly that the ghosts of Hemingway and Anais Nin had anything to do with our being there. We published a literary magazine out of the mouldy upstairs of the new Shakespeare & Co. bookstore, which was an excellent perch from which to see the girls who stopped by with back-packs on their European tours.

It was so fine to say to these tired and lost girls that we were living in Paris, and it was so fine to steer them to cheap hotels and meet them for dinners in inexpensive restaurants. The girls were usually homesick, and they welcomed the offer, eventually, of a couch to sleep on in our apartments. For three or four days we could be their hosts and sometime lovers, and their wonder at our shabby lives increased our pride in our fifth-floor walk-up *chambres de bonne*. We too were only temporary visitors, and we hardly pierced French society beyond the pleasantries exchanged with grocers and bakers, but for a time it seemed to us as if we were above the despicable acquisition game of North America.

Rus was our unproclaimed leader, by virtue of his having lived in Paris the longest and by virtue of his French girlfriend. He also fronted the money for our literary revue, so he was the first among equals. Rus was cockier than the rest of us. He was the one who told the retired American consul that his fiction was lousy. But Rus was a lamb compared to his brother Steve.

If I or any of the others thought about Steve at all in those days, it was as the image of the worst of America, and everything we despised. Steve was an international banker stationed in Paris. He had a big apartment, a country house, and money. If we were aggressively literary, he was grandly and proudly philistine. I remember the night when he came to Shakespeare & Co. to attend a reading, and while the rest of us were Paris-chic in our old leather jackets, he was staunchly establishment in his three-piece suit. And he had a mouth. He laughed when somebody read a bad line of poetry, and he made gagging sounds when he tasted the wine we were serving.

He liked to patronize us, though, and when the reading was over, he and his French wife took Rus out to a restaurant, and at the last minute, invited a few of the rest of us to go along. He paid for the dinner, but he made us listen to him, which was payment enough. "Mummy stop sending cheques?" he asked when David said he was thinking of going back to California. Claudine, his French wife, was appalled at the strays her husband had invited to dinner, and she kept staring at a distant point on a wall as if she were a plaster inspector.

"Do you think I've sold out?" Steve asked me when my turn for the application of his irony came. They were the first words he had ever directed at me. He was swirling wine around in a glass. Cowlick on his crown forever in place and voice as sincere as could be.

"Absolutely," I said, and I reached for another brochette of beef before any of the other diners took it. In our group, one had to eat fast because the food on the table disappeared quickly and the French portions were small.

"Don't you feel bad about eating food bought with dirty money?" Steve asked me as I chewed.

"I'm milking the system," I said with my mouth full.

Steve laughed and ordered two more bottles of wine. He loved to think of himself as "the system", even if it meant being milked. And he had this strange kind of grace about him. He could see the humour in the way we despised him. It amused him. He could be generous, and it stood out all the more in France, which is not a generous country and whose people are determinedly tight-fisted.

This generosity to pen and ink revolutionaries may not stand out as such a grand act, you might say. No reason for inclusion in the *Lives of the Saints*. But if you read the *Lives*, you'll see that many of the saints lived unremarkable lives full of good works. Most of the saints didn't make big splashes with miracles and fiery martyrdoms. Saints just make ripples. Maybe ripples are enough.

I next saw Steve a year later. Steve's wife, the plaster inspector, had left him by then. Like a good Frenchwoman, she was both dramatic and practical. She claimed domestic life was crushing her soul, so she needed to get away from all the family to find herself. But not too far away. Steve paid her seven thousand francs a month, he and the kids moved out of the apartment to give her breathing room, and she got free access to the summer house.

I'd heard about all of this from Rus. We were having dinner at Rus's and I expected Steve to show up depressed or in a sulk. Rus's door opened straight onto the kitchen, and when Steve arrived he lifted tops off the pots on the stove while he still had his coat on and his bag of wine bottles in hand.

"I brought some very expensive wine, and I just want to make sure the food is worthy of it."

I make him sound annoying, and he certainly was that, but everything he said had an underlying sense of good humour, and it made it difficult to be very angry with him. I'd spent a week's grocery money to bring oysters to the dinner. Rus was cooking a jugged hare.

"Do you have any champagne?" Steve asked when he'd put down his bag. "The bank's sending me to the Ivory Coast in two weeks."

"Promotion or demotion?" Rus wanted to know. Only a brother can ask a question like that.

"Any move is a promotion in my business."

Rus always had champagne in the fridge. Well, not champagne. It was cheap vin mousseux, but we all called it champagne and the cork popped the same way the real stuff did.

"Can you get me a girl too?" Steve asked while Rus was at the fridge.

"What for?" Rus asked.

"I want to get laid and I want to be loved."

"First one's easier than the last."

"Yeah, well I want both if I can get them."

Rus's girlfriend Pierrette started phoning around to her friends to see who would accept a last-minute dinner invitation. The rest of us sat on the mattress on Rus's floor and listened to Chick Corea records.

"What are you going to do about the kids?" Rus asked.

"The bank'll pay for a private school in the Ivory Coast. We'll manage all right. They'll like the beaches."

Rus and I went to the kitchen to open another bottle.

"I bet he asked for the transfer," he said. "That way the mother will have an excuse for not visiting her kids. The way it stands now, they can't understand why she never comes around."

A goofy-looking American who liked good wine and wanted to get laid. Hardly a character worth veneration, you'd think, but I liked what he was doing for the kids.

Pierrette finally got hold of Annie, a friend who had nothing to do on a Saturday night, and when the girl showed up at the door she was carrying a couple dozen more oysters so she wouldn't feel too much like a last minute stand-in. I remember that the plastic bag she had in her hand was torn, and some drops from the oysters were dripping onto the floor. Annie was about twenty-three, dark-haired and lovely in a way that all young women are lovely. But she had a slightly hunted look to her, as if she was not sure that she wasn't going to be humiliated for being so available on such short notice. It was raining that night, and her straight hair curled up slightly at the edges as she stood in the doorway trying to save her self-respect. Her chin jutted forward a little to show her defiance, her "I don't give a damn what you think of me."

But Steve acted unobtrusively, if you can imagine, as if the Virgin Mary herself had appeared in a glorious vision, except that this virgin was clearly of the modern type: one that had to be given a glass of wine, one whose feet had to be shod in an extra pair of Pierrette's slippers, one who had to be made to feel at home. Who else but an American saint would have tried to make a vision feel comfortable?

And what made the venerable Steve different from any Lothario on the make? How was he anything more than a seducer? Maybe it was Steve's desire to be loved by her, this wet girl who had stood so unsteadily in the doorway. Maybe it was in his desire to bring her into the room and warm her and give her his heart.

Rus was not so understanding. Four hours later, Steve was in the bedroom with Annie, and only Pierrette and Rus and I were in the living room. Maybe Rus was uncharitable because he would probably not get his bed back that night, or perhaps he was angry because Pierrette was sitting on my lap.

"The trouble with Steve is," he said, "that he confuses his dick with his heart."

But even then I knew he was wrong. Rus glared at me as Pierrette caressed my thigh. Steve wanted to love very much, to be in love all the time. I can understand this in a young man; every one of us has an age when we write poetry or feel we could, but Steve was well beyond his twenties. Rus said that Steve's age meant he should have known better, but I said that if Steve was somehow arrested in his development, then he was arrested at a magnificent age.

I saw Steve again three years later. I had returned to Canada, and then, in a fit of nostalgia, gone back to France to see Rus again. Rus and I were at Steve's house near the Pyrenees, recuperating after two days of fiesta at Pamplona. The old farmhouse was partially renovated and had a magnificent great hall with a ceiling perhaps eight metres high. Ropes hung down from the exposed beams for the kids to climb upon. The baking oven in the kitchen was big enough to be a small apartment in itself. And yet, for all the grandness of the old country house, the furnishings were poor - the remainders of apartments long-since vacated, a cheap set of foam chairs with the covers torn and the foam crumbling at the edges, mattresses on the floors and curtains slung over doorways.

It was a summer night, and we saw the lights of the taxi zigzag up and down as it approached the house along the rutted drive.

"Pierrette, get some money for the cab, will you?" Rus asked.

"Steve's broke?" I asked incredulously.

"I lent him fifteen thousand francs to get started in Paris, but you know Steve. That kind of money's nothing to him."

The kids came bursting through the door first. William was twelve and Sonia ten and they tore towards the knotted ropes that hung from the rafters. Sonia swung on one and William climbed the other to the top. They had the exuberance of American kids, but their language of preference was French. Next came a coffee-coloured woman I'd never met before. She was about thirty and she carried a baby wrapped in blankets. Pierrette introduced her as Steve's fiancé and the child was their son. Rus and Steve came last, dragging suitcases and talking about the disrepair of the house.

"Every time I go out of the country, part of the roof blows away," said Steve. "Oh well. Stick a bucket under the hole. Hello Leo, come to France to relive your youth? Kids! Down off the ropes. Kiss Lena goodnight and get up to bed. Any beds in their rooms Rus? Come on. Give her a kiss."

William and Sonia had been unwilling to climb down the ropes, and they were even less willing to kiss Lena. She barely noticed the icy touches of their lips on her cheek. She smiled as if she was thinking about something else. Pierrette took the baby out of her arms, but Lena stayed where she was, smiling.

"Get me something to drink," she said to Rus. "Something stronger than wine."

"Nothing else in the house," said Rus.

"I've got a bottle of Canadian whisky," I volunteered, and Rus frowned at me as Lena said that would be fine.

Steve had quit his banking job in the Ivory Coast and then tried to open a business dealing in spare parts, which practically didn't exist there. It had cost him most of his savings to find out that there were no spare parts because it was impossible to get them into the country without paying off a lot of people. Too many for the business to be worth it.

Lena drank her whisky and nursed the baby and kept on smiling at her private thoughts. Rus and Steve circled the house with a flashlight and tried to assess the amount of repair work that was necessary and how much it might cost. Pierrette tried to talk to Lena but it was hopeless. The only responses she got were "yes-dear" and "no-dear".

So little was saintly in that scene. The devil's advocate would pounce on Steve for making his children kiss their stepmother-to-be when they clearly did not want to do so. She was his weakness come to roost in his house. A beautiful woman too contented with whisky. Wine annoyed her because it took so long to take effect, and this was all the worse in France because the drinkers of whisky and brandy are so noticeable in that country. Wine drinkers could hide their addictions at the dinner table, but whisky drinkers took their glasses without food.

Even before the marriage, anyone could see that it would not last. But Steve walked directly into it, not in blindness, not even in myopia. He could see the trouble in Lena and the pain it would cause his children, but he had a belief in redemption. Who believes in redemption any more? Maybe he saw more clearly than anyone the capacity for love in the women he chose, and certainly he never imagined he would be unable to tap that capacity.

Of course you will say that the only reason he married her was because they had a child together, and of course you will say that the gesture was nothing more than misguided chivalry, an old-fashioned gesture. But no. I think redemption was the motivation. Hers and his.

Another five years passed before I saw him, and this was the last time, the time I came up to Paris for Rus's wedding. Rus and I had changed - grown older and fatter. Rus was a reporter and I was a teacher who dabbled in editing. The cafes of a decade before had changed or closed down and the old crowd was gone. Only Steve remained unchanged: the tuft of hair still stood up at the crown of his head and he wore the same gold-rimmed glasses. How was it that he retained that same smile and easy conversation? Lena had left him a year before and the baby in her arms was now almost six.

"Better for a kid to live with its mother for the first few years," said Steve. "I call every morning to make sure she remembers to send him to school."

So Lena was still drinking. He did not blame her for it. Things were like that. People forgot.

Rus's apartment was full of family that had come into town for the wedding. Children raced around the place and knocked over wine glasses. I was interested in their parents, I mean Steve and Rus's mother and father. The mother, thin and blond, nervous and rude, was standing by the kitchen door. "Get out," she said to anyone who came near. I thought perhaps Rus's cool Swedish fiancée (Pierrette was long-gone) was crying behind the door - I smelled family scandal - but it was only a Swedish brother-in-law making meatballs. "You get out too," the mother said to me before we were introduced.

"Where's your son?" I asked Steve.

"In a school in Nice. He needed to get away. We had a talk last fall and I told him I didn't care about anything as long as he got his grades up."

"He's getting C's?" the mother asked from her station at the door. Like all mothers, she had very sharp ears.

"Mother, if he got his marks up to C's, I'd be thrilled."

Sister Teddy was a health-food wholesaler in Phoenix, and the bride's brother was a Swedish farmer who spoke diplomat's English and smoked Dunhills. Rus's son and daughter by Pierrette surprised me from behind and wrestled me to the floor. His daughter gave me a hug before she chased her brother off and chased him into another room. Steve and Rus's father was enthroned in an easy chair in the living-room. He wore a navy blazer with a crest. There were no other chairs, so I squatted on the floor beside him.

"Interesting crest," I said.

"International Peace Force."

"Are you a veteran?"

"No. A golfer."

The Swedish farmer's wife brought around caviar on crackers. The little black eggs were spilling off the crackers and littered the tray.

"Eisenhower's idea," said the father.

"What?"

"Well, you see son, he had this idea that people around the world would understand one another better if they shared their common interests. Now the general was a big golf player, so he started the International Peace Force for golfers of the world to get together and play in tournaments. I've played in Japan, Hawaii, Scotland, England and Ireland. Never played in France, but I come over to see the kids when there's a game across the channel. I do it to make sure Rus's brain is all right."

"His brain?"

Rus's son had tipped a cracker onto the floor. I wet the end of my finger and picked the fish eggs off the rug.

"You see," the father went on, "Rus took a lot of LSD when he was young, and I've never gotten over the worry that it's all going to flash back at him one day. I'm afraid he might do something more foolish than usual, so I come over from time to time to see him."

"Rus'll have a new wife to watch out for him now."

"Hmm."

"And his brother Steve lives here too."

"Oh. Him." The old man made a dismissive wave with his hand. "Hey Steve," he called out across the room. "Are you making any money?"

"I don't need to yet. I'm still good for a few months of living on loans."

"See what I mean?" he said.

Someone had miscalculated and there wasn't enough food for the guests. It made everyone a little edgy. That and the placement of Rus beside his father at the table. Rus wasn't talking to his father. "Not too much!" the mother said as Rus put food on the plates and passed them around. What she really meant was that we weren't supposed to hog the food. Luckily, there was a lot of wine to drink, and the mother became, after a while, like one of those electronic watches that bleeps every fifteen minutes. Annoying at first, but forgettable eventually.

Rus and I went down to the cellar to get more wine.

"Steve living with anyone now?"

"Not just yet. There's a girl he likes a lot but she wants to sleep with other men too and Steve doesn't think the kids would like to find strangers in the house in the morning."

"He never used to hesitate when he loved a girl."

"No."

"What about your parents?"

"What about them?"

"What do they think of Steve?"

"They don't show their appreciation too easily."

Rus was married an hour late the next day because the maid of honour hadn't been informed of her duties ahead of time. A friend stood in when the minister started getting nervous. Then over to the Parc de la Bagatelle where we drank champagne in the horse barn, and afterwards dinner at Steve's apartment.

It was near the Pompidou Centre, a good address. Steve's place was a triplex penthouse with a view of the Centre off one balcony, and of Sacre Coeur off another. It was furnished in Steve's style. There was a small, out of tune piano, wicker lounge chairs with cushions so deep that you folded up when you sat in them. The bedrooms had mattresses on the floors and the upper storey an unassembled IKEA wall unit and table still in their cartons. It was the kind of apartment that showed one had a successful career, but it was furnished the way a student might do it his first semester away from home.

"Get out!"

Steve's mother was at her position by the kitchen again. Steve was carving salmon and lamb and opening champagne bottles that his son, William, carried around the room. William had grown. He was muscular and tanned, like a Californian, but he spoke English with a French accent.

Over the previous years, Rus had become an arms specialist with a sideline in Middle-Eastern politics, and he and his other friends were talking about Canada's need for nuclear submarines and the reputation of Exocet missiles. They claimed to work for Peace Institutes, but they all knew their hardware. I wandered the apartment.

"Where are you from?"

The father was standing ramrod straight at a doorway with a glass of bourbon in his hand. He was wearing a different blazer, but this one, a maroon model, had the same crest.

"Toronto."

"In the textile business?"

"Me?"

"Yeah."

"No. I teach."

"If ever you get into textiles, mention my name at Dominion. I used to get to Toronto a lot before I retired, and there are people there who still know me. Should get you a ten percent discount."

"Thanks."

"Remember now."

"I will."

Within an hour everybody had eaten and the arms men huddled around one table with Rus to talk artillery. William walked the room with a champagne bottle he was supposed to use to top up drinks, but he lounged in the doorways and drank from the bottle instead. Steve was picking up plates and opening new bottles of champagne in the kitchen.

"Get out!" said the mother, but she didn't bite when I walked past her into the kitchen.

"Big spread you put on for your brother," I said.

"Well, he won't get married too often, so I guess he deserves it the first time around."

Soon the party thinned, and we found ourselves up in the top of the triplex, sitting under the glass roof and listening to the rain.

I saw it happen under that roof again, even though I could not hear the words being spoken because of the drumming of the rain. The Japanese Third World Aid Consultant was a stunning woman with a pale yellow scarf on her neck that could have been pinned there by Yves St. Laurent himself. She was the one who gravitated towards Steve, and I saw the spiral of her movements as she drew closer to him. There were younger men, more successful ones, and certainly more eager ones there as well, but it was Steve who attracted her. He had a rare smile, I'll admit, but of course there had to be more to it than that. Even in a room where not a word could be heard, his love of women, his love of love pulled her towards him. I could sense his heart opening already, and his desire to please her, and I knew that disaster would await him in the end.

Those were the glimpses I got of Steve, the brother of my friend. I wonder now, if they're enough to bring up his case before the court of beatification? Some saints were never well-known; bits of trivia passed down through the ages about them. That was good enough for Rome in some cases. Why shouldn't it be enough for him?

But is a chaotic, undisciplined life enough? I don't know. Steve's life was always a mess, one way or another. Too many women - children running wild - apartments half lived in and jobs taken and left. Parents a horror.

And yet.

It was raining harder than I'd ever seen it rain before. All of us were sipping champagne. Somebody turned off the lights and the rain felt close.

"Steve, lend me thirty francs."

"What'll I get in return?"

"I'll make you famous."

"That's a good deal."

"The best."

"You're on."

Chapter 9

The tundra was shedding its darkness, and yet there was no sign of the sun. It held back coyly, prolonging the night. Stan stood up and hauled another piece of tree to the fire. It was an untrimmed trunk, with a few branches and dry leaves, and the whole mass was so big it spread well beyond the centre of their fire. The thin branches cracked and the tiny curled leaves caught fire first, and then the flame rushed in toward the centre.

"What's the point?" Victor asked. "Dawn is almost here and we won't need that firelight much longer."

"Keeps away the bogeyman," said Stan, and he sat back down again.

"Butler, what's the score?" Victor asked.

"I can't keep score of stories. They're not like hockey games."

"You know the score Butler. Deep in your heart, you know."

And he did. Nothing anyone had said yet had made the world worth saving.

"You still have time," said Victor. "One story - maybe even two. They could make all the difference."

The strange roar sounded somewhere near them again. Simon looked nervously over his shoulder and Stan stood up with his rifle in hand to scan the horizon. The others huddled closer to the fire. Alice Waver's children shifted uneasily on their mother's lap.

"What *is* that sound?" Andy asked. "It's giving me the creeps."

The sound came again, a painful and outraged roar that seemed to be located nowhere and everywhere.

"My guess is that the bear had a mate, and she's not too pleased that he's gone," said Stan.

Victor looked uncomfortable for the first time that night. He pushed his eyeglasses up on his nose and then repeated the action.

"What's the matter Vic?" asked Stan. "Don't you like bears?"

"No I don't," he said irritably.

"Well what do you know. It's human."

Andy had stood up from the place where he had been sitting by the fire. He jangled the car keys in his pants pocket and looked at Victor nervously. He cleared his throat.

"Would you try to stop me if I left?"

"Of course not. You could get in your car and drive to Winnipeg for all I care. It'll make no difference in the long run. My nerve gas will drift down there eventually. As a matter of fact, I can picture it. I can picture the people behind you starting to drop, and there you'd be, driving faster and faster to stay ahead of the cloud. You'd be watching the fuel tank to see how many more klicks you'd have to go before you ran out. But you'd have to stop eventually. Then it would get you. I don't know any details about the particular gas in this tin. It might be fast-acting or it might be slow. You might drop without knowing what hit you, or you might linger in pain like someone who's swallowed strychnine. One way or another, the gas will get you. Why bother to run away now, just as we're nearing the climax?"

"I think I'd like to give it a try anyway," said Andy. He did not look at any of the others around the fire.

"Be my guest," said Victor. "You can all leave if you like. I'll wait for dawn before I give the world a spritz from my can here. Audience or not, it makes no difference to me. On the other hand, you might want to try another story or two. You might still be able to avoid the end. It's not likely, I'll admit, but I suppose it's possible."

"In that case, I guess I'll be seeing you."

Andy walked towards his car. He moved like a man who tried not to show he was in a hurry.

"What do you think?" Simon asked Alice.

"We owe it to the kids to give it a try."

Simon lifted the boy from her lap and draped him over his shoulder. Alice carried the girl in both arms.

"Good-bye!" Simon called over his shoulder. "Good luck!"

Some of the others rose too, Lionel and Eve among them. They muttered their goodbyes to their shoes. They left behind half-finished drinks and hurried to their cars. A miniature traffic jam started as drivers turned the tight circles necessary to get off the stone on which the cars were parked.

"I really don't think you can afford the time to watch them go," said Victor. "Use the time to save yourselves."

The roar came again and Victor cringed when he heard it. "Make it fast."

"Now hold on Victor," said Odds. He was scratching at the strawberry birthmark on the side of his face. "It doesn't seem right to me that we should go out without some kind of fanfare. You know, a few effects. Sure, we might convince you yet, but you don't seem to be a convincible kind of guy."

Victor tapped his foot irritably.

"You're wasting everybody's time," he said.

"Anybody object?" Odds asked, and when Stan told him that it probably didn't make much of a difference one way or the other, Odds stood up and straightened the candy-stripe jacket on his shoulders.

"Now, if I'd thought of this earlier, I would've put on a show of fireworks. You wouldn't believe what I've got in the back of the Winnebago. I've got the fireworks that were supposed to celebrate the Shah of Iran's birthday. Imagine, the work of a hundred Persian firework artists, and all of it went to waste because the Shah ran away. It was a long time ago, mind you, but fireworks don't grow old. The only problem is, the sun's not too far off from rising, and I wouldn't want to waste the best fireworks built by man on a daytime show. Better to show them on a dark, clear night, or else not at all. If you have your way, Victor, it'll be not at all. Real shame."

"Get to the point."

"Well, seeing as how I can't show fireworks, maybe I ought to do something a little different. Let me see..."

Odds put a finger on the side of his nose and thought for a long time. Victor tapped the side of his aerosol can impatiently.

Odds looked up. "I could make it snow for you."

Nobody around the fire had seen snow for ten years at the very least.

"I made a snowman once, when I was a kid," Mike said wistfully.

"See what I mean?" Odds asked. "Just the thing to lift our spirits."

"You can't make it snow," Victor snapped. "Nobody can."

"When I was a kid, we still had a couple of White Christmases," said Teresa. "Or maybe they weren't Christmases - I don't know. But anyway, I remember there was still plenty of snow then. When I turned eighteen we went up to a friend's lodge to go skiing - it was the last year there was enough for skiing - and we got snowed in. Just two girls and two guys, a fireplace and enough rum toddies to last us three days."

Butler wished he knew how to ski. In compensation for the lack of ability, he poured Teresa another gin and added the last of his tonic. She was pale in the pre-dawn glow, yet to Butler the whiteness of her face made her seem all the more desirable.

How ridiculous to fall in love now, he thought, but it would be an appropriate end to a ridiculous life. Too bad there would be no time to do anything about his love.

And then Butler grew tired of mourning.

What was it about the light on the last morning that made everything so clear? So clear and so monstrous. Elaine had taken him in her arms and led him out of the seminary. Oh, he had wanted to leave it all right, but if it had not been for her, he might still be wearing a collar, most likely as a teacher at a Catholic College. He would have become a drinker of evening port or sherry, and he would have developed esoteric aesthetic tastes - say a fondness for the songs of castrates. It had been absurd to spend a lifetime writing about fish, yet somehow less absurd than the priestly route. Elaine had given him a better life than the one he had been shuffling into, and then she had died.

She would have expected better of him than to waste away over the years as he had. She would have been disappointed to see him becoming so timid with women again.

And he was not timid in his heart, damn it. He wanted Teresa passionately, but his voice and his body failed him. He could not say the right things, nor make the right gestures.

How awful to find oneself shy on the morning of the apocalypse.

"Teresa." He said it quietly. Her mind had been elsewhere, and it was late in the morning.

"Let's do something."

"What do you have in mind?"

"A bet."

He spoke quietly as he could, trying to speak below the level of Victor's acute hearing.

"I've already got one bet going tonight, and I don't think I can keep track of two of them."

She did not sound interested. Damn it, he would say it anyway. What did he have to lose?

"If Odds makes it snow, let's celebrate."

"What did you have in mind?"

Damn it, she wasn't making the thing any easier on him.

"We might go for a walk."

"You call that a celebration?"

"Just the two of us."

"We won't get far before Victor zaps us."

"No need to go any farther than my car."

There. He had said it. Now she would either put her arm around him, or else she would call him a rude name. Loudly. So the others could hear.

"I'll think about it. Okay?"

He thought at first that he would die. Think about it? That was what reluctant girls did at the high school prom. And yet she looked like she really was thinking about it.

Odds was speaking.

"Don't be such a sceptic! Making snow is child's work compared to ending the world. All it takes is a machine, and I've got it."

"Yes, I know," Victor said sharply. "Ski resort owners used to use them, and I don't doubt you have one hidden in the back of your department store. But all those machines do is throw out a fine spray of water. They still depend on cold air."

Odds nodded sagely and rubbed his face some more.

"Well, that was true of the older models, but not of the new ones. You see, some of the more desperate ski resort owners developed a new machine. It doesn't just blow mist, it blows real snow. Cooling mechanism's right in the nozzle. Now, it doesn't last too long at first, but the snow does eventually start to pile up. Stan and Mike, you can help me set up. You too, Butler."

"What about the stories?" Victor asked. "Are you going to waste your time with a machine when you might be saving the world?"

"Nothing I'm doing will stop anyone from telling a story," said Odds. "We're going to be working right here, and we'll hear everything you say."

"You may not remember this, but I've got a busted-up ankle," said Mike. "You three set up the machine without me. I've got a story of my own to tell."

"That's the spirit," Margaret whooped. "Give him a wild-West kind of tale, will you? Perk the man up."

"The story I was thinking of isn't exactly Wild West," said Mike. "You might even think it's a downer, but Victor here is too sophisticated to pay much attention to narrative elements. He just wants a good story, and I'm not sure if this is one of them, but it's the only story I know. Should I start?"

"Be my guest," said Victor.

BREAD
Mike's Story

The old Buick's dashboard oil light came on while I was driving home from the city with Rita one night. The Buick used to belong to my brother, and he gave it to me when he bought a new one. I couldn't really afford to run the Buick because I didn't have a job and the insurance payments were eating up my savings. I'd tried to repair some of the rust spots, but I'm not too good at that kind of thing and the body looked lumpy where I hadn't sanded down the filler enough. Everything was going wrong with that car.

"Something's wrong with the oil level. I've got to stop," I said to Rita.

"I'm tired. A few more miles won't make any difference."

"I'll burn out the engine if I don't stop."

Rita just looked out the window. It was an early March night, a dog's night, when the rain couldn't decide if it wanted to be snow and the drops on the cooler parts of the hood were turning to ice. I turned off the boulevard and we parked on a side street. In Toronto, most of the gas stations in the city close at six, and it was about four more miles to a station in the suburb where we lived. Rita kept looking out the window.

We'd only been in Toronto a couple of months, ever since I lost my job in Vancouver. Rita had never gotten around to finding one there in the first place, and we came back home with twenty-eight hundred dollars. Toronto was expensive. Fifteen hundred went for first and last month's rent, and another three for the first instalment on the insurance. Rita found a job as a telephone canvasser for the *Toronto Star*. She made a hundred and fifty a week plus commission, but the commission never amounted to much. I was still looking for something to do. The Manpower office told me I should take a real estate course, but it lasted six weeks and I wasn't ready to get into that line of work. I would've had to buy a lot of new clothes and drive people around in my car to show them houses. The old Buick would have lost me all my customers.

"Maybe I should call a cab."

That made her laugh out loud. It could have been worse.

"Ben lives around here. Maybe he could lend us some oil."

"Ben doesn't own a car."

"Who knows?"

It was better than sitting in the Buick. I'd had to turn off the engine and it was getting cold. Rita shrugged and we got out of the car. Half an inch of wet snow on the ground soaked through my shoes by the time we'd gone half a block. Rita wore high heels and her toes were wet but her heels were dry. It wasn't all that much consolation. The only good part about the weather was that it kept all the creeps indoors.

Parkdale was not exactly a rough neighbourhood, but it could still be bad. Creeps lived in the halfway houses and bachelorettes. Anyone who couldn't get into a psychiatric hospital or was near the end of a prison term got put into a halfway house in Parkdale. It was supposed to ease their re-entry into society, but there were so many halfway houses in the neighbourhood that the place was like an open-plan asylum cum penitentiary. Next door to the creeps there were some young professional couples, the kind who'd speculated that Parkdale was ready to boom as soon as we climbed out of the real estate slump. I didn't see it that way. No way there was going to be a real-estate boom in a neighbourhood full of creeps. Other kinds lived there as well, people on the way up and people on the way down; students who'd moved out of their parents' places and drunks who'd sold their homes and moved into rental units and were drinking away whatever money they had left.

Ben lived in a semi-detached three-storey house with a porch that made you think you were stoned every time you looked at it. Two guys on the neighbouring porch ignored the cold to share a joint, and they watched Rita and me as we walked up the steps to Ben's place. Ben's door had a built-in bell, like the bell on a kid's tricycle, and we had to turn it about twenty times before anybody inside could hear us.

Ben himself opened the door. He was a big guy, over six feet, with a barrel chest and curly beard and long hair. He looked like a biker, but he was a script-writer. He'd been writing scripts for seven years without getting one of them optioned. His wife Terry held down a full-time job.

"Come on in," he said. "I'll get you some socks."

The house was cold. Terry had it all in her name, but Ben ran the place for her and he kept the heat down low to save money. He gave extra socks and sweaters to people who came to visit. Ben rented out rooms to his friends, and the income carried the mortgage and paid the utility bills. He even made a bit extra. Everybody except Terry was in the living-room watching Gord's colour TV.

Gord and Terry were the only two in the house with regular jobs. He drove cab while he thought about what he wanted to do with his life. He'd been thinking for five years. He was the only one who had any real money, so he was the one who bought the TV and he always had a couple of bottles stashed in his room. Gord was a nice guy, but he wasn't stupid. He sometimes gave away a bottle, but he kept the liquor cabinet in his room locked up tight.

"I'm making bread!" Terry shouted out from the kitchen, and I went in to talk to her. Terry was blonde and skinny and a compulsive collector of supermarket coupons. She only ate whatever was on sale, and I guess she had to because her job at Big Steel didn't bring her in a lot of money. She could type fifty words a minute, so she could have been making more. But she was holding out for a job with a future, not a secretarial pool or anything like that. She was patient. She figured that if Ben could wait for seven years for a big studio to option one of his scripts, she might as well wait for a really good break too.

There was flour all over the kitchen, and a little mountain of it beside a hundred pound sack on the floor.

"You nuts?" I asked her, and she laughed.

"One of the guys next door sold this to me for eight dollars. He wanted ten, but I talked him down. And get this, he even has yeast at ten cents a pack. I'm going to be like my granny and bake up a storm."

"I thought the guys next door stole car radios."

"One of them got a job at a big bakery and he takes home a little something every day."

The hundred pound sack looked funny, like some sort of beast Terry'd hauled in, and the sight of it made me laugh some more. Terry was kneading a big loaf, and there were pans with dough for bread and cinnamon rolls. She'd made footprints on the flour on the floor.

"You go watch TV with Ben," she said to me. "He's lonely these days and he needs somebody to talk to."

"Lonely?" The house was always full of people.

"He's got something new to show you."

I tried to think of something else to say so I could stick around for a while, but she just shooed me away. I always felt like she made me leave before we'd finished talking. I wanted to talk to her all the time.

Everybody was sitting around the TV in the living room, watching a rerun of the Incredible Hulk. Rita had a big pair of gray wool socks pulled over her nylons. Dianne was drinking a glass of wine and Gord and Sal were just watching along with everyone else.

Rita looked over at me a couple of times as if she was wondering when I was going to ask about the oil, but it was still early and I liked the feel of all those people sitting around in the same room, so I didn't rush. I knew I'd pay for it later, but it was worth it.

"Hey Ben," Dianne said during a commercial. "Show them the skull."

Gord made puking sounds. "Not now, eh. Terry's making bread and I don't want to spoil my appetite."

Rita gave me a couple more looks, but I knew we couldn't just stand up and leave right then. Ben went upstairs, and Rita's look got more and more panicky. He came downstairs with what looked like an old-fashioned hat-box. For a second, I thought it was going to be like some late night horror movie, and he was going to pull a severed head with bloody veins dripping off the neck. He sat beside Rita. Ben was never the sensitive type.

He opened the box and folded back some tissue paper. Then he took out the skull.

I thought skulls were supposed to be white, like the ones you see in doctors' offices on TV. This one was kind of brown, but not dirty. Half the teeth were missing, but it wasn't creepy like I thought it would be. I'd seen so many on TV and at amusement park horror rides when I was a kid, that the real thing was kind of an anti-climax. In a way, it was kind of reassuring to know that the owner of the skull, who'd once had a head full of problems, now had no problems at all. Rita didn't jump off the couch the way I'd expected her to.

"Do you keep this in your room?" she asked.

"Yep," said Ben, and he lit a cigarette. Ben didn't smoke much, but he was a screen-writer and he used the cigarettes like props.

"It's his great grandmother," said Gord, and barked a short laugh, nervous.

"That's right," said Ben.

"What do you keep it in your closet for?" Rita asked.

"My father gave it to me last week. He turned sixty and he's had a couple of by-passes and he figured it was time to give it to me. He said as Armenians, we should never forget what happened to our people. She was butchered by the Turks in the Armenian holocaust. My grandfather found the skull and dug it up when he left Armenia."

I thought for sure that Rita was going to explode. Not loud, you know, that wasn't her style. She'd just stand up and say we were going. Instead, she took the skull and held it in her hands the way you might hold a piece of driftwood.

"Don't you find it depressing?"

"Are you kidding?" Ben answered. "The way I see it, this is my muse. I've been working all these years to breathe a little life into my scripts, but I've got dick on a stick to show for it. I'm situated now. I've found my centre, so I can finally pull things together. I'm talking the big time."

The smell of baking bread began to fill the room. I'd heard about the smell of baking bread, but I'd never smelled it myself. Not in a house. Cake mix, or muffins, sure, but my mother never baked anything else. Once or twice I drove past big bakeries, but it's not the same when you smell the bread from the inside of your car.

Rita was looking over the skull, studying it, and all I could think of was how good the bread smelled.

Gord was lighting up another cigarette, and I wished he wouldn't do it because it ruined the smell of the bread.

"Ben claims this skull brings him luck. We could test that our with a poker game."

"Poker," said Sal, and his eyes lit up.

"Poker," said Ben.

Terry called to us from the hall. "I'll get the cards. In about fifteen minutes you'll have hot bread with margarine."

Rita hated cards, but she seemed willing enough to come into the dining room with everybody else. She didn't play, but she sat close beside me. Ben put the skull beside him on the table and I fished out the few bills I had. We played for quarters.

"You show them how to play," Terry said to Ben. She kept coming in from the kitchen and going back again.

She brought out thick slices of bread on little plates. She only had hard margarine, so she couldn't spread it because it would tear the bread. We got steaming slices with a piece of margarine in the middle that was melting fast. We ate the bread as we played cards, and after a while the deck got greasy and Terry made us all get up and wash our hands in the sink before she brought out another pack. She mixed up some powdered milk and it tasted good after the bread. I hadn't drunk milk from a glass in fifteen years.

"That's my man," Terry said whenever Ben won a hand. She hugged him around the neck and he beamed.

And all the time there was this skull on the table. Cards and money and glasses of milk too. It didn't seem strange after a while. We got used to it.

Ben was on a winning streak. "That's my man," Terry said every time he won a pot and raked in the quarters.

By the end of the night, I'd won nine dollars and Ben the lion's share of the rest, maybe thirty. We would've played longer but Terry started to tug at Ben's arm. "He's got an appointment," she said and then laughed. She laughed the way you might in private, when nobody was listening. A goofy laugh, but she didn't care.

"I suppose you'll say the skull brought you luck," said Gord.

"Sure it did. I could have lost instead of you."

Rita and I were getting ready to leave when I remembered we needed oil. Ben said I could buy some at the all-night variety store. With my winnings, I could get two litres and a pack of cigarettes as well. Rita and I walked back outside. It had stopped raining slush, but it had cooled down a lot as well. The sidewalks were slippery and she held onto my arm all the way to the store.

"You've got an appointment too," she whispered in my ear as I was paying for the oil.

When we got back to the car, Rita didn't climb in first the way she usually did. She stood beside me as I opened the hood and unscrewed the oil cap and she stood right there as the wind off the lake blew under her skirt and down her neck. My fingers were so cold I was having a hard time punching out the foil seal on the top of the oil containers.

"What are you doing?"

The guy had appeared out of nowhere, and now he was standing beside Rita. She started, and moved closer to me when she heard him. I should've known he was a creep, but it was dark where we'd parked between the street lamps and I didn't get a really good look at him.

"Putting in some oil," I said. Rita walked away and got into the passenger side of the car. The big door of the Buick made a heavy sound when she slammed it shut.

He wasn't a big guy, but he was solid. The kind of guy who lifts weights in prison to put on muscle so he won't get shoved around too much.

"Do me a favour?"

I should've told him to screw off then and there. But I still had my head under the hood and for some reason I had this vivid picture of it slamming down on me. Hard. I didn't say anything.

"The beer store closes in ten minutes. It's not far, but I'll never make it if I try to do it on foot."

Rita rolled down her window. "You've got an appointment. Remember?"

"Come on," the guy kind of whined.

"Take a cab."

"I haven't got the money."

I would've had to turn my back on him to get into the car, and I didn't know if Rita had her door locked. I motioned to her to get out of the car.

"What are we doing?" she asked when she stepped out. She sounded scared.

"You get in the back seat. We're going to give this man a lift."

The guy offered to get in the back seat. He said Rita would be warmer in the front, but I wouldn't go along with it. He sat in the front.

The roads were slippery with new ice, so I started off slow. It wasn't far to the beer store, and I hoped he wouldn't ask for a ride back. I could just leave when he went inside.

The guy kept his hands on his lap. They were big hands for a guy that small, and he kept the fingers locked together as if he wanted to hold them prisoner. Hard to tell if the hands were soft or hard, but I guessed hard. They had to make up for the pretty-boy blonde hair, long and shiny down to his shoulders. Hands like a bricklayer's and hair like a girl's.

"Got a cigarette?" he asked, and I gave him one. I was trying to take a small road up to the main street, but someone had abandoned a car on the road ahead of me, and there was no way around it. I turned around to look out the back window as I backed up. Rita wouldn't look at me. I got a little confused back at the intersection, and headed off on a small street that was taking us in the wrong direction.

"I've got a knife," the guy said. When I looked at his lap again I saw the blade.

It wasn't a big knife, but it looked evil enough. It had a thin blade on a long, dark handle. Not a switchblade and not a hunting knife. The first was for punks and the second was for amateurs, and this guy was neither.

He didn't say anything more about what he wanted. Maybe money, or maybe the car. Maybe he just wanted to impress me with the blade. He was so quiet about the whole thing. He acted like the knife wasn't even a part of him, or if it was, he had no control over it. It felt as if I didn't have to be afraid of him, but I had to be afraid of the blade.

"This knife's cut three people already. One of them bad."

The guy talked as if Rita wasn't in the seat behind him. He talked like we were the only two people in the world. Intimate.

I've seen a couple of knife fights in my time. From a distance. I never went looking for that kind of thing and until then it had never come looking for me.

I wasn't sure what he was going to do. Maybe he was just showing me the blade. Maybe not. I could hear Rita breathing hard in the back seat.

I stiffened my arms as much as I could and hit the brakes hard. I didn't have a seat-belt on and I almost hit the windshield. He did. But not hard enough because I couldn't some to a sudden stop. It was slippery outside and the car went into a sickening, slow-motion glide.

"Shit!" he said, and he pulled his head away from the windshield and put one hand on his forehead to feel for blood. He still held the knife in the other hand. The car kept right on sliding and Rita started crying in the back seat. I could hear her whimpering.

"Shit!" he said again. Mad this time. Really mad.

The car slid gently into a tree. It wasn't going fast, but my arms still buckled and my chest hit the wheel. I heard Rita fall against the front seat and the guy's head hit the windshield again. This time hard. Cracks sprouted on the glass. The knife fell onto the floor.

My chest hurt, and the guy fell back with his head on the head-rest as if it was too heavy for his neck to support him any longer. His face looked too white in the light that came in through the windshield. His eyes were only half open and they looked glazed. He was young - maybe nineteen. I reached across him and opened the passenger door and then I shoved him out onto the street. He was like dead weight, and he didn't fall far enough away for me to be able to close the door again. I slid over to the passenger side and kicked him away from the car. He didn't make a sound.

The engine was still running even though the front end was smashed up. I could hear the hiss of steam where the broken radiator was leaking. I edged the car back from the tree, careful not to run over the guy. He was lying half on the road and half on the sidewalk. I started backing up the street away from him.

"The knife," Rita said shrilly.

I reached down to the floor without stopping, and I sideswiped another car as I was doing it. But I had the knife in my hand and I held it there until we backed up to an intersection where I could turn and head off in another direction. I didn't want the knife lying on the same street as that guy. I threw it onto the median when we reached the boulevard.

I drove home, not even stopping when the temperature light shone up red on the panel. I had that funny feeling you get in your knees when you've been scared. I wasn't sure if I was going to pass out or not. My chest was hurting bad and the engine kept hissing as the coolant leaked out onto the block and turned to steam.

As soon as I got into the driveway, I turned around to look at Rita. Even in that light, I could see her hair was a mess and her make-up was all smeared. She was still. Really still. I was wondering whether or not I should call the cops. There might be trouble either way.

"We can't go back there," said Rita.

I nodded, but she could see I didn't understand.

"I mean Ben's house. We can't go back there. Not in spring, not in summer. Never." She started to cry. I was afraid too. I was afraid that maybe the guy got a look at our licence plate. I was afraid he might be dead.

It was getting cold in the car, but we kept on sitting there. I was in the front seat and she was in the back. It would have been too hard to move. Too hard to do anything. The steam from the radiator hissed for a long time, shooting out a plume of white into the cold air.

Chapter 10

The brightness of the early morning could no longer be denied. Colour filled objects that had been gray in the pre-dawn light and a chorus of birds chirped and whistled and sang as if it knew there would be no time for an encore. In the distance, an arctic fox loped by and then stopped to sniff the air for the smell of people and the remains of roast bear. It sat down on its haunches and waited.

"You bastard." Margaret was bleary-eyed and holding a glass of gin in her hand. She had not bothered to ask for tonic. In the night she had seemed to be so vibrant and alive, but now it looked as if she were very close to death.

Victor laughed. His voice sounded like an obscene tear in the fabric of early morning.

"Don't blame him. He told us the story of his life, the life of a loser. And we are all losers one way or another."

"How could you give him a story like that one just before dawn?" Dianne asked. "You were always the outdoorsman among us, the upbeat one. We respected you and looked up to you, and now you've killed us all."

Mike had looked sorrowful when he finished his story, but now his face changed.

"The whole fucking thing has been a joke from beginning to end. Do you think this lunatic can really kill us? He's cracked up in the heat of the mid-day sun. He sits there with his little can and terrorizes the rest of us, and we sit here like a bunch of cowards and let him do it. And that's not all. Even if he does have the power to do what he claims, why should I go searching through my life for some Disneyland story of joy? That's just not the way my life was or is. My life is one, big, long complicated mess, and sometimes I like it, and sometimes I hate it. The thing that galls me is this man here, this so-called Victor wants me to be responsible for the fate of the earth. Shit, I could barely handle the responsibility for keeping my bills paid in the old days, and I can barely handle the responsibility for finding enough food to eat these days. How come I'm supposed to be the one who bears fate on my shoulders? They're just not broad enough for that."

"My point exactly!" said Victor. "The shoulders of humanity have not been broad enough for the job, and now it is time to collapse beneath the weight."

"And you enjoy the whole damn thing," said Margaret. "That's what I blame you for. You're like a voyeur or something."

"I do enjoy it. I suppose it's a weakness I have, but the reason I enjoy the end so much is that there was a time when I believed in redemption. I actually thought it was possible for people to change, and then I became bitter when I realized that we were not only weak, we were stupid as well. It gives me some pleasure to destroy a stupid race."

The camp ground looked shabby in the new light. Tanqueray gin bottles were strewn about and disposable plastic glasses lay all over the wet grass. A few flies buzzed around some discarded bits of bear fat. Butler looked at the pale faces around the fire and thought that all except one looked as though they they belonged to the dead. Even the gin was not enough to colour the pastiness of frightened faces.

"Now don't get all silent on me yet," Odds shouted at them from the machine he had set up. A long plastic tube ran from the pool of the fresh-water spring to a machine-gun shaped apparatus that had a condenser the size of a refrigerator off to one side. The nozzle of the outlandish machine pointed off to one side of the camp-fire. Odds pulled a rope and the gas motor started to chug smoothly.

"There, you see? That's what I call quality. Hasn't been used for ten years and it starts in a snap. Hear that gurgle? That's water coming up the tube from the spring. This is a self-priming pump designed by the last of the great Japanese mechanical engineers. I've pointed the machine a bit to one side so we can have a show but not get frozen at the same time. Anybody got mukluks with them? No? Ha ha. I've got a full line of winter gear in the back of my Winnebago, so just give me a shout when you want something. Hudson's Bay blankets, lumberjack coats, down vests. All the best of Eddie Bauer and L.L. Bean."

Teresa sat beside Butler, and she watched the set-up of the machine in a maddeningly detached way. He could not tell if she wanted it to work or not. He was not even sure if their bet was on. The fatigue had loosened the muscles in her face, but instead of making her look tired, she seemed strangely calm and appealing, more appealing, if possible, than she had looked all evening.

Butler shifted to disguise his erection. This isn't normal, he thought. He was on the point of being murdered, obliterated, and his hormones were acting as if he were a seventeen-year-old boy.

"Nice fox," said Victor, looking over at the creature that was still watching them from a distance.

Strange, thought Butler, that Victor should admire a fox at a time like this. Perhaps he was the kind of nihilist whose detestation had gaps in it. Butler had known others of the same kind. They were men who despised mankind, but bore an affection for dogs or budgies or bag ladies. The trick was to find the trace of humanity in Victor.

A fine, cool mist landed on Butler's face, and as he wiped it off, he noticed that others were doing the same thing.

"Damn it Odds," said Victor, "nobody is interested in your snow machine, especially if it doesn't work."

"What's the matter Vic, afraid you'll catch your death of cold?" Odds chuckled. "It's just warming up, that's all. Takes a few minutes for the snow to start kicking out. Now I'm sorry if the aim isn't quite as it should be, but the machine's way too heavy to move once it has water in the system. Seems to be a bit of wind coming up. It's carrying the spray into our faces. Never mind. If it gets too bad, I'll drain the pump and move the nozzle over so it sprays to one side. Just keep your eyes open when it starts to snow. You'll see industrial magic before your eyes. Remember, I've got everything in that Winnebago of mine, so if you want something, just give me a shout. I'm always ready to trade."

Butler thought hard of a way to stop Victor, but the residue of gin in his veins and arteries made him sluggish in thought. And what oxygen there was in his blood was being sidled out by hormones that rushed about more madly as Teresa leaned against his side. She draped an arm over his shoulder and looked at the fox on the horizon. She seemed oblivious to the danger of Victor. She acted as if she had found a new lover, and that was enough for the moment.

"I am her lover," thought Butler. He had never thought of himself as anyone's lover before. His vision of himself had always been tragi-comic. He knew only too well how a mirror could bring back the ridiculous image of a chubby, balding man in middle age. And yet there was Teresa beside him, with one hand on his shoulder.

The others all watched Victor carefully, trying to guess when he would move. They had no doubt that he intended to move sooner or later.

Butler saw Stan's hand slide carefully on the rifle to complete a small action. The safety. Stan had slipped back the safety on his rifle. He was a good shot. All he had to do was raise his gun quickly and shoot, and Victor would be dead. Maybe it was easier said than done. Victor had the spray can in his hand and he could probably give a short squirt faster than Stan could shoot. Probably.

"Sometimes I wish I had a space ship," said Victor.

Odds rolled his eyes. "Looney Tunes," he said, and adjusted the dial on the nozzle. The mist became finer.

"What for?" Butler asked, trying to draw Victor out. Teresa's hand on his shoulder caressed him lightly.

"You see, there might be a few worth saving. Not many, I'm sure, but a few anyway. I wish I could put them on a space ship and send them far away somewhere to avoid the holocaust. Maybe they could start again on another planet and avoid the mistakes we made."

"But there are no space-ships," Butler said seductively. "There is no way to save the few, so you'd be destroying them with the others if you actually did what you said."

The mist of wet rain changed into wet pellets of ice that started to shower down on them as the wind picked up.

"It'll be here any second," said Odds. "Just hold onto your horses. This damn dial is frozen open and I can't reduce the flow."

And as he spoke the spray of wet ice turned into a jet of snowflakes that burst out of the nozzle in a tight stream and then got caught by the wind. The snowflakes twisted and turned in spirals like autumn leaves that rose high into the sky before falling back to the earth. A collective "ooh" escaped from all mouths, even Victor's. He had been born in Florida and never seen snow, not even in his childhood.

The flakes made a spectacular daylight firework, but they melted as soon as they touched the earth. The wind kept blowing the snow right into the centre of the circle where they sat. Hot logs on the edge of the fire hissed as the snowflakes fell on them.

"This isn't a side-show!" Victor shouted to get their attention. "Look!" and he pointed to the sun which had inched up above the horizon.

"I wonder," said Victor slowly, now that he had their attention, "if dawn is officially here when the sun breaks the horizon, or if it's when the bottom tip of the sun comes up. I want to be fair," he added, almost as an afterthought. He spoke loudly. The machine chugged and whistled as it spewed out the snow.

The roar of the widowed polar bear sounded above the machine, loud and painful. Stan stood up to scan the horizon, but his view was clouded by the thickening snowflakes. "I can't figure out where that roar is coming from," he bellowed.

Teresa's hand reached further over Butler's shoulder, and her other hand came up in front to join it. She hung onto him as if they were in water and she did not know how to swim.

"One last story," said Victor. "Hurry. You have to start it before the bottom tip of the sun breaks the horizon. One last chance to swing the balance in your favour. Butler here will do a score as soon as it's over. Quick, quick. It's time to begin before it's too late."

It was a call to action, but no one knew what arms to take up. It was hard to think of a story so fast, especially with all the distractions. It was snowing for the first time in years and that polar bear was out there some place. It made them nervous. Even worse, if one chose to speak up, the story might not be good enough. The fate of the earth was in the balance.

The sun, ragged through the cloud of snow, rose until the barest slice of it was below the horizon.

"I'll give you a story," said Dianne.

Some of them sighed with relief, and others sat forward to listen carefully. They had all liked Dianne, but she was just a cook, and who could tell if her story would be any good?

Butler opened his notebook, but Teresa flipped it shut again.

"A few minutes after she starts, I'll go aside to take a pee. Wait a couple of minutes and follow me. I'll be by your car." She licked his ear as she finished, and Butler's erection gave a quiver.

"It's another story about Lithuania," Dianne began, but she did not have time to go on before Margaret interrupted her.

"I think we've already had one story on that subject dear, and it didn't leave a very good impression."

"It's set in Lithuania," Dianne insisted. "It's a story my father told me about the times before the Soviet Union began to shake apart. Anyway, it doesn't really matter where a story has been set. There are only so many places, and it might as well be there. Listen."

The bottom tip of the sun reached above the horizon, but as she began before that moment, Victor let her go on, as if permitting the game for the fate of the earth to go into overtime.

THE HUMAN COMEDY
Dianne's Story

The cold war was ending, of that there could be no doubt. The old fears were dying, and new fears had not yet had time to grow. It was one of those very brief moments that occur perhaps once in the lives of men, when it seems as if there might be cause for hope.

My father was a journalist, and Joe Curtis was his name. The last name had originally been spelled differently, because his parents had

come from Hungary, and Joe grew up with all the horrors of the
Hungarian revolution of '56 as part of the family lore. An uncle had
died attacking a tank with a molotov cocktail. But Joe couldn't
remember anything of Hungary himself. East European politics had
been a kind of background music in his lifetime. Sometimes the
music was low, as it had been throughout most of the early sixties,
and then it suddenly became loud, as in 1968 when the tanks rolled
again in Czechoslovakia. I say background music, because Joe was
not especially keen to be recognized as Hungarian. East Europeans
who insisted on it were not popular. Their politics were too right-
wing. The only advice anyone had asked of Joe, based on his
nationality, had been where to get good chicken paprikash.

He still spoke some Hungarian, and on the basis of that he
became designated an expert at his newspaper when Eastern Europe
began to be news. He covered Hungary, East Germany, Poland,
Czechoslovakia. Each country was a little different from the other,
but the pattern quickly became clear to him - the Soviets were on the
way out. Things were not quite so simple in Lithuania. People were
still tentative in the fall of 1988. They were still afraid, and some of
their fear was catching. Dictatorial regimes in their death throes
could be dangerous.

Everywhere else in the East, the end of the old regimes was in
sight, but Lithuania lay behind the Soviet Border. Some of his
subjects refused to be interviewed, and there were still dissidents. The
very word felt out of place, an anachronism. In Moscow, former
dissidents were making speeches in the Kremlin.

In Lithuania, it was different. Joe felt uneasy in the badly-lit
Vilnius street, where a pair of drunkards slouched in a doorway in
an alcoholic embrace. He walked in the centre of the pavement to
avoid the yawning entrances to courtyards where burning cigarette
ends betrayed the bored, yet silent teenagers. It was not yet late, but
the November evening was dark, wet and windy. The man my father
was going to interview lived in the old part of Vilnius, the former
Jewish ghetto. The renovating hand of the civic authorities was slow,
and the outlines of Hebrew lettering still tried to make themselves
visible below the lamps that lit the entrances to the courtyards.

He found the right street number, at last, and as he turned to
enter the courtyard, someone called his name.

The voice was accented, and the single syllable of his name rose at the end like an ironic question mark. It was unnerving to have his name called out in a strange city in a foreign country.

Joe did not look back. He hurried into the courtyard. Beneath his feet, the cobblestones had been pulled up from the ground, and planks were half-submerged in the wet earth below. He went to a door under a stone arch, knocked, and then strained to listen for footsteps on the street behind him. He heard nothing.

"Open the door, open it!" he said quietly. His heart was racing.

He had had the sense of being followed that day and had put it down to needless anxiety. At least until his name had been called.

A girl of about eight opened the door. She had hair in two ribboned pig-tails and she wore an orange sweater and matching skirt. The child smiled, and said a few words in Lithuanian, and then remembered something she'd clearly been taught. "How do you do?" she asked in a thick accent, and then she curtsied.

From behind, in the dark, Joe heard his name called again and unnerved, he stepped right inside and closed the door behind him.

He leaned his back against the door and held the interior door knob in his hand to keep it from being turned. The girl was looking at him strangely. Joe reached into his pocket with his free hand and took out a small log of bubble gum. The girl giggled at him and called out to someone inside. Her father appeared.

"Ah, Mr. Curtis."

It was Tomas Vastokas, Joe's dissident, and not for the first time in his journalistic life, Joe was astonished that a man he had read about and talked to on the phone looked so different from what he had imagined. Tomas looked like a pre-WWI diplomat. He was short, and in his early forties. He wore glasses and a goatee. He was wearing a dark, worn suit and he held a burning cigarette. Joe took all this in as he listened for noises outside the door behind him. He still held the door-knob in his hand.

"You look pale, Mr. Curtis," said Tomas.

"Someone out there called my name as I came in."

A look of recognition and understanding flashed across Tomas's face.

"You see, the Kremlin is crumbling, but here in Lithuania they are still playing their little games. Let me throw the bolt on the door behind you so you can let go of the handle." He kept speaking in a soft voice as he took off Joe's coat and hung it on a hook and then guided him into room. The voice was comforting.

"When they first begin to play their tricks, you can't help but be nervous, but after a while you get used to it. Their intention is to make you feel frightened, so you must learn not to fear them. Otherwise, they will have won a victory, and that is one thing you must not let them have."

Tomas took him into a room that looked as if it might belong to a Parisian student. The walls were peeling stucco, books lay stacked on the floor, and the furniture was very badly worn. A large ceramic wood stove was embedded in one wall, and clearly extended through the wall into the next room.

Tomas pulled a curtain aside and pointed out to the courtyard.

"You see the window up there? The one with the lights on?" Joe looked up at a curtained window with a light behind it. All the other windows in the courtyard were dark. "All the other apartments are empty, but they have a listening post there. They can hear everything we say in this room." Tomas bent down and butted his cigarette in an ash tray that already had half a dozen cigarette ends in it. "I feel very honoured that in the midst of a Soviet-wide housing shortage, this entire building has been emptied so that my voice will not be confused with that of the neighbours."

"I thought they weren't doing that kind of thing any more."

"Oh, they stop, they start. In your country, they build roads when unemployment is high. Here they hire more KGB men and then they have to keep them busy."

Another, younger girl had come into the room. She too was dressed in the same garish orange as her sister, and she was studying Joe curiously. Joe took another package of bubble gum from his bag and gave it to the girl, and as soon as she had it in her hand, she ran into an adjoining room saying something in Lithuanian, of which "Mama" was the only word he understood.

"Mr. Curtis, this is my wife Karolina."

She stood in the doorway holding the hand of her daughter. At first Joe did not recognize her because the little girl at her side made her look so motherly. She had long, dark brown hair and was at least a decade younger than her husband. Her eyes were large and deep and not made up at all, as they had been the last time Joe saw her. Did she recognize him? She gave no hint of it, but reached forward to give him a light handshake.

"Do we still have that bottle of Bulgarian wine?" Tomas asked. He was lighting another of the foul-smelling Lithuanian cigarettes from a pack on the coffee table.

"I'll bring it," said Karolina, "and I'll make something to eat."

"I've already eaten," said Joe.

"Just something light," said Tomas. "I hope you can bear the smell of this smoke."

"I have some American cigarettes," said Joe hopefully. The smell of Tomas's cigarettes was unbearable.

Tomas's eyes lit up. "Then it'll be a party."

The two girls played around the door of the room, looking at Joe shyly. European kids, thought Joe, they seemed to be born with a kind of discretion that was absent from the American atmosphere. Hair in ribboned pigtails, they looked like pictures from a story-book. If only they had not been in those ghastly orange outfits designed by some Soviet clothier with a hangover.

Joe took out his notebook and tape recorder.

"Please, let us have something to eat and drink first. We can do the interview later," said Tomas.

But Joe stuck with his tools. In Lithuania, if he waited until the wining and dining was over, he would be too drunk and full to do the job. Karolina's appearance in the apartment disturbed him. The one question he wanted to ask, he could not, so he started with biographical questions.

"I was first interrogated when I was sixteen years old," said Tomas. "What for? I wore a tie and a jacket to school one day. You see, it was February the sixteenth, the old Lithuanian independence day, but none of us were supposed to know that. We lived in an upside down world where history began in 1940, when the Soviets first came in here. I had a teacher who told some us that the prewar independence day was on the sixteenth, so in a kind of private protest, I got dressed up and went to school.

"Nobody could show they knew what I was up to, but everyone understood. This was a country of taboos and open secrets. I was called into the principal's office and ordered to go home and change into a sweater. This is how my life of 'dissidence' began. Two days later I received a note to report to the Ministry of the Interior for a talk.

"I was sixteen, remember that. The guard at the door of the ministry told me to wait, and a uniformed man took me to a room, showed me in, and locked the door behind me. There were only two chairs in the room, and both of them already had men in them. One's nose was puffed up, and he still had traces of dried blood around the nostrils. The other's face was puffy too, and his hair was wild, and I could tell he was an alcoholic. We have many of those here. Imagine me, a high school boy in his best pants and sweater, locked into a room with these men.

"They were barbaric men, those two. One had hit his wife over the head with an iron, and the other was a bootlegger who had grown too fond of his own product. But depraved though they were, they still had a spark of humanity in them. They sympathized with a young man who was entering the maw of the beast for the first time.

"'Do you have an address book?' the one with the broken nose wanted to know. I did. He told me to eat it. "We'll help you," they said, and I tore out pages three at a time, and we chewed them in a kind of prison ritual. When I told them what I was in for, they called me a fool and laughed. But they liked me. In their eyes, the drunkard, the ruffian, and the protester were all of the same school. If the state was my enemy, then I was their friend. I think that in their own way, they were protesters who had gone wrong. They hated the world they lived in too.

"Think, Mr. Curtis, of a drunkard and a ruffian, each taking me under his wing for the morning. They taught me the one important principle of the Brezhnevist world. There were laws, usually secret laws, to make the system seem humane. I mean that on the books, there were rules, but no one would tell you what they were. They asked me, for example, if I was a high school student, and I told them I was. The one with the broken nose informed me that a high school student under interrogation had the right to go home for lunch.

"Imagine such a law! Such codification of barbarity! I banged on the door and told the guard I had a right to go home for lunch. He did not like it, and he looked at my fellow-prisoners with anger, but he made me sign a registry and let me go home.

"This is what you must understand Mr. Curtis. The entire country was a prison, and we lived our lives in a panopticon, visible to our teachers, the storekeepers, the colleagues at work, and we participated in this upside-down world where we were both prisoners and jailers at the same time.

"None of us liked this world, but some became accustomed to it. I could not. I wanted to live in the kind of world you do, you Westerners, but I did not want to leave my country. I wanted to bring the West to Lithuania by taking this country out of the Soviet Union."

A few years earlier, perhaps even a few months earlier, Joe would have labelled the man a dreamer. The goateed chain-smoker in a run-down apartment wanted to change the Soviet Union - more - he wanted to take his country out of it. But men such as he were winning in Poland and Hungary and Czechoslovakia - the bohemians, the writers, the religious - they were taking governments into their hands.

Karolina came in and began to set the coffee table with plates and glasses. She set out sandwiches spread with an unidentifiable meat paté and sprinkled with equally mysterious flavourful seeds. Tomas opened the wine and poured it. Karolina sat down across from her husband and listened as he spoke.

"I knew I would never be allowed to continue my education after high school. What was the point in applying to the university when my 'charakteristika', you know, my file, would have 'bourgeois nationalist' written all over it? I did not wait to be called up for military service. I volunteered for it.

"I was known by then, so they sent me to the far East, on the border with China, where the soldiers lived in the most miserable conditions. We stayed in tents winter and summer, and we had to bring our own utensils or have our relatives send knives and forks from home. I ate with my hands for a month. The men were covered with fleas because it was hard to heat water to wash our clothes, and there was never enough powder to kill them off. The conditions were terrible, but no more terrible for me than for the other soldiers.

"Even there, I ran up against the system of secret laws again when one of my fellow soldiers caught fire. I suppose he may have had some gasoline on his pant leg, we were filling the trucks with gas, because when we went for our break and he tossed a match after lighting a cigarette, his whole leg lit up and the clothes on his back started to burn as well. The poor young man began to yelp like a dog, and he ran as if he could get away from the fire. But I caught him, and rolled him on the ground to smother the flames, and when that did not work, I used my jacket to put them out.

"For this act, I received a commendation. More, in the highly codified world of the Soviet Army, I was to receive a week's pass and airfare home, for that is the reward for saving the life of a man on fire. But they could not let me go home. I was a dissident, you see, and they would get in trouble with the authorities if I returned. My sergeant had to deal with me, and he was a good man, a Ukrainian, and he asked me to sign a document saying I'd renounce my nationalist activites. It would be so easy, he said, both for him and for me if I did so. He pleaded with me, my sergeant, to make life easier for both of us. But I could not sign. Not only would I not sign, I deserved a week's pass, and I demanded that I get it.

"Such trouble for the authorities! The officers scowled, until some bureaucrat saved them. It seems that the law said I had to be granted either a week's pass, or a reward of three roubles plus a medal. They did not want to give a dissident a medal, but I believe they found it the lesser of two evils. No ceremony, you understand. I simply went to the paymaster one day, and received a large brown envelope with a medal and a three-rouble banknote.

"Comedy, Mr. Curtis! Life here was hilarious, if you could only step back from the smothering forces and look at what they were doing."

The older of the girls in orange was tugging at Karolina's sleeve, and she leaned forward to whisper in her mother's ear.

"The children would like to do a little something for you Mr. Curtis."

The two girls stepped into an open space near the coffee table. They were holding hands, and the older one counted carefully to three, and then they began:

"I'm a Yankee Doodle Dandy,
Yankee Doodle all the Way...."

The goateed Tomas smoked and smiled as the children sang, and he looked at Joe as only a proud father could.

Joe clapped when the children finished, and he fished in his satchel for more packages of gum.

"That should keep the listeners busy with their dictionaries for hours," said Tomas.

"The listeners?"

"Yes, the KGB, remember? They can hear everything we say here. For all they know, you might be my CIA chief, and the children might be giving you a coded message."

Tomas laughed, but Joe could only manage a weak smile. He thought of the man who had called his name out in the street. He might still be out there.

"Children, to bed," said Karolina, and she rose and took the girls by their hands. They curtsied to Joe and giggled as they left the room.

"Mr. Vastokas," Joe said in his best journalist's voice, "*Le Monde* has said you are the type of man who will walk into the heart of a bonfire if he believes his cause is just, and *Die Zeit* says you have lived so long with your head in the jaws of a lion that you know every one of its teeth. What gave you the courage to act this way?"

Tomas blushed a deep red and made a dismissive wave with his hand.

"Such hyperbole! Perhaps all that time in the lion's mouth I've learned which of the teeth is rotten and where the gaps are, so when it brings its jaws together I can find a safe place to rest my neck. When the lion opens its jaws again and finds that my head is still attached to my body, it begins to feel ashamed. It asks itself, 'What kind of a king of the jungle am I?' And then it begins to doubt. Then it becomes afraid. Perhaps eventually it will skulk back to its den and leave me and my poor country alone."

"But the things you have given up," Joe insisted. "All these books here. You should have gone to a university, taken a profession..."

"And joined the Communist Party and written trash and informed on suspicious colleagues. Better to have the job I do and be free to act as I wish."

"What is your job?"

"I am a lighting man at the theatre."

"And that satisfies you?"

"You are beginning to sound like one of the men at the KGB offices. Be reasonable, they said to me. Think of your career, think of your family! You could have a nice apartment with hot running water and an elevator. Just stop writing for the underground press. We don't ask you to betray anyone, although you would be doing your patriotic duty to tell us your friends' names. Just sign this paper. Say you will be quiet, and everything will be fine."

"And weren't you tempted?"

"Of course I was tempted! Don't you think I want my children to get a good education? But listen, all of you reporters from the West are the same. Forgive the generalization, but it is true. You fly in here for a few days and ask us if the new Lithuania we want to build is going to pay sufficient attention to human rights, and then you ask us if we are not being unkind to poor Mr. Gorbachev. You did not have to live in a web of lies all of your lives, balancing and counterbalancing to keep from falling into a semantic trap that might cost you your career. You never had your children made to stand in school and have the teacher laugh at them for going to Church the Sunday before. You were never a writer who had to change all the yellow sunsets to red ones to make for more patriotic literature. This systematic deformation of decency has turned us into a nation of liars and thieves, and I for one cannot bear the thought of living in a country whose basic premise is a lie. The Soviet Union claims we joined in 1940, but they came and killed our people, took the farmers off their land, and even made the priests into KGB apparatchiks. I know one. Perhaps it would make a good story for your paper. 'I was a priest for the KGB'. This fundamental lie is impossible for us to live in, so some become drunkards and some become dissidents and some learn to accommodate, but they live with a dirty conscience that embitters them. I just want to live in a society without lies."

Joe could have pushed him on that. The ridiculous admiration these Easterners had for the West. Instead, he asked another question.

"Aren't you ever afraid for your life?"

Tomas took another cigarette from the package on the table, even though the smoke in the air was burning Joe's eyes and searing his throat.

"You exaggerate. The years under Brezhnev were bad, but we usually did not have to fear for our lives."

"What about Father Pliumpa?" It was Karolina. She was standing at the door. "Why don't you tell him that the leading cause of death for priests is car accidents? Why don't you tell him what happened last year on February the sixteenth?"

"A comedy," said Tomas dismissively.

"Not a comedy," said Karolina, and she came in and sat at her chair by the coffee table. She wore no discernible perfume, but Joe believed he smelled something fresh about her, something that drew her toward him. As he looked at her, the first few words remained unheard. Her eyes were lovely.

"They kidnapped Tomas and took him to a forest. Three men - KGB. It was February 16, the old independence day, the anniversary of his first protest. They drove him deep into the forest to kill him."

"How can you know this? They were just trying to frighten me as they have tried so many times before."

"Do not joke about this. They were going to kill you. They were ready to kill you."

"Then why didn't they?"

"Because something went wrong. Perhaps the officer who was supposed to give the order was drunk."

"But listen, Karolina, that night ended as a comedy too. They drove me to Byelorussia and dropped me off at a small town, and then they followed the bus that I took back home to Vilnius."

"Please Tomas. No more jokes about this. I'm tired of your *human comedy*."

But Joe had his notebook and they talked much longer. Karolina was silent for most of time, except when she provided him with dates and times that had slipped his mind. She had an excellent memory.

It was well after midnight when Joe had finished. Tomas put on his coat as well.

"I'll walk with you to the taxi stand and we can wait together."

Karolina touched the tips of her fingers to his hand at the door.

Outside, the night had grown colder and it smelled as if it might snow. The light was still on in the window that gave onto the courtyard. Joe was awkward as Tomas linked arms with him in the European fashion, but then it comforted him to have another body so close as they walked out of the maze of small streets and into the square in front of the state art gallery where there was a taxi stand. They stood quietly for a while.

"Fewer and fewer people are afraid now, Mr. Curtis," said Tomas, just as a late night cab came around from behind the gallery. "And that is a good thing, because the Soviet Empire is rotten, and in its dying spasms it might still do us great harm."

Joe got into the cab.

"It is easier when not so many are afraid," Tomas said through the open window, and then he gave directions to the cabbie in Russian.

The hotel doorman made a great show of checking Joe's registration slip when he came back in. The Hotel Lietuva was built something like a Holiday Inn. It was the only tourist-class hotel in the country, which meant that the rooms were clean and the phones usually worked. Joe went straight into the Black Bar on the ground floor. It stayed open until dawn.

There was not much business. Two Germans spoke drunkenly to one another in a corner booth and an olive-skinned woman, perhaps an Armenian, sat alone in another. She wore an evening dress.

The bartender greeted Joe effusively by name.

"A cocktail Mr. Curtis? A gin and tonic? A glass of champagne?"

"Do you have any Bulgarian wine?"

"Ahh, you know all our secrets."

The bartender brought a bottle of wine and one glass. Joe asked for a second one.

"Expecting company?"

"Perhaps."

He sat in the bar for two hours, and drank three-quarters of the bottle, but no one showed. When he got up to go, the bartender put the cork back into the bottle and gave him a bag so he could bring the remains up to his room.

Joe was on the fifteenth floor, in a modest two-room suite that overlooked the old city of Vilnius. It had a view of the cathedral and the ruined castle on the hilltop. The elevator was slow, as usual, although there were no other guests using it. He padded down the hallway to his door, unlocked it, and stepped inside.

At first, he thought he'd gone into the wrong room, the room of a particularly messy person. The couch cushions were lying on the floor, the refrigerator and drawers of the chest were open and the television was on, though there was no sound because the stations were off the air for the night. His bedroom was equally messed, with the sheets pulled off the beds and his notes strewn about. His mini-cassette tapes had been pulled off the spools and the door to the balcony was open.

Joe gripped the neck of the wine bottle as he walked towards the balcony, but there was no one there. He closed and bolted the balcony door and pulled one of the beds up against it. He put the chain on the door and stacked some bottles so that he would hear it if anyone pushed the door open. He checked the bathroom, shower, and closets, and then began to straighten out his belongings.

No use in calling down to the reception desk. They probably already knew about it.

For an hour he cleaned and ordered the rooms. Nothing had been stolen, but then he carried his passport and camera and cash with him. But it was not a robbery anyway. He was sure of that.

When everything was more or less in order again, he tried to go to sleep, but he was too shaken. His bed faced the window to the balcony, and he felt exposed if he left the night lamp on. The curtains were semi-sheer, and a watcher from outside would be able to observe him. On the other hand, he was not comfortable with lying in the dark. He was afraid.

That was what they wanted, and Tomas had told him not to give into it. Realistically, what would the KGB do to a journalist? Stalin was long dead, and Westerners did not disappear. At worst, they might not renew his visa if he wanted to return to the Soviet Union, but it was not his normal beat anyway. So there was nothing to be afraid of.

Joe sat up the rest of the night, taking small sips of the Bulgarian wine. He even smoked two of the cigarettes from packages he had brought with him as gifts for the locals. He was not used to smoking any more, and it tasted bad, but the cigarettes comforted him.

The dawn came late in November, yet even so, he waited until the sun was well up above the horizon before he went to bed.

He dined early the next evening, and returned to the Black Bar and ordered another bottle of the Bulgarian wine. The taste grew on him. He was in a corner booth, and the waiter had taken the hint with the five dollar tip and left him alone. Joe had to call him over at ten when he wanted another one.

Karolina came into the bar at eleven. She came to his table when she saw him, and she sat down. Joe poured her a glass of the wine, but she did not touch it.

"I thought you liked Bulgarian wine."

"You think you understand me, don't you?"

She said it bitterly. Karolina was wearing a black dress and her face was made up in the Soviet fashion - too heavily.

"Where do you keep your clothes and make-up? Doesn't he suspect?"

"I have a friend."

"What if someone sees you the way I did? Vilnius is not such a big city."

"Nobody we know comes to this hotel. I am out of context here. Give me a cigarette."

He lit it for her and waited, but she did not speak.

"Do you need the money that badly? I could give you a couple of hundred dollars. Maybe I could even send you some money from time to time."

She laughed at him, low and bitterly.

"It's not the money, Mr. Curtis. You come from a capitalist country, so you think it all comes down to that. I'm not a.... *kurva*."

"That other night. I saw you leave this bar with a man."

"Yes, I know. He is waiting for me outside in the lobby."

"Maybe he'll get jealous."

"He knows all about you. He knows everything. You do not."

"So let me in on the secret. Why is the wife of Lithuania's leading dissident hanging around hotel bars with strange men?"

"I shall tell you, but you must promise me that this is not just another story to you. You must promise me that what we say will never appear in print, in one of your newspapers in the West that the embassy people clip and send back here to the Ministry of the Interior."

"I'm a journalist."

"And I am the wife of a dissident. Step out of your role for a minute."

Joe shrugged, and she took it to mean he agreed.

"I have two children, Mr. Curtis, and life is very hard for them. The teachers at school single them out. Their father has been called a criminal in the press. We try to make them understand, but I am afraid for them."

"He isn't afraid. He seems willing to throw you into the fire as well. Just another scrap for the human comedy."

"He is a good man. I won't hear you speaking ill of him."

"Then why are you doing this? If your press ever found out, and they will, he'll become a laughing stock."

"The press will never run this story."

"How do you know?"

"Because I have my connections too. Now listen, because I will only tell you once and then I have to leave. Lithuania is going to be a free country Mr. Curtis, and it is going to be so because of men such as Tomas. They have to be protected."

"Go on."

"I have been interrogated as well. There is a certain KGB colonel, Eimantas is his name. He interrogated me often enough, and he flirted often enough as well. He is a young man, virile, and I hate him very much. He is the one who is waiting for me out in the lobby. You see, that night last year, when they took Tomas into the forest, Eimantas came to our apartment. He had a bottle of champagne, and he had a driver wait for him in a car outside. I told him to leave. I told him Tomas would be home any time, and I told him the children were asleep in the next room. He was not worried in the least. He told me they had Tomas, and he told me they were going to kill him. Of course I did not believe him, but he waved at someone out in the courtyard and the man brought in a small radio. Eimantas told me to wait. I did, and he opened the bottle of champagne. He drank half of it, and we waited, and then a sound came over the radio. There were two voices, it seemed, as if two men were hunched over a radio somewhere. They said they had Tomas.

"Eimantas was very cruel. He asked the men about his condition, and they said they thought they had broken a rib, but he was otherwise all right. Eimantas asked if they were ready to kill him, and they said they were. They might bury the body there, or leave it out for hikers to find. They would say he had been robbed, or else one of the criminals he worked with had turned on him.

"Eimantas told me to choose, then. I could sleep with him, or Tomas could die."

"Knowing Tomas, he probably would have preferred to die," said Joe.

"And what good would that have been? I'd be alone with the two children, if Eimantas didn't kill me as well."

"Of course."

"We live in such a world of lies here. He could have been trying to trap me, so Tomas would find us in bed when he returned, or he might have wanted to film us and use the pictures against us later. Anything could have been true. But I did as he asked. He radioed his men and told them to drop Tomas in a village in Byelorussia, and make sure he had enough money to get a bus ride home.

"But it did not end there. I must still see him sometimes. He demands it. And I come to this place, just as you saw me here the first time."

"Take me out to the lobby and show him to me. I'll kill him."

"Ach, you men talk so stupidly."

"You're in very great danger, Karolina. This place is falling apart. I've seen it happen in Hungary and Poland, and when the old regimes fall, they leave files behind them. Your Tomas is going to win, and when he does, your file's going to be dug up by someone. Tomas will find out then."

"But by then the country will be free. I just have to do this for a little while longer. No thank you, Mr. Curtis, save your solutions for your Western world. It is different here. Each of us survives as she can."

Chapter 11

Butler had left the fireside a few minutes after Dianne began her story. By that time, the snow was blowing thick and wild and no longer melting when it hit the earth. He was leaving footprints in an inch of snow. The blizzard was curiously heavy for something that came out of a machine, yet if he looked straight up, he could see the yellow sun with a halo of shifting white.

Teresa was waiting by the four-wheel drive with a fresh gin and tonic in her hand. Butler was still carrying his book.

"Going to keep notes?" Teresa asked.

Butler laughed. He felt ridiculous to be standing beside her with the book in hand, and he found himself strangely wordless. Teresa waited.

"Aren't you afraid you'll miss something?" she asked. Her voice sounded a little defiant.

The weight of the book in his hand seemed to grow until it became unbearable. He tossed the book onto the snow-covered hood of his car, and then he put his arms around Teresa. She liked that.

"What's your name?" she asked.

"You know my name."

"Tell it to me again."

"Alban."

"Unusual. Alban. Albey? That sounds nice. Al? No, that's not you at all. Maybe I'll just stick with Alban. It sounds so British. You could have a school named after you or something. St. Alban's Hall - a training school for boys."

He kissed her. Her face was wet with melted snow and he was unsure if she shivered at the kiss or the cold. Butler kissed both her lips, and then he tasted each one separately, carrying on from there to her cheeks and eyelids. He felt breathless. He had forgotten how to breathe and kiss and the latter seemed so much more important than the former.

"Did you learn that in books?" Teresa asked. He pulled his face away from her and looked. Her eyes were half-closed, sleepy and attractive.

"I'm going on instinct."

"You should trust in your instinct more often," and Butler knew it was time to kiss her again.

"We haven't got much time," Teresa said when he was finished, and Butler took her around to the back of his four-wheel drive. He had gear packed almost to the ceiling, but there was a narrow space among the sleeping bags and satchels where he had an inflated air-mattress.

"Are you a virgin?" Teresa asked as they slid awkwardly inside, trying to avoid projecting tent pegs and loose tools that tumbled off the pile and fell onto the mattress.

"You know I was married once."

"But since then?"

He said nothing.

She nodded as if she understood something better, and then began to take off her wet shirt. Butler helped her with fingers that had become magically adept. The back of the truck smelled of canvas and tools. It was cool at first, but Butler pulled an open sleeping-bag down upon them, and they warmed themselves quickly. The snow had made a curtain on the windows of the jeep, and no curious onlooker would have noticed anything usual from the outside. The sound, the roar of the angry polar bear which had lost its mate, did not penetrate the snow-covered jeep. Inside, there was a very small, yet very complete world. Only two of them belonged in it.

The springs of the four-wheel drive rocked gently.

Even as they lay in one another's arms, they knew that they had very little time left. "Time will have its fancy," he said sadly, and traced a finger over Teresa's lips. Butler was happy and tired and he would have liked to sleep, but it was not possible. Not now. They began to dress.

"Why did you do it?" he asked Teresa as he slipped his arm into his shirt.

"Because of you," she said, and continued to dress. The answer was obvious, but he had wanted to hear her say it.

"And for another reason as well," she added, tucking in a shirt. "I ovulate today. I've kept records for a long time in case I ever wanted to get pregnant. I felt like it this morning."

"Pregnant?"

It seemed so odd. "Do you think that's appropriate?" Butler could hear his old, school-marmish voice coming out. He did not like the sound of it, but he could not be turned into a new man in half an hour.

"Act of faith, love," she said, and kissed him gently on the ear.

Butler began to dress more quickly just as Teresa stopped what she had been doing.

"Can it really be time?" she asked. And Butler would have loved to make love again.

She could have picked someone like Stan. He would have been the obvious choice. A man of action. Not a reflective type like Butler. But now Butler knew there was no more time for reflection.

Teresa put on one of Butler's heavy sweaters, and each of them wrapped a blanket over their head and shoulders. When they opened the back of the four-wheel drive, a mixture of wet snow and grit blew against their faces and made them wince. The wind was so high they had to lean into it, and within seconds their heads and shoulders were covered with snow. Butler held tight to Teresa's hand.

"The world's going to end and I won't even be there to see it," thought Butler. They were lost in the tiny blizzard.

"Why don't we separate?" Teresa asked.

But it made no sense to do so, and Butler would not permit it. He held her hand more tightly and tried to walk in a straight line. Suddenly the snow thinned, and they stepped beyond the bounds of the blizzard.

Beyond the range of the snow machine, the sun was as hot as ever, though gray behind a cloud of dust. A great wind was blowing and the air was dirty with earth and grit. Butler and Teresa stood for a moment on the muskeg and stared at the strange mass of snow that swirled and twisted and mingled with the dust blown by the wind. It was like looking into another world.

"We've got to get back to the camp-fire," said Butler. "I've got the book with me, and he'll want to do some kind of tally of the stories."

Teresa nodded, and, holding hands, they stepped back into the snowstorm to search for their friends. The wind was from the north, so as long as Butler felt it on the same cheek, he knew he was going in approximately the right direction. By the time he caught sight of the figures around the camp-fire, his shoes and pants were wet straight through, and he could feel Teresa shaking beside him.

At first he thought the people at the camp-fire were dead or frozen, for they were fixed and still. But they were only listening to Dianne, who finished her story of the dissident as Butler and Teresa returned.

Margaret was sitting up with tears streaming down her face.

They had all huddled more closely in order to hear what she was saying. Mike had two inches of snow on his head because he had not thought to wipe it off as she was speaking.

"Exceptional," Odds said again and again. He was the only one dressed for the weather. He had on a gortex Skidoo suit, lined leather gloves and a Chamonix toque. "I've never heard another story quite like it. Look, you can come on over to my Winnebago and I'll give you ten percent off anything. Your choice. What am I saying? Make it fifteen percent. Across the board, Dianne. You name the pieces you want and they're yours."

"How was her story?" Butler asked as he and Teresa slipped in beside Mike.

"I liked it, but I'm not a critic," said Mike. "Critics are a cranky bunch, and Victor's the king of critics."

So maybe they had won, Butler thought.

"Well Victor," said Stan, "If it was close before, it's all clear now. Dianne's story was just what you were looking for. We won, right?"

Victor said nothing, and if he had not brushed the snow off his shoulders, he would have looked asleep, or so wrapped up in his thoughts that nothing anybody said came through.

"We won, right?" Stan shouted.

But Victor seemed strangely unmoved. His face was sterner than it had been the entire night, and he looked frozen and somehow magnificent in his impassivity. He was Solomon, willing to cut the baby in half; he was Peter at the gate, watching the backs of sinners he had turned away and sent to begin the descent to hell; he was a schoolteacher assigning a ten-thousand word essay on the Dewey Decimal system.

"What's the problem Victor?" Odds asked.

"You assume too much. We have to check the score. Butler!"

Butler felt his feet grow even colder inside his Reebok runners. It felt as if he were standing on a patch of ice and the cold was running up through his soles, through his Odour Eaters and through his acrylic sox.

"I wasn't here for the story," said Butler.

"Ahh," said Victor. "Well then, we'll have to judge the fate of the Earth on the stories that were told before. The last one has not been recorded."

"You asshole!" Mike shouted at Butler. Butler could feel his cheeks turn hot even as his feet continued to freeze. "Of all the times to get your rocks off, you had to choose now. If there's anyone left to remember this, you'll be famouser than Nero. You fucked as the world ended. Jesus, it pisses me off."

The wind screeched and Mike batted at the snowflakes as if they were flies. The fireside party was beginning to end.

"Lay off him Mike," said Stan. "This isn't Butler's fault - it's Victor's. He wants to cheat his way to the apocalypse. Seems kind of slimy to me."

"Too late," said Victor. "You can't judge the judge."

"I don't think it's too late," said Butler. The others looked at him.

"Just let me flip through my notes here, will you?" And he turned the pages of his soggy notebook carefully, studying each page and wiping off the snowflakes before turning to the next one.

"Looks like a draw to me," said Butler calmly when he was done.

"A draw?" Victor asked incredulously. "Impossible."

"You said I'd have this sinking feeling in my gut if we lost," Butler answered. "Well, I don't have a sinking feeling. Actually, I feel pretty good. You made me the scorekeeper, and I'm telling you the results. No arguing with the scorekeeper."

"Oh yes there is," said Victor. "I say that your stories were not good enough. This is the end. No letters to the editor - no defence of the work by friends in high places."

Victor moved slowly as he spoke, until he had withdrawn from the circle and was facing them all. He spoke loudly so the others could hear him above the wind.

"I'm not afraid," said Victor, "And you shouldn't be either. I'm just going to hurry along the end, finish us off and spare us the misery of rotting cancerous flesh and parched earth. The snowstorm is a toy, an illusion. The real world is burning up. Butler would soon stop loving his Teresa if the skin cancer were there for him to see - it's just too early, and I'm saving you the horror. Think of liver spots that rise up above the level of the skin and then begin to fall off. And it's not just her. Think of the children scouring the earth for a blade of edible grass, and finding only burnt stalks. I pity you, and I pity all the people who would have to live in such a horrifying future. I do them all a favour by ending it now."

"Christ," said Margaret, "It's bad enough to be snuffed like this without having to listen to a sermon first. This guy is Vincent Price and Bela Lugosi rolled into one."

"Shh!" said Butler.

"Thank you," said Victor. "I have a few more words to say."

Stan made his move. In a sweep that would have made Wyatt Earp proud, he raised his rifle from his side, aimed, and pulled the trigger faster than it took to spit.

Nothing happened.

"Damn trigger is frozen," said Stan.

Victor laughed, and the inside of his mouth looked like a black maw with all of the snowflakes in front of it. He seemed to roar, but the sound came from the circling polar bear, searching for its lost mate.

"Listen to that roar," said Victor happily. "I like to think of it as the last sound of outraged polluters who can't reach their lobbyists in Washington. The lines have been cut, AT&T has collapsed. The earth's credit rating has been exceeded and the gas company is turning off the flow for lack of payment."

In the great swirl of snow, Butler though he saw a movement of white against white.

"Tell us some more," said Butler.

"More? I was finished. I'm about to press the button."

"You must have a story of your own. You never told us."

"It's too late now. The sun's up."

"How about a synopsis? A coming attractions teaser?"

"There is only one coming attraction," said Victor, "and this is it."

Victor depressed the nozzle of the can in his hand.

Instinctively, Butler held his breath, as if doing so would save him from the nerve gas.

Nothing happened.

"Damned nozzle is frozen," said Victor, and he started to blow on the top of the can to thaw the depresser.

Teresa touched Butler's hand, and he knew immediately what he had to do. He dove forward as if thirty pounds and twenty years had been miraculously taken off him. He reached for Victor's wrist and tried to knock the spray can free.

But Victor was strong and his determination was stronger still. He held on to the can and tried to knock Butler down, and the two of them tumbled onto the snow. Even in the midst of the struggle, Butler could hear the shout.

"Everybody run!"

Butler did not have time to think about it. He had Victor under him, and with both hands he took the wrist of the hand holding the spray can and tried to bend Victor's arm back in an arc. But where there should have been nothing but air and snow, he struck something solid - something white, furry and warm.

The bear had returned for its mate.

It turned to see what had struck it in the flank, and its mind registered two things. Enemy and food.

In shock at the closeness of the bear - he could feel its hot breath so near - Butler released Victor's wrist. Victor was on the ground beneath Butler, and he could not see behind him. He raised his hand in attempt at giving the nozzle another try.

The can struck the bear in the snout, and in one quick, clean motion, the animal took Victor's hand and the spray can into its mouth.

Butler leaped off Victor and started to struggle away in the snow. Everyone else had fled, and he did not know which way to go. He looked over his shoulder and saw the bear shake its head. As it did so, Victor's hand began to come away from his arm. The bear seemed to swallow, and then reached forward so that it had Victor's arm in its throat as well.

Butler saw a peculiar look come over the bear's face - one of suspicion. Victor's face was a picture of shock. The rest was lost in the swirl of snow.

*   *   *

It was mid-day before the snow machine ran out of gas, and those who had hidden in their cars began to unlock their doors and come out. The wind was still high, and very quickly it covered the snow field with dust. They waited for the snow to melt so they could see what was below.

"You sure the bear swallowed the can?" Stan asked Butler.

"Sure I'm sure."

Teresa was holding his hand as they waited for Victor's body to be revealed. But by late afternoon there was only a little snow left in the shade of the Winnebago. No body, no bear, and no spray can lay in the muck that remained after the snow had gone.

"Must have dragged him away someplace," said Stan.

"What about the spray can?" Margaret asked.

"I don't know," said Stan. "Maybe the bear's gastric juices will melt it down. If they do, then one day it's going to fart and finish the job that Victor wanted to do all along."

"I don't think so," said Teresa. Butler looked at her.

"I think we've been saved."

It was hard to believe what she said when the late afternoon sun was an angry hot orb in the sky and the muck around the camp-fire was beginning to dry into a hard crust of earth. It was hard to believe when the sting of the wind-blown grit against Butler's face made him wince with pain. But there was something comforting about the words, and something comforting about the warmth of her hand against his.